THE ARCHANGEL'S HEART

Realm of the Immortals
Book Two

By Juliette N. Banks

COPYRIGHT

Copyright © 2021 by Juliette N. Banks. All rights reserved.

No part of this book may be reproduced in any form or by any means, electronic or mechanical, including photocopying, recording, or by any information storage and retrieval system without the written permission of the author, except for the use of brief quotations in a review.

This book is a work of fiction and imagination. Names, characters, places, and incidents are either products of the author's imagination or are used fictitiously. Any resemblance to actual persons, living or dead, events, or locales is entirely one of coincidence. The author acknowledges the trademarked status and trademark owners of various products and music referenced in this work of fiction, which have been used without permission. The publication and/or use of these trademarks is not authorized, associated with, or sponsored by the trademark owners.

Author: Juliette N. Banks
Editor: Happily Ever Proofreading LLC
Cover design by: Sheri Lynn Marean of SLM Creations

ABOUT THE AUTHOR

Juliette first published with Random House in 2013. After three decades as a marketer, Juliette felt the time was right to share the stories and characters who were taking up residence in her imagination. 2020 gifted her with the time to write and learn about the independent author landscape, and by early 2021, Juliette had released her first paranormal romance series, the Moretti Blood Brothers, and then the Realm of the Immortals.

She lives with her Maine coon kitty in Auckland, New Zealand, frequently travels to the United States, and reads the same books as her readers.

Connect with me:
www.juliettebanks.com
https://www.instagram.com/juliettebanksauthor
https://www.facebook.com/juliettenbanks

Facebook Readers Group:
https://www.facebook.com/groups/authorjuliettebanksreaders

DEDICATION

To my archangels,
I hear you and I thank you.
Juliette x

ALSO BY JULIETTE N. BANKS

The Moretti Blood Brothers
The Vampire King (novella)
The Vampire Prince
The Vampire Protector
Book four coming late 2021

Realm of the Immortals
The Archangels Battle (novella)
The Archangel's Heart
Book three coming late 2021

PROLOGUE

England, Planet Earth Year 1843

Flapping its wings, the magical creature struggled to maintain invisibility as the surrounding gods battled. Swords clashed and bolts of lightning flashed through the air as war waged in the skies.

She dodged one bolt not meant for her as she flew over the vast mountain range. The air was misty as she flew down into the tree line, hoping to find shelter. Archangel Michael had sent them and the angel warriors to Earth to protect humans while the Titans and Olympians fought.

For three days now she'd been chased by Ares, god of war. He wanted her magic. Worse, she'd overheard him say she was the last of her kind. Powerful though her kind may be, nimble they were not. She knew there had been casualties, but not to this extent. Not to extinction.

She landed on the ground, found a puddle of dirty water, and lapped up what she could, knowing this reprieve was short. She'd been hunted for days and needed to rest and regenerate. Only then would she have the energy to return to Heaven.

How Ares had discovered her species' unique powers, she did not know. Aside from God, their creator, and the seven archangels, no one was supposed to know. It was one of Heaven's most closely guarded secrets for good reason.

She could not be captured by the Olympians. For her sake, and for the safety of Heaven.

She walked through the forest until she came to a small town. People were milling about the streets, dressed in tailored suits and long gowns. A little boy chased a dog, giggling, while his mother waved her hand to keep him in order.

They walked toward a building she identified as a place of worship, the large cross sitting proudly on its roof.

The boy raced back to his family, and in an act of defiance, took hold of his sister's hand and shot his mother a glance. The sister tsked him but squeezed his hand and looked at her mama, both of them sharing a knowing smile.

The young woman looked to her right and stared directly at the magical creature, her eyes widening.

Startled, she looked down to see her power was weakening, and along with it, her cloaking abilities.

Help me, my Lord.

"There!" she heard above her as the gods descended.

Armed with swords and eagerly marching toward her, she knew they wouldn't kill her. They would imprison her and siphon her powers, using them for…well, nothing good if she knew the Olympic gods.

And she did.

Panicked and nearly depleted of energy, she made the only decision available to her. Returning to her spirit form, she bolted toward the young woman and entered her body.

Slamming into the human, she felt her fall to the ground and heard the young boy and mother cry out. The human's strong, capable father picked them up and carried them inside the church.

She heard the gods cursing, invisible to the humans and unable to reach her. Ares didn't have the power to extract a soul from a body.

Safe for now, the creature relaxed inside the human and let herself recharge, awaiting the moment it would be safe for her to depart.

The moment never came.

Ares hovered and tracked her and the human woman, Isobel, over the next few weeks.

One day while Isobel was picking berries in a nearby field, he approached. Hand flying to her chest and dropping her basket, Isobel screamed.

"Quiet, human," he demanded, then waved to the two males with him. "Go ahead, warlocks. Make it quick."

Isobel stood terrified and silent as the male witches muttered words which meant nothing to her. But the creature knew and was powerless to do anything.

"You want to hide in there, be my guest. I am patient. Okay, I'm not, but sooner or later I will be your master. When that day finally comes, the Archangel Michael will finally kneel before me," Ares sneered.

The curse swirled through the human's body and then took hold. Isobel stood, shivering.

"Who…who are you?"

Ares ran his eyes up and down her youthful, slender body. "Tempting. But not today. I have a war to win."

Isobel dropped to the ground, shaking.

"You have something I want. Give up your life and release what is mine."

Suicide, the creature realized. She hadn't taken that into consideration. When a human took their own life, its soul—and hers—would be released and linger long enough for it to be imprisoned.

The girl shook.

"Until then, you're trapped in there," he said, speaking to her and ignoring the human. "The human won't last long before…" He ran his finger across his throat sardonically and laughed.

"Who's trapped? What are you talking about?" Isobel bravely asked despite her fear.

"Shut up, human. God, I'd love to lick you from head to toe, but there's no time. Go, live your shitty life, and I'll come back for what is mine."

As the gods flew up into the sky, Isobel collapsed to the ground. The creature cried quietly, realizing she'd achieved the one thing she'd been trying to avoid.

Entrapment.

CHAPTER ONE

Earth, 2020

Sara fell to her knees.

"I've had enough," she cried, her throat dry from the adult tantrum she'd just thrown. A tear fell down her cheek and she wiped it away with her fist.

She'd cursed Buddha, God, Jesus, the archangels, and then added the universe in for good measure. She wasn't religious, so she didn't really know what she was doing—she simply wanted to yell. She didn't expect any response because, again, she didn't believe in any of these entities.

But who else did you yell at in these circumstances?

At thirty-five, Sara Jacobson had endured a hard life by anyone's standards. Her life had been one of constant bad luck. If she fell in love, her boyfriends either cheated or left her without explanation. If she got promoted, she'd lose the job. She'd quickly find another one and land a manager who bullied her. She'd find a great rental property, and then the owner would give her notice. One year she'd had to move three times. On and on and on it went.

Sara had spent years blaming herself and trying to understand what she was doing wrong. She'd lost count of how much money she'd spent on therapists, healers, astrologers, and every guru you could imagine. In the end, they had all been as bamboozled as her.

Nothing made sense.

More recently, a psychic had told her things would turn around and for her to speak to her angels.

Christ. It had come to this.

Sara had driven home that day and rolled her eyes, mostly at herself. It was time to stop searching for answers and grow up. Clearly, she was destined to live a hard life, likely something to do with her childhood. She'd had no intentions of talking to her angels—as if that would help—and had instead gotten on with her life.

Until a month ago.

The World Health Organization had declared a global pandemic. Everyone's lives had spun into chaos.

2020. No one's favorite year.

The New Zealand government had gone into the strictest shutdown on the planet. Sara lived in Auckland, the country's largest city, with Tilly, her Maine coon kitty. Together, they were what was being called a bubble. Once you decided on your bubble, no one else was allowed in. And no one knew when things would change.

No one.

Supermarkets, pharmacies and gas stations were open, but everything else was forbidden to trade. It felt like they were in a damn zombie apocalypse movie. Sara could exercise in her neighborhood, but not in parks or on the beach.

The silence was eerie; peaceful, yet it felt unnatural and wrong. There were no planes flying, barely any traffic, and the economy was all but shut down.

People were scared.

Sara was scared.

And she was on her own.

Worse, the company she had worked for had made her redundant—illegally—and no one was hiring. She had some savings, but no one knew how long this would go on for or how the economy would fare at the end of it.

Oh God.

"For crying out loud. This is not fair!"

Sara had always believed people created their own lives

with their beliefs, thoughts, and actions. She blamed no one else for her chaotic life. But all this time to sit and think…and think…and think had given her no other option but to reflect on what was really going on in her life.

And so far, zip.

Nada.

Nothing.

"No one else I know deals with the same amount of drama I have in my life. Over and damn over. Come on!"

She'd concluded she was either cursed, or fate had dealt her a terrible hand. And if they could do that, then they could un-freaking-do it.

"Seriously, you angels need to help me or I will mess you up, you fuzzy-winged fuckers." She let out a snotty laugh. "Oh God, listen to me. I'm a lunatic." She shook her head at herself. Again. And because she couldn't help it, she added, "And don't send me some moron. I want Archangel Michael."

To be honest, she'd pulled that name out of thin air because she didn't know any of the other archangels' names.

Oh wait—wasn't there a Gabriel and Raphael?

She shrugged.

If memory served right, Michael was the big cheese, so he'd do, not that she was expecting him to email her an invitation to a video call or anything.

She snorted.

"Alright, girl, get your life together."

She wiped her tears away and groaned at how pathetic she was, especially given how she was such a strong, independent woman. Sure, everyone had their moments of breaking down, and this virus was testing them all, but she usually prided herself of keeping it together.

With a sigh, she glanced at her bed and began to get ready to sleep. She washed her face and slipped on her favorite white silk negligee.

"Fucking virus," she mumbled as she climbed into bed. The cat jumped up and curled at her feet. Completely exhausted, she slid down the covers, punched her pillow, and turned off the light.

"Goodnight, Tilly. We'll be okay."

I hope.

Archangel Michael was making his way through the Great Hall when he suddenly heard a loud female voice bouncing off the walls.

He stopped dead in his tracks and looked around.

Farther ahead of him, Raphael was unclasping his cape, having just returned from Earth. He had also stopped to look around.

"What the hell?" Raphael said.

"It appears to be coming from…"

"Archangel Michael!" the female voice cried, and he raised an eyebrow.

"What on Earth?" Raphael asked.

"Exactly." Michael crossed his enormous arms as his brother walked the length of the hall, his expression mirroring his own.

The voice was definitely a human female, there was no doubt about that. Humans prayed for his help all day, every day.

Not all of them were polite, either.

However, never in all his existence had a prayer echoed like a stereo inside the Great Hall in Heaven. The archangels received prayers inside their minds, and for the most part, the seven of them answered them with the ease of breathing.

"You can hear her?"

Raphael smirked. "I can. She sounds fiery. Let's take a look."

Frowning, Michael flicked his hand in front of him,

and the air shifted. A blur of blue energy twirled in circles until it cleared. Raphael snorted as a life-size vision of a young woman sitting on the floor of her bedroom ranting and yelling appeared.

"You archangels, gods, or whatever you are, get your asses down here and help me, you fuzzy-winged fuckers."

Michael failed to stop his grin.

Raphael snorted again.

"How is she doing this?"

"Is she just a human?" Raphael squinted and leaned in.

"She appears to be," Michael answered, wondering if only the two of them could hear her. Despite the breach, he was impressed by her sass and was hoping she would look up from the floor so they could properly see her.

He smiled.

This human was going to get a huge surprise when she learned she had been heard. Not that he would go himself; he'd send Raphael. Michael rarely went to Earth. It was more his brothers' jam.

"Well, calling on the gods will do her no good," Raphael said with a little laugh, and they shared a knowing grin.

"She is afraid, though, Raph," he told his favorite brother. Michael could sense her anguish. "Something is not right here."

Michael watched as the upset female lifted her head so he was finally able to get a good, clear look at her. She wiped her tears, and as her hand fell away, his mouth fell open.

"Fuck me," he whispered under his breath, taking a sudden step back.

"What?"

"What?" He ran a hand over his face and turned to Raphael as if the guy had only just appeared. "What? Oh. Nothing."

Raphael's eyes narrowed at him, which he ignored.

His eyes went straight back to the woman who was

now getting ready to sleep. With a dry mouth, he clenched his fist as a tear escaped and ran down her cheek.

This was his female. No. Not his. THE female.

From his dreams.

At last.

CHAPTER TWO

Michael drew in a deep breath. He couldn't believe he'd found her.

For nearly two hundred years, she'd appeared in his dreams, where he'd been haunted by her beauty, and worse, by the sight of her dying as she screamed his name. He had eventually consulted the Oracle and been told she hadn't been born yet, but she would be important. And now he had found her.

Or rather, she had called to him.

He didn't believe in fate. He was an archangel. His Father created life, and they were ruled by one primary law: free will.

Michael didn't know what his role would be in this delicate yet fiery woman's life, but he knew she had called to him personally for a reason.

And he was going to find out why.

He waved away the vision.

"Hey!"

He glanced at Raphael with a raised eyebrow.

"What? She's entertaining." Raphael grinned. "Alright, fun police. I'm heading back to Earth in a few hours, so I'll head to her house and check this out."

Like fuck.

Raphael, Archangel of Healing, was busy with Earth's pandemic; not that they could interfere. Free will yada, yada.

Michael shook his head and made the rare decision to head to Earth for the first time in a long damn time.

Centuries.

"No. She called for me, so I will go."

"Really? To Earth?"

"Yes, Raphael. To Earth." He rolled his eyes.

Michael was the Supreme and led the seven archangels. When necessary—which was often—they respected him as their leader. But he was also a brother, so whenever they could—and that was also often—they did what brothers did: bullshit banter, play fights (it was lucky they were immortal), and teasing the shit out of each other.

But at the end of the day, he was the head of God's army, and none of them ever forgot it. Or at least he didn't let them forget it. They called him grumpy. He called it leadership.

Over his shoulder, Raphael called out, "Let me know how you get on. I'm intrigued."

So was he. And concerned. No human should have been able to breach Heaven's walls like that, and yet, she had.

Michael wanted to meet this human.

He needed answers after hundreds of years of seeing her in his dreams and the impact she'd just had physically in Heaven. He threw on a pair of dark jeans which clung to his large, solid legs, pulled on a blue Huffer t-shirt, whoever Huffer was, and added some sneakers.

Splashing water on his face, he looked in the mirror. Michael was large, larger than his brothers, and at six foot five and two hundred and sixty pounds of muscle, he was substantially bigger than most humans. The thought of intimidating the woman worried him, but also sent a thrill running through his body.

Pushing away the unfamiliar feelings, he reminded himself that he did not fornicate with humans.

Ever.

This human needed him, and he would help her. Perhaps even save her life.

He stretched out his wings, the ethereal white, glistening feathers spanning wide, then lifted into the air.
At last.

CHAPTER THREE

Sara rolled over for the hundredth time, and the cat jumped off the bed, irritated by all the movement.

"Ugh, now I can't sleep."

She stared into the darkness, feeling the shadows fall around the room, and shivered. She felt like she was being watched, which was ridiculous.

"Well, big mouth, you just conjured up every divine being in the universe," she berated herself.

She turned on her lamp and pulled out her diary. Turning to her last entry, she realized it had been over a year since she'd last written. That had been the day she'd discovered her fiancé had been unfaithful. She'd kicked him out a few days later, and while nursing her broken heart, she had been given notice by her landlady.

She had story after story of tragedy and bad luck in her life leading back to her childhood. Her mother had died when she was five. Her father had emotionally abused and neglected her until, finally, she had cut him out of her life, knowing he would never change. Alone with no family, no partner, and no financial security, Sara had felt worn down and mentally exhausted.

Sara flipped to the back of her diary and looked at the list she'd made that day. The one which remained the same even today. She didn't want much. She wanted what most people wanted and, it seemed, most people achieved.

Own a home.

Meet the love of my life.

Have financial security.

"Can't you just help a girl out, for crying out loud! Haven't I suffered enough?" She sniffed. "I give to charity. I'm a good, kind, and loving friend. I recycle and care for animals. Come on!"

Well, it was worth one last shot.

Letting out a long sigh, Sara put the notebook away. She turned off the light and suddenly felt a warm, protective, comforting feeling wrap around her. Like she'd been hugged by her grandmother who had long since passed.

"Who's there?" She felt something against her arm. "You better not have sent a damn cherub to placate me."

Was that a snort?

"Oh, man, I am losing it. What is wrong with me?"

She really was losing it. It wasn't as if some magical creature was going to show up in her bedroom with a goody bag and a signed apology from the cosmos. Though it would be a good start if they were thinking about it.

She slid down under the sheets.

"Angels." She snorted. "Total load of rubbish."

She'd think of a better plan tomorrow—she had plenty of time on her hands now.

Michael stood at the end of the bed, watching the female he'd dreamed about for almost two hundred years mumble. While it was mildly amusing, he was distracted by his curiosity about her.

She was a human. He had no doubt about that. He'd been expecting to find traces of witch energy or perhaps something else, but he had not.

But he had found something.

His own ever-increasing desire to protect and comfort her. Observing her in a state of fear and anguish was uncomfortable. He wanted to touch her, but she had already sensed him once, so he clenched his fists.

He ran his eyes over her body and took in her long, dark-blonde hair which spread across her pillow. As she turned to get comfortable, her nightgown twisted and exposed a hard pink nipple. He clenched his fists tighter and let out a soft curse.

Never had he desired a human, male or female.

Perhaps it was the buildup from seeing her in his dreams for so many years and now here she lay, her soft, creamy skin, angelic hair, and lightning spirit.

She was alive.

And he planned to ensure it stayed that way.

He didn't know if his dreams were a premonition or a powerful message that he needed to protect her, but it was clear he would be doing the latter. He was drawn to this human in such a strong way, he couldn't have ignored her even if he'd wanted to. And he really didn't.

Michael didn't believe in premonitions, even though he had visited the Oracle to understand his dreams—or nightmares, as they'd become. One minute he would be enjoying her body; the next she would be lying in his arms, dying.

It had to be a message.

She had called to him for help. How she'd done it so directly raised a big question, but there was a link here, and he'd find it.

For now, he'd watch over her while she rested.

"Sleep, little one," he whispered, brushing angelic light over her. "You have my protection."

"Hmpphh," she mumbled as if wanting to have the last word, then dozed off.

This time, he smirked.

Michael gave himself a moment to push the strap of her nightgown back up onto her shoulder. His finger lingered.

Shit. She was so soft and delicate.

He pulled his hand away and made a fist. No more.

He needed to do as he promised. Focusing, he closed his eyes and scanned her life history. After a moment, he shook his head. This human had led a challenging life. Not one of war and violence but one with an unreasonable quota of bad luck, abuse, and lack of love. He scanned for curses or evil entities and found none.

His eyebrows furrowed. Something didn't add up.

He'd noticed her energy field was incredibly bright when he'd arrived, and yet, she was still only human; a standard, off-the-rack human being.

As an archangel, Michael viewed life in multiple dimensions; he saw things as energy. After God, archangels had the brightest light, whereas humans had a smaller energy footprint. They were like staring at the lights of a city from an airplane. Most humans looked like the average suburban home.

But Sara was different; she shone like a large city in comparison, dominant and dazzling.

He shook his head.

She was a mystery he was going to solve, one way or the other. And that meant revealing himself to her and asking some questions.

He stared at the stunningly beautiful woman before him and realized he'd have to use a good deal of self-control around her. He was infamous for his willpower, but he suspected it was about to be tested.

He'd never wanted to touch a female as much as he did right now. Hopefully, her smart-mouth would turn him off, but he doubted it. If anything, her sass made him smile.

It would serve him well to remember his dreams of her had not been real, that they had been for a higher purpose: to send him to her so he could solve his mystery and protect her. He had no doubt.

And so, Michael decided to appoint himself as her personal archangel.

Now, that was a first.

CHAPTER FOUR

The next morning, Sara stretched blissfully across the entire bed. She'd just had the best sleep she'd had in years.

"Good morning, Tilly."

Curled up at the bottom of her bed, the cat yawned and rolled onto her back, looking as content as she felt.

Sara showered and dressed in a pair of denim shorts, T-shirt, and a pair of white sneakers. Hands on hips, she stared at her average height and slim figure in the mirror. She tilted her head. She had new curves, courtesy of all the banana bread baking she and half the world were doing to ease lockdown boredom.

She shrugged. She had bigger problems than her jean size right now.

"Another day in lockdown paradise, Tilly. What excitement can we get up to in our little prison today?"

Sarcasm was one of her superpowers, but it was wasted on the cat, so she wandered through her home, opening up the curtains, letting the sunshine pour in.

Sara was grateful to have found such a sunny, north-facing home. In the southern hemisphere, everything was the opposite, so Kiwis lined up looking for the best positioned home to capture the sun from the north, while news of a southern breeze made them shiver. Antarctica wasn't far away, and a shifting wind could plummet temperatures quickly.

Feeding the feline, Sara started mixing the protein shake she drank every day.

"Hold on to your hat, Tilly. Things around here are about to get wild. I'm adding cinnamon today." She laughed as the cat yawned.

She stepped out onto the large, sunny deck and sat in the sunshine. Around her, pretty flowers blossomed and palm trees swayed in the warm breeze.

Memories of her breakdown the night before returned, and she groaned. She knew she should be grateful, and she was; it would just be nice if things didn't turn chaotic so frequently. It was giving her whiplash. Surely one person couldn't have this much bad luck.

Then, feeling righteous once again, she made sure any universal beings who were paying attention knew she was serious about her threats. She lifted her hand skyward, giving them the middle finger.

Leaning on the doorframe nearby, Michael grinned.

God, this little human had spunk, and he was trying really damn hard to ignore how incredibly beautiful she was.

She'd been in his dreams for an awfully long time, so to be standing here with her was surreal. He had expected to feel protective of her, and yes, there had been passion in the dreams, but he'd never thought he'd feel this strongly in real life. She was human, after all. He had never been attracted to a human before last night.

Over the years, he'd imagined all kinds of scenarios to why he was seeing her. He had imagined a disease or an accident, perhaps even a war. Michael had assumed his role was, as Lord Protector, to save this female, and free will be damned, he had intended to do just that.

He believed in his Father's plan. He wouldn't have sent her to him in his dreams for no purpose. Sure, he'd been surprised when he had first started shooting awake screaming her name, his chest covered in sweat. But over time, it had created such a bond between the then unborn human and himself that he couldn't imagine standing back and allowing her to die, if that was actually what would take place and not just a metaphor delivered through his dreams for another purpose; then, he had no idea what it could be.

Now here he was, trying to keep his damn cock down so he could present himself to the beautiful female.

If he'd been any one of his other brothers, he knew they'd have strutted straight out, stiff cock and all. Absolutely no shame. Massive pride. Yeah, they copulated with humans on the regular.

Michael, on the other hand, kept to a healthy diet of goddesses, angels, and a handful of other species. And when he said handful, he meant an archangel-sized handful. He was never short of options. He was the Archangel Michael, the most powerful being in the realm.

And yet, after being pleasured by some of the most stunning creatures across the universe, it was the human—or at least, he was 99 percent sure she was simply human—in front of him who held his attention more powerfully than any other being he could remember.

He had waited for her morning ritual to end, but was now out of patience. He walked out onto the front lawn and made himself visible. As he was just out of her line of sight, Michael waited for her to put her glass down before he spoke.

"Good morning, Sara." He failed to hide his smile as she sprayed water out of her nose.

Coughing and spluttering, Sara wiped her mouth against her arm and stared at the incredibly large and handsome man standing on the grass.

"Holy shit, you gave me a fright." She coughed, pointing to her mouth. "Not coronavirus, just water."

"I know." He grinned.

"How did you get in here?" She dabbed at her mouth with a napkin and noticed the gate was still closed.

She was struggling to focus. It wasn't like she was a fumbling fool around good-looking men—okay, maybe she was—but there was something about his presence which simply took her breath away.

He was one of the largest men she'd ever seen. His arms were like tree trunks; really smooth, tanned, muscular trees with equally solid thighs. But his eyes were what captured her. They were the bluest, most surreal eyes she'd ever seen. Even from this distance, they stood out bright and clear. Obviously, they were contacts, as there was no way they were real. Vain much?

The man stood with his legs wide and hands jammed into his jeans pockets.

"You invited me," he replied.

"I…what now?" While her brain caught up, she realized they were breaking lockdown laws. "Actually, we probably shouldn't get too close, so if you could just stay over there."

He might be hot as hell, but he wasn't allowed in her bubble. Nobody was.

Fucking bubbles.

Once you'd defined who was in your bubble at the beginning of lockdown, you weren't allowed to add anyone else. Her bubble included her and Tilly, and that was it.

"I am Michael." He smiled calmly at her again, and she wondered if he might be simple. A shame, she sighed. It's always the hot ones.

"Nice to meet you, Mike, but I'm afraid I'm going to have to ask you to leave." She stood up and waved as if to see him off the property. "Bubbles and all that. We'd better not get caught."

One of her neighbors only had to ring the police hotline and report them. And they would. People all around the world were taking this very seriously.

The man didn't move. He simply stood there, looking at her.

Irritated because there were only so many steps she could take before breaking the six feet social distance rule—goddamn this fucking virus—she put her hands on her hips.

"Look, Mike. I'm sorry, but you can't just come onto my property, especially during a pan-fucking-demic. So can you please go, or should I call the police?"

Frankly, she was out of patience with everyone right now. Even if he was drop dead gorgeous.

Damn it.

His smile fell.

Finally, some progress.

He took a step toward her, and calm washed over her like she'd drunk a supercharged cup of chamomile tea. Dosed with kava. Suddenly, her body relaxed in places she didn't know were tense.

"Let me introduce myself properly. I am Archangel Michael. Last night, you made a very loud demand of me. So here I am."

What the hell?

Sara felt her legs wobble, and the world went black.

CHAPTER FIVE

Michael had been expecting her to faint.

As archangels, they rarely declared themselves to humans. His brothers socialized with them often, yes, but under the guise of being humans. There was rarely a good way to go about doing it without a shock, so he'd just come straight out and introduced himself.

He'd caught her before she hit the ground, and now carried the sleeping beauty inside. He laid her down on the sofa and moved to sit in the opposite chair. Waving a hand, he woke her up.

Her eyes flickered, and then slowly opened.

Michael watched as she took in the room around her before spotting him. She leaped to her feet.

"What did you do to me?"

"I caught you and carried you inside." He leaned back in the chair, attempting to look less threatening, which was ridiculous, considering how large and powerful he was.

She sat back down, glaring at him while rubbing her forehead. "Great. Bubble burst."

"I am an archangel, Sara. We cannot get, nor share, the virus."

Sara crossed her arms and frowned at him.

Michael tried not to notice her top lifting, showing off the tanned skin underneath, or the white tassels on her shorts contrasting against her sexy legs.

He really tried, but he failed.

Licking his lips, he forced his eyes to her face and

noticed she was slightly flushed with a blush he recognized as attraction.

He swallowed.

God, he was happy she was blushing. Too damn happy.

"Archangel," she muttered as if trying the word out.

He nodded.

Her eyes narrowed.

"You don't believe me." This wasn't his first rodeo, so he'd expected Sara to have doubts.

"Of course I don't."

Michael looked around and spotted a box of tissues on the coffee table. He looked at her, and she looked at him. He looked at the tissues, then back at her. She looked at the tissues and then gasped when they disappeared and reappeared in his hands.

"Oh my God." Her hand flew to her chest, and she jumped to her feet.

"Close." He winked, unable to help himself. "But you'll have to deal with me today, I'm afraid."

"I didn't…" Her mouth was gaping. "I said…"

He stood and moved across the room to stand in front of her. "You did, and yes, you do. Please be calm. I won't hurt you. You're safe, Sara."

She leaned away from him, and he sent another shimmer of calming light over her.

"How do you know my name? Hey, stop doing that!" she exclaimed, waving her hand around.

"You can feel that?" he asked, his eyes widening in surprise. Michael knew of no other human who was able to sense energy as she just had.

"Yes." She glanced at him, looking nervous.

He stared at her a moment before deciding to let it go for now. He would learn what he needed to in time, and time was something he had in spades, being an immortal and all.

"It's just to calm you. Now, let's get down to business. You called for me personally. Why?"

"I honestly didn't, well…" She shrugged. "I really don't know any of the others' names."

Oh. Okay. Not offended.

Much.

"Okay, never mind. Let's just skip right to your list." Michael's fingers were tingling with the need to reach out and touch her. For so long he'd watched her in his dreams, and now she was here, in front of him.

And far bolder than he'd expected.

"Give me a minute," she said, running her hands through her long hair. "Anyway, if you are who you say you are, then you received my wish list last night."

He raised an eyebrow at her.

"Alright, demands."

Michael moved back to his chair and looked at her pointedly. "So, Sara, you have the Supreme Archangel at your disposal. What do you want?"

To his surprise, the sassy human raised her eyebrows and said, "You know, I expected a little less ego and a bit more humility."

Michael let out a huge laugh.

CHAPTER SIX

Seriously, what a douchebag.

The man in her living room might be incredibly gorgeous and one of the most muscular men she had ever seen, but he was also the most arrogant. And a lunatic.

He was no angel.

She rubbed her head. Clearly, she'd hit it when she fainted.

"Sorry to disappoint you." He continued laughing.

"That's fine. I've never been hugely religious." She shrugged. She needed to get him out of her house. For one, they were breaching lockdown rules, and two, he was clearly a little bit deranged. Playing it cool, she stood up and stretched, walking toward the front door. "But look, thanks for popping down to Earth. The only wish I really have is for this pandemic to be cleared up fast, so if you could sort that out, I'd be very grateful."

Michael lifted his ankle up onto his knee and got comfortable. He wasn't going anywhere.

"We cannot interfere with the free will of humans, so I'm sorry, Sara. What else is on your list?"

"Figures," she mumbled, unable to help herself.

"Sara, please sit."

Every word out of his mouth was authoritative. He had a power about him that was starting to freak her out. She looked around for her cell phone and began patting her pockets.

No phone.

It was probably out on the patio where she had fainted.

Even if she could get to it, he looked strong enough to tackle her. A trace of regret at the fact he was potentially dangerous crossed her mind, because damn, the man was hot.

Sara glanced outside and wondered how quickly she could run to the neighbor's house.

Not fast enough.

Okay, new tactic.

"Look, Michael, or whatever your name is, you're a pretty hot guy, but we really shouldn't be in the same room together right now. Perhaps you can give me your number, and we can have a drink after lockdown."

Over my dead body.

He didn't move.

"Let me see you out; it's no big deal." She waved her hand around her face, all totally cool.

Michael stood and stared at her for a moment, then began walking toward her.

What were the chances of him walking right past and waving on his way out? Nil, she suspected.

He stopped in front of her, a foot away, and as he stared down at her, she reminded herself to breathe. His stunningly big blue eyes sparkled as they held her in a near frozen state.

She swallowed.

Her mind was torn between getting the stranger out of her home and having a huge amount of trouble ignoring the chemistry flowing between them.

He wasn't the first man she'd felt immediate lust for, but it had never been to this degree. She could barely remember her name.

"I'm trying not to scare you, Sara, but you obviously need more proof."

A shiver ran through her body. When she began to protest, he took a step closer, then his hands were on her face, and a delicious warmth replaced the chill.

She wanted to hum. Or purr. Or both.

"You're safe. Open your eyes, Sara."

She hadn't realized she'd closed them, but as her lids lifted, she saw he was glowing. Not like a candle; it was more like the corona during a solar eclipse or the glow around the sun at sunset. She reached out and touched him to make sure he was real.

"This isn't possible," she said, blinking.

"You're a tough audience," he replied with a small smirk. "I can only show you so much, Sara. The human mind can only...wait, how about this. Ask me for something."

"What?"

He took her hand in his. "Ask me for something. Anything that could fit in your hand right now. Something random I could never guess in as much detail as you can. Anything."

"Um, a diamond bangle?" She grinned and quietly prided herself on her fast thinking. "Diamonds around the entire thing. Not spaced out, side by side. In white gold."

He raised an eyebrow.

"Anything else?"

"Yes, please make it oval; I don't really like the round ones."

Okay, where had that all come from?

"It is done. Watch, little human."

He raised his hand, and sparkles flicked from his fingers as he twirled them before suddenly catching something in midair. She followed his hand as he placed the bangle in her palm and closed her fingers over it.

The wheels in Sara's brain jumbled as her mouth fell open. His firm hand enveloped hers around the piece of jewelry. She closed her eyes and focused on her breathing until she felt a finger under her chin.

"I'm real," he whispered gently.

She nodded and felt him place the bracelet on her arm.

Opening her eyes, she looked down at the bangle for a long moment.

"Sara, look at me."

Tipping her head up, she swallowed and began shaking.

"Are you okay?"

She nodded and felt energy flow between them as they gazed at one another.

Then it hit her.

"Oh God, I'm sorry," she apologized. "You're an archangel. And I yelled."

Michael nodded and gave her a small smile.

She lifted her hand and looked at the bangle. "And also—holy shit!"

It seemed ridiculous to focus on the piece of jewelry when she had an archangel standing in front of her, but she'd heard shock did weird things to your brain.

Also. Diamond bangle. Hello. She was in shock, not dead.

She had wanted one of these her entire life.

Suddenly, she felt embarrassed about her attraction to the archangel. And yet she couldn't ignore the fact that he still appeared to be the most muscular and gorgeous man she'd ever seen.

But he wasn't. He was one of God's archangels. She wasn't religious, but even she knew that was a damn big deal. Plus, she needed to stop saying damn and a bunch of other words now.

Damn it.

Ugh.

She'd work on that.

She realized they were standing inappropriately close, so she began to step away.

"Don't," he commanded, voice thick, before cupping her cheek.

Sara's gaze found its way to his lips then back up to his

sparkling blue eyes. The air around them sizzled, and she drew in a breath, waiting, she realized, for him to kiss her.

So damn wrong.

But would he?

His mouth opened slightly as he moved closer, their bodies nearly touching. Heat blazed between them, and everything else around them blurred into oblivion.

Her heart began to race as her lips parted...

"I need to go," he said suddenly, shattering the moment. He stepped away, shaking his head. "Now. Right now."

She coughed. "Sure, yes, right. You should go."

He ran a hand over his face and looked at her again, his expression one of frustration. "I will return. Be ready with your list of demands, Sara."

She nodded, her bottom lip stuck between her teeth.

He stared at her for a moment longer, then vanished.

Vanished.

She crumpled to the floor.

CHAPTER SEVEN

Michael paced back and forth in his chambers. He'd flown around for hours before feeling calm enough to head home.

But he had been wrong. He wasn't calm at all.

I nearly fucking kissed her! he berated himself.

The problem was, he wasn't sure if his regret was because he had nearly kissed her or because he hadn't fucking done it.

The usual flow of prayers had flowed in, and he had tended to them the best he could, but for the first time in his existence, Michael had felt completely out of kilter. Eventually, he'd delegated his prayers to the other archangels, as they did from time to time, so he could regain focus.

Worst move ever.

With more time to think and no distractions, he was even more aware of how his body craved to be near her. After seeing her in his dreams for so long, he hadn't expected to feel like this.

Protective? Maybe.

Attracted? Never.

Who am I?

More pacing.

I have never desired a human.

And not because he was dead inside. Michael had a rich and active sex life; all seven archangels did. They just weren't monogamous. He'd always assumed it was because they weren't able to procreate.

Still, he craved touch, sex, and pleasure like all other living beings. Just never with a human. That he'd dreamed of this female for so long and felt such a strong desire was unnerving enough. But there was something else. A feeling unlike anything he'd felt or understood before.

He wanted to protect her and...possess her. First with his lips, then with his body. Then? Deeper. Something he didn't understand and wasn't ready to look at.

So he had fled, for both their sakes.

Sara was vulnerable and in need of angelic assistance. He would return as promised and fulfill her prayers. One thing Michael would not do was take advantage of her.

She deserved better.

Letting out a huge laugh, he realized his arrogance. Likely she'd allow him a kiss, but Sara was no pushover. Assuming he could fuck her? Well, that would be at his own downfall.

And damn, that turned him on.

For millennia, women had desired him. The male in him knew Sara was attracted to him, but she would never beg. Nor did she need to. No female—goddess, angel, or otherwise—had had such an impact on him.

He sensed his brother Jophiel before he burst through the doors.

"Bro, what's going on?"

"Nothing. Why?" Michael turned, frowning.

"You redirected all your traffic my way. I'm always happy to help, but I can't take the total load, Michael."

"What do you mean?"

"You sent me all your prayers. All of them."

Michael narrowed his eyes. "I apologize."

Shit.

He felt like an ass. As the most powerful archangel and the most called upon, his load was heavy. Michael thought he'd divvied it up across all six of his brothers.

His head was so filled with Sara he'd stuffed up.

He never stuffed up.

"Is everything okay?"

Michael wondered what Sara was doing right now. If she was upset after he'd left her. Or was she confused?

He shouldn't have left. He should return.

Jophiel cleared his throat.

Crap.

"Sorry, brother. I've been distracted. Let me…" Michael reached out energetically for his connection to humanity.

What the actual fuck?

Nothing happened. He heard nothing. Not a single prayer.

"What the hell!" he growled, his hands dropping to his sides.

Raphael appeared in the doorway. "What's going on?"

Yeah, exactly what I'm wondering.

"I've unplugged from humanity. I can't sense anything," Michael replied between gritted teeth. The two brothers looked at each other for a second, then turned as Gabriel entered the room.

"Hey. You on holiday or something?" Gabriel grinned cheekily.

This was bad.

Really, really bad.

He'd only meant to redirect his prayers for a few hours while he got his thinking straight. Instead, he'd dumped it all on poor Jophiel and had completely disconnected, something he'd never done in his entire existence.

"How is that possible?" Raphael asked.

"I will fix this," Michael said firmly.

Uriel pushed through the three angels standing in the doorway. "Did someone forget to invite me?" He winked. "Where are we going?"

"There's no party, Uri. Michael's on unpaid leave,"

Gabe teased, not yet realizing the seriousness of the matter.

Michael crossed his arms and faced all four of them, expecting Zadkiel and Chamuel to show up any minute now. He loved all his brothers, and like any siblings, they bickered and teased each other a lot. But right now, he wasn't their brother; he was their leader.

This was serious.

If he had unplugged from humanity, then what other powers had he lost? As the Supreme Archangel, this wasn't a joke. Heaven could be at risk.

"I cannot hear any of humanity's prayers, and who knows what else. Give me a few hours," Michael said as authoritatively as he could. "I'm…"—he cleared his throat—"I'm dealing with an unusual case."

"Is this about that girl?" Raphael, the big mouth, asked.

"No," he answered too fast, and they all grinned at him.

"No!" he repeated more forcefully, and the grins turned to smirks. Michael put his hands on his hips.

"I'll fix this." He looked them in the eye. "Will you be okay, or do I need to call Father to help your pussy asses?"

Quickly, they all shook their heads and groaned. It was never a wise move to include God in anything unnecessary.

"We'll be fine. Go get your girl."

"She's not my gi—look, it's just an unusual case."

"Had one of those in Houston recently." Gabriel nodded knowingly, and Raphael choked on a cough.

Michael shook his head. They tested his patience some days.

Most days.

"Get out of here," he ordered, and they all smiled before sauntering off.

Son.

At last. His request for an audience had been answered. Humans imagined the archangels were able to speak to God at any old time. It definitely didn't work that way. No open-door policy in Heaven—except for his own chambers, it seemed.

He appeared in front of his Father. "My Lord."

"Michael."

"I need your help."

One never knew what environment they were going to appear in when they met with God. Today, it was an old-fashioned library filled with books and scrolls. Ladders leaned against floor-to-ceiling shelves as light filtered in from a glass skylight.

God walked to a desk and sat down. "No, you don't."

Oh, great.

He was in that kind of mood.

"Father, I don't have time for this. I've disconnected from humanity." As soon as the words left his mouth, he wished he could turn back time, but unfortunately, he didn't possess that skill. Getting an attitude with God never achieved very much. "Look, I'm s—"

God held up his hand and stopped him. "Son, I feel your anguish over this."

Then he stared.

And stared.

Maybe time was in fact able to be manipulated. He waited and waited for God to speak further.

He didn't.

Michael arched an eyebrow, which got him a smirk. Finally, he sat down on the couch, lifted his ankle over his knee, and sighed. "She's human."

"Yes."

"It's totally inappropriate."

"Is it?"

"Are you telling me to copulate with humans, Father?"

There was no way he was, but Michael couldn't help taunting him. It was a family trait. God wasn't a fan of the archangels' playboy tendencies, but couldn't stop them. Sometimes, free will was a bitch for everyone.

"She needs your help, Michael. Return to her."

Before he could respond, Michael found himself back in his chambers.

And humans thought they had daddy issues.

He let out a groan.

CHAPTER EIGHT

Nope, that did not happen.

"It didn't happen. Nope. No way. Impossible."

Despite the bangle on her arm, Sara was still finding it difficult to believe the man who had been in her home the day before had been Archangel Michael.

But who went around handing out twenty-thousand-dollar diamond bangles? Assuming it was real, and Sara was pretty sure she knew a real diamond from a fake.

Standing in the shower, she touched her cheek where his hand had been. "Please tell me I didn't make him up in my head."

Drying off, Sara put on a white, midlength sundress and long cardigan. She ran her fingers through her hair and added some lip balm.

"No bras in lockdown, Tilly," she said to the cat twirling around her legs as her screen lit up with a FaceTime call from her bestie.

"Hey, gorgeous!" Sara answered.

She had met Lisa when they worked together nearly ten years ago. She was a natural salesperson, and boy, could she talk an Eskimo into a big bag of ice. Or ten.

"How bored are you? I'm dying here."

Lisa was also a social butterfly. While Sara happily curled up with a book on the weekends, Lisa was out hitting the city's hot spots and going to all kinds of events. But despite their differences, they were like sisters and shared a love of cafés, hiking, and shopping.

And yet, she strongly felt she should keep her visitor a secret. Also, saying, "Oh, hey, super busy here with archangels popping in and out," would have made her sound crazier than she already felt, so she opted for the safer conversation.

"So bored. Have you heard from Dave?" Lisa's current boyfriend. Or lover. She was never sure where the relationship was at.

"Yes, we've been catching up on Zoom every day," her friend replied. "I'm not sure about him anymore, though."

Sara sighed and sat on the edge of her bed. Her friend went through men like she did paper towels. But at least Lisa was out there dating—Sara had all but given up on men. Or at least human men.

She hadn't been able to stop thinking about Michael. Aside from questioning her sanity, her body had wriggled for hours in bed the night before as she recalled the little shivers she'd felt as his stunning blue eyes gazed over her. Eventually, she'd slipped her hand between her thighs and found her sensitive spot.

"Don't make any decisions right now. These are unprecedented times. Life is just weird."

"Wise advice, my friend. So what are you going to do about work right now?" Lisa asked.

"I don't know." She chewed her lower lip. "The job market is pretty much dead."

"I'm sorry."

"Well, you know my luck."

"Girl, you do have the worst luck. But you also bounce back. You'll get through this."

Not for the first time, Sara wished she had her friend's optimism, but as her therapist had once said, "Lisa had loving and available parents, which created a security and sense of self you never had." It affected a person. A lot.

But it didn't mean she couldn't create it herself. It just took work.

"I will. This too shall pass."

"Well, girl, I was just checking in on you. I'm off for a run. Talk in a few days, okay?" Lisa said, and a few air kisses later, they hung up.

Sara's stomach growled, reminding her it was time for breakfast. She wandered into the living room, where she suddenly ground to a halt.

"Oh, damn."

"Hello, Sara," Michael greeted.

"I was kind of hoping you weren't real."

Michael stood with his legs spread and huge, muscular arms crossed. He smirked. "Is that true?"

No. But she wasn't about to feed his ego, so she shrugged. A wasted effort, as they both could feel the sparks flying between them. Her tummy filled with butterflies as a delicious shiver spread through her body.

Damn it.

A crease appeared at the corner of Michael's blue eyes, and they sparkled with amusement.

"It appears I need to finish what I started." He walked toward her, his eyes never leaving hers.

She swallowed.

He took her hand and led her toward the dining room table.

Wait.

Had she misread him? She blushed and began to question herself. Perhaps all archangels emitted a sexual charge, and every damn female they came in contact with reacted like this. She was just another human desiring him. He felt nothing for her.

Ugh. What an idiot I am.

It must be like the vampires in the books she read. Did archangels have some magical mojo to make women want them?

Well, she wasn't about to make more of a fool of herself, so she took a deep breath and ignored her traitorous body as Michael sat facing her. He looked all serious, which just confirmed she had read the entire situation wrong.

Sex was definitely not on his mind.

Wait, do archangels have sex?

She felt herself blush even brighter.

"You okay?"

"Yes." She shook her head, then nodded stupidly. "So, you're real."

"I am."

At least she wasn't crazy. A small consolation.

"Well, thanks for coming back." Sara felt like she was having a meeting with her bank manager. A really damn hot bank manager—whom she would not think of as hot anymore.

"I promised I would." He looked away from her and scratched his jaw. Despite all her efforts, her body tingled, and she wanted nothing more than for him to reach out and touch her. Kiss her.

Oh hell, I hope he can't read my mind.

She let out a little laugh.

"What?"

"Nothing." She shook her head.

Michael narrowed his eyes a little, and then they dropped down and ran over her body.

She shivered.

Finally, he closed his eyes.

"Sara. I'm here to answer your prayers. And I want to discuss with you how you reached me so in Heaven," he said, opening his eyes. His gaze was deep and heated.

She nodded, blushing.

Stop lusting after the archangel.

Michael leaned forward. "You're not the first human to yell at me. There's no need to be embarrassed."

"No." She shook her head. "I'm not embarrassed."

She didn't want him to think she regretted anything she had said that night. Regardless of her inappropriate attraction to the archangel, Sara really felt she had been served a raw deal in life. Something felt off, and she had this gift of an opportunity to ask for what she wanted. She wasn't going to waste it.

"Yet you blush. Why?" he asked, leaning back in his chair.

Oh.

No way was she going to tell him she was highly attracted to him. Did he not know? The guy was giving her whiplash. One minute he looked at her like they were in a business meeting, the next, like he wanted to lick every inch of her. But she wasn't going to say any of that. She'd rather die.

"Coronavirus fever," she replied, shrugging.

He narrowed his eyes and frowned. "You're not infected with the virus."

"Look, it doesn't matter. Shall we continue?" she said flustered, flinging out her hands.

"Tell me or I will read your mind," he demanded.

Her eyes widened.

Hell no!

"You can do that?" she asked, panicked. She was in serious trouble if he could. She might, in fact, actually die of shame if he read her mind.

"I'm an archangel. Of course I can."

"Are you always such an asshole?" she asked, shaking her head.

He grinned.

"No. Well, maybe." His grin disappeared. "Nevertheless, it appears you bring out the worst in me. Now spill."

She glared at him.

She had two options: tell him she was attracted to him and apologize, or let him read her embarrassing thoughts.

It was better if she edited them.

"Fine," she moaned, dropping her face into her hands. "I thought you were going to kiss me the other day. I'm not religious, but I'm fairly certain that's not good. For you or me. Because you're an angel."

When there was simply silence, she peeked between her fingers and found Michael staring at her in what appeared to be pain.

"Obviously, I was wrong. Sorry. I'm an idiot."

Michael groaned then ran his hand through his hair.

And she was a nuisance, obviously.

"Let's get one thing clear. I did nearly kiss you."

Oh.

Sara's eyebrows shot to her hairline.

"It's something I've never, ever, done before. I apologize. It won't happen again," he added.

Sara was speechless. The archangel had nearly kissed her. Her. And never anyone else.

What did that mean?

Michael stared at her with his jaw clenched as her mouth gaped open.

She swallowed.

"It won't happen again," he had said, and she had to remember that.

"Okay," she replied quietly. "Then I guess that's…shall we get started?"

He glowered at her before his eyes dropped to her lips. Without thinking, she licked them and heard him groan. His eyes flew back to hers, a storm now brewing in them.

He may be an archangel, but Sara knew powerful chemistry when she felt it, and theirs was out of this world. Heat pooled in her core, and she tried to ignore it, but with his eyes all over her, it was impossible.

They needed to get this over with, and fast.

The good thing was, she wouldn't bump into him at the mall once he left.

CHAPTER NINE

"I am not an angel."

"What?"

"You called me an angel. I'm an archangel."

She frowned at him, and Michael felt like an idiot, something foreign to him. He didn't know why he had said it—well, that wasn't true. He hated being called an angel, and humans often mixed them up.

Call it a pet peeve.

He knew he was trying to distract himself from the powerful and overwhelming attraction flowing between them. What he really wanted to do was pull her body against his and claim those gorgeous, plush lips.

"I'm sorry."

He shook his head. The quicker he did this, the sooner he could leave. "Okay, let's get to your prayers, Sara."

Trouble was, he didn't want to leave.

He wanted to touch her, find out what was under that sundress and...fuck it, he wanted to bury himself deep inside her.

But he had to focus on the bigger picture here. His attraction to Sara had caused a complete shutdown from humanity, and he had to fix this. He figured if he answered her prayers and then found release on his own or with another female, he'd reconnect.

It was a theory.

Strangely, the thought of taking another female didn't appeal to him. He wanted her. So his hand would have to do.

He still had no idea why she had come to him in his dreams and haunted him for so long, or why her energy was greater than other humans' energy. But if he stayed too long, he wasn't sure he would be able to control himself or if he really wanted to.

Which messed with his brain because he never, ever, copulated with humans.

So why now? Why this attraction to her?

He swallowed a groan.

"Let's start at the top. Why were you screaming at us? Me?"

"Cats."

"Cats?"

Michael's eyes furrowed as he looked down at the cat sitting at their feet. The long-haired feline followed her everywhere.

"Yes. People are killing their cats. I heard on the news people can't afford to keep them because of this damn virus. I snapped. It felt like the last straw. But what I really want to do is speak to someone about the bad luck in my life."

Michael felt the ripples of her sadness flow over him. That was new. Usually, he had to tap into a human to feel their emotions. More unusual was the desire to pull her into his arms and comfort her.

As the Lord Protector, it was natural for him to care for humans, but this felt different. More intimate, just between the two of them.

He ran a hand over his face. He felt like he was losing control. What was going on with this female?

He took a breath. "Okay, first things first—"

"Let me guess, you can't stop people from hurting their pets because they have free will?"

Smart and beautiful.

"Correct." He nodded. "Or the virus. It's something

you have all cocreated."

Sara groaned and shook her head. "Great. I have the most powerful archangel at my disposal, and even you can't help these innocent animals. Goddamn."

"I'm sorry, Sara," he apologized, meaning every bit of that sentiment.

Tears built in her eyes, and he clenched his fists in his lap.

Do. Not. Touch. Her.

"I figured that was the case. I know I can only control my life, and it appears I've made a big mess of it so far. So I want some help."

Damn this human tugging at his heart.

"Why do you see your life as a failure?"

He had scanned her life history and knew many of the facts, but he wanted to hear them from her. What he knew was that Sara's mother had become extremely ill soon after she'd given birth to her. Sara had had no one to nurture her, as her father had been cold and unemotional, neglectful of his parental duties. Sara had brought herself up emotionally, and as a young woman, had ended up in relationships with the wrong men, desperate for love.

Those men had taken advantage of her, as had many people in her life. But she had one wonderful friend in a woman named Lisa.

Michael wondered if Sara was aware how all these experiences had made her grow into the beautiful, strong woman she was right now. Along the way, she had learned to love herself, and the broken people who had taken advantage of her had fallen away.

Away from all the people, family, and situations she would no longer put up with, she felt like her life was empty when, in fact, it had simply created space for new, much healthier relationships to show up. However, the pandemic had come along, and, in her vulnerability, her last thread had snapped.

Despite all his efforts, Michael was struggling to ignore the powerful need within him to protect this human. To hold her in a very nonparental way.

He knew what she was going to ask from him today. All archangels knew. On her list was a lover. A husband who would love her forever.

Michael clenched his jaw. Archangels didn't have monogamous—or romantic—relationships, yet he wanted to keep this human to himself. An irrational and selfish emotion he'd not experienced in…ever.

"Well, let me see. I have no financial security, I'm out of work, and the economy is shutdown," Sara started, her passion rising. She rose and began pacing the floor. "I was serious the other night. I've been dealt a tough few cards in life and have had enough of it."

She turned and pointed at him. "You have to help me, Michael. I deserve happiness, just like everyone else."

Michael.

Raph?

Raphael appeared in the living room behind them, remaining invisible. He spotted Sara.

I see you have your hands filled with this one. No begging?

Nope. Not at all.

She has suffered, Raphael noted, tilting his head.

Michael nodded.

"My requests are pretty simple. All I'm asking for is some financial security. A job, a windfall. Something." She fell silent, glancing away for a moment before her eyes returned to him. "And love."

He glanced away from her.

What is she? Her light is enormous.

Human. I can only sense humanity within her.

Then why are you so tense?

Why are you here, Raphael? he asked, ignoring his brother's question.

"You don't think I deserve love?" Sara asked, glaring at him as she sat down. His chest tightened.

"Everyone deserves love," he gritted out.

Leave us, Raphael.

"But not me?"

Michael stared over her shoulder at his brother. Raphael crossed his arms and smirked.

You like her. You really like her.

Leave. Now.

Raphael shook his head and vanished.

Sara stood up in a hurry. He stood and began to follow her, but she turned back to him, and they bumped into each other. He gripped her arms to steady her, and his hands burned as they held her soft, supple skin.

"I'm sorry." He felt her begin to shake.

"No. Sorry, I…"

He stared down at her using all his immense power to stop from lowering his lips to hers.

She swallowed.

He took a step away and immediately felt an enormous feeling of loss. He had to reconnect with humanity and get back to his eternal life.

"Is this your list?" He lifted a notebook off the table. "Come, show me. I must return to Heaven, so let's create a happier life for you."

Sara smiled sadly. "Of course, you have a lot of other people to help."

She doesn't want me to leave?

Why did that make him so happy?

"Yes. I'm an archangel."

"As you've said," she teased, a cheeky smile hitting her lips.

And damn, he wanted to pull her against him and kiss her.

He smirked.

"It's a pet peeve, okay?"

"Good to know."

They laughed and stood staring at each other, attraction between them flowing like a damn river.

How was this possible?

Michael wanted to snatch her up and flash her back to his bedroom. Of course, that was impossible; she would die if he did. It was Heaven, after all. Mortals could not enter.

He held out the notebook.

"Okay." Sara took it from him, smiled, and sat down. "I, um, didn't expect to read this out to you directly, of course, so it's pretty detailed."

He took in the blush on her cheeks and found himself delighted by her show of vulnerability yet again. She was beautiful, strong, and had just enough cheek to make him want to smile for hours. That, and his cock stood to attention whenever he was in her presence.

"So, I'd like my own house by the ocean where I can hear the waves. I want to be able to walk on the beach and dig my toes into the sand. I want to be debt free and have enough cash to last me a lifetime so I can follow my dreams instead of a paycheck."

He nodded. All of this he could give her and more.

She dropped the notebook and stared at him nervously. "These are just my dreams. I'm not sure what is possible, but whatever you can help me with today, I would appreciate."

Michael scanned her mind, taking in all the details of her dream home and the amount of money she truly wanted.

"It is done."

"Now? All of it?" she gasped.

"Yes."

He smiled and reached out a hand, pulling her to her feet.

Sara gripped Michael's forearm as her head spun for a moment.

Gone were the walls of her old home. Gone was the old ranchslider, and in its place, beautiful French doors led out to a garden, and beyond, the ocean. The house was larger, with two stories and a mix of her own and new furniture.

She pushed him away and raced outside.

"Tilly. Oh my God, Tilly, where are you?"

Sara swooped the feline up as it ran to her. "Oh, thank God. How did…?"

She turned to face him with tears in her eyes.

"You really are an archangel."

Michael found himself staring in wonder at how ridiculously happy it made him to please her. He'd never felt more alive than he did right now. The number of prayers he answered a day were infinite—he shouldn't feel such euphoria.

"Had we not already ascertained that?" Michael laughed and sent her a bold wink. She blushed, and his jeans tightened. His need for her grew stronger by the minute.

He groaned, knowing that if she looked down, she'd see his obvious growing bulge.

"Let's go take a look," he said, guiding her outside to a backyard full of rose bushes, a swimming pool, beautiful new outdoor furniture, and at the end, a gate which led straight down to the beach. Palm trees swayed overhead, and birds sang happily. "Your furniture, belongings, and car are all here. Tilly knows it's her home and is safe."

Sara let the squirming cat down to run around.

"So this is mine? I own it?" she asked in awe.

He understood her reluctance to believe she was safe. She'd been unable to truly trust anyone in her life.

"Yes, you own it outright. Plus, as requested, your bank

account has enough money in it to last you the rest of your long life."

Tears flowed down her face, and he reached out, wiping one away. He couldn't help himself. He smiled gently. "Just don't buy an island, or you might run out."

She let out a little teary laugh, and another knot tightened in his chest.

Fuck.

He had to leave this beautiful being. But there was one last thing he had to do for her.

And he would give anything not to do it.

CHAPTER TEN

Sara turned around and looked back at the two-story, white wooden structure she would now call home. She'd dreamed about this moment for years and couldn't believe it had finally come true. And not in a way she could have ever anticipated.

One minute she'd been in her old house; the next, she was here. If that wasn't magic, she didn't know what was.

She was grateful beyond words.

Yet, despite the gift she'd received, Sara couldn't help feeling a desire for the man standing in front of her. Desire on more levels than she wanted to admit.

He made her smile. He made her squirm. He made her feel all warm and gooey inside, like that first kiss when you were a teenager.

But he was an archangel who was going to vanish into thin air, and she would never see him again.

Was it completely unreasonable to want him to kiss her? When they had touched, her body had burned from the inside out. Michael had looked, in that moment, like any man desiring a woman, torn between wanting to act and knowing he couldn't.

Would he be punished if he touched a human inappropriately?

It didn't matter. It was hardly like they could have a long-distance relationship. It even sounded completely insane as she thought about it.

No. She deserved a forever love.

Which brought her to her last wish.

Love.

The sexy archangel may have exhibited everything she desired in a man, but he was not hers. But he could help her meet the right one, and she'd be a fool to let her desire for him stop her from asking.

"So," Sara said, and Michael dropped his head. He knew what she was going to ask for now.

"So," he repeated, his eyes darkening.

"My last wish."

"Yes." Michael abruptly looked away from her, out over the ocean. "Love."

"Michael?"

"Let's go inside," he said, taking her hand.

"Look, it's okay. I understand," she started, "you know, if there isn't anyone."

He hated hearing her lack of confidence in herself. She was such a beautiful woman worthy of great love and commitment. Yet, he couldn't bring himself to comfort her. Not when he wanted to shake her and tell her he could never bear to watch another man touch her.

Inside the house, he stopped, turned, and placed his hands on his hips. And yeah, he knew he looked intimidating, but still couldn't stop. "Tell me. Who is this great love you desire?"

"Are you mad at me?" she asked, voice small.

"I'm not mad. I'm…you just didn't give me any details. I need more information," he replied defensively. "Perhaps you aren't ready to find love yet?"

Her mouth fell open.

"You don't get to decide that for me. I do. I am ready to love and be loved."

"Yet you have no idea what you want." He turned away, angry with himself.

"Wait. I do know." Sara reached out and grabbed his

arm, her hand burning into his skin. They both stared at the point of connection, and then their eyes met, blazing.

Sara swallowed and dropped her hand.

"Read me your list," he ground out, fists clenched at his sides.

Sara closed her eyes, and he felt her begin to visualize the man she wanted. She turned away from him and walked toward the glass doors, facing outside.

"Perhaps I should talk to a different archangel?"

"What the fuck? No," he growled.

"Then…"

Patience was his weak point, he knew that, but waiting for Sara to speak was painful. Every second felt like a knife to his heart.

He still had no answers about why he had dreamed of her. In fact, he had more questions than before he'd met her. Why was he so powerfully attracted to her when no other human had ever caught his attention? Not of his cock, in any case.

Why did he feel so powerfully protective of her? Was it because he'd dreamed of her death? And had his interference in her life now changed that?

Michael simply didn't know if his dreams were foresight or just dreams—nightmares, really. All he could do was fulfill the human's desires and hope he reconnected with the rest of humanity so he could continue doing his job, what he had been created to do. God may not be concerned, but he was, as were his brothers. Which in hindsight was probably why Raphael had visited. Still, his favorite brother had poor timing.

In a few minutes, Michael would return to Heaven, leaving Sara and taking all memory of him from her. One day not long from now, she would be held by the man she was currently imagining.

Fuck.

"He's tall."

His chest tightened.

Sara's words were now connected to his celestial powers, allowing her to manifest her dreams as she had done with the bangle and the house they now stood in.

Michael's head dropped as she listed all the attributes she wanted in a man. Her list was good. She wanted a strong man to love, support, and cherish her for the rest of her life. All things she deserved.

He should have kissed her. Just one beautiful kiss he could have savored.

What if he kept her? Just for a little while?

"Tall and broad. He's really big. His dark hair curls around his ears, and he has strong, commanding features. He has blue eyes which sparkle with love and adoration when he looks at me," Sara said, continuing with her description.

Suddenly, a shiver passed through him.

What the hell?

"His hands are large and strong, and he's confident, loyal, and supportive."

He took a step forward, her pull incredibly powerful.

"He respects my independence, but he's protective. Wildly protective. We laugh, we talk, and he understands me. He makes me laugh and giggle."

Michael felt her joy.

"He desires me with great passion. He possesses my heart, my soul, and my body. As I do his."

Her energy turned hot and pulsed into him as he stood flush behind her. His hands were inches from her hips.

"Our chemistry is palpable. Explosive. Our kisses, mouthwatering. He makes love to me with strength and passion. He's gentle, yet possessive. His cock..."

She paused.

Michael froze, his lips nearly at her neck.

"Sara," he whispered, his voice full of gravel.

She shivered visibly.

"He..."

"Be very clear, Sara."

He could hear her shallow breathing as he towered over her. His fingers were burning to touch her, the fire between them raging.

Sara tilted her head, exposing her neck to him. He closed his eyes.

"He is powerful. So powerful."

Then he knew.

Michael placed his hands on her hips, and they both groaned. He turned her around and stared down into her beautiful hazel eyes, full of desire and heat.

"Do you choose him?"

"Yes," she answered breathlessly.

In the next moment, everything around them ceased to exist. His mouth claimed hers with such passion, he thought for a moment he may have hurt her. Neither of them halted. He pulled her into his body and placed his hand on the back of her head, plunging his tongue inside. When it met hers, fire exploded.

He'd never known such desire and need to be inside a female.

"All I can give you is this," he rasped as their mouths momentarily separated. "Say yes, Sara," he demanded. "Now. Say it."

"Y...yes."

She's mine.

He groaned as the words struck him. No, she couldn't be.

Just for today, she's mine. He'd make it up to her, but right now, he couldn't walk away from this beautiful female who had been inside his mind for nearly two hundred years.

He needed to be inside her, and he was done fighting it. Nothing and no one but God could stop him.

Picking her up, he wrapped her legs around him and

carried her into the bedroom. He dropped her to the floor and vanished both their clothes so they stood naked and breathless.

"Are you allowed to do this?" she asked.

Michael cupped her cheek. "Yes, and if anyone tried to stop me, they'd...well, they couldn't."

Their mouths connected again with a roaring passion he was fast becoming addicted to. He placed her hand on his shaft and groaned when she began stroking him.

He lifted her up and placed her on the bed.

"You're beautiful. So fucking beautiful, Sara."

His body would not wait long to be inside this female. He nudged her legs apart and pushed his fingers through her wet folds. And God, she was wet.

Michael wanted to take his time, to savor this, but it was fast becoming obvious neither of them could. His cock was twitching, and she was aching with need as she writhed on the bed.

Sara cried with pleasure as he inserted first one, then two fingers. He pressed a kiss on her lips before moving down her body; he needed to taste her need for him. When he did, his body flared with desire.

Pressing his hands on the back of her thighs, he opened her wider and circled his tongue over her clit. Sweet heavens, she was delicious.

"Oh my...fuck," Sara cried out, throwing her head back and arching into him.

His cock demanded its turn. As he lay back over her, Sara ran her hands over him, and he wanted to purr. Her small hands—compared to his enormous body—moved up his pecs and over his shoulders, the burning look in her eyes telling him what she wanted.

"Do you want me to fuck you, Sara?"

"Is it not obvious, archangel?"

He grinned and tugged her against him, positioning his cock at her entrance. "Beautiful girl, you are incredible."

Never in his entire existence had he wanted a female this much, or this simply. Just the desire to be inside her had his head in a blur, blocking out everything else in existence.

"Don't look away. I want your eyes with mine," he requested and she nodded, her mouth open in that sexy way. He lowered over her and took her bottom lip between his teeth.

"Tell me if I hurt you," he said as he began to press into her.

"Ohfuckohmyyes," she cried out, and Michael wanted to roar with delight at how much she loved feeling him.

"You're mine, Sara. I'm sorry, but you're mine," Michael groaned as he thrust in deep.

Then he felt his soul burst apart.

CHAPTER ELEVEN

A burst of energy enveloped them. Michael had never experienced or seen anything like it in his long existence.

He gazed at his human in complete awe.

Conscious of his power, he had flipped her on top of him, where she had ridden him, with his help, to orgasm twice. When she collapsed on his chest, Michael laid them down and wrapped his body around hers. She twisted to face him, and his lips found hers without thought, like a magnet.

"You're delicious," he said, wrapping a leg around her hips, pulling her closer. Sara flinched, and he sat up in question.

"Are you okay? Did I hurt you?"

"Yes. No. I'm a little tender. It's been a while."

"I don't think three orgasms requires an apology." He ran his hand over her bottom. "Rest, beautiful."

Michael lay holding her in his arms, enjoying the warmth of her body and listening to her breathe. It was an intimacy Michael had little experience with.

It was available to him; he just didn't seek it out.

Sensing tension in her body, he opened his eyes and looked upon her slight frown. He ran a thumb over her lips. "What is it, little human?"

"That was just, well, amazing."

"And?"

"Nothing."

"Mind reader, remember."

Sara shook her head. "You are annoying."

He grinned.

"It's just sad you have to leave."

Fuck.

He did the only thing available to him: he nodded. Because he did have to leave. But he didn't want to. He really fucking did not want to leave the warmth of this beautiful female that set his body, heart, and soul on fire.

But telling her that would not make any difference, so he kept his thoughts to himself.

Sara gave him a sad smile as her fingers drifted over his chest. He loved her touch and the feeling of her in his arms. How could he just return to the heavens as if this had never happened?

Could he just forget about her?

No.

He sat up suddenly.

"Holy shit." He quickly apologized to Sara, who was staring wide-eyed at him.

"Where's the fire?"

"I can hear the humans again. Thank fuck!" he exclaimed, flopping back down onto the pillow and pulling her into his arms.

"You stopped hearing us?"

"Yes."

"Were you sick?" She smirked. "It was probably coronavirus."

He laughed and twisted until he was lying over her. "No, cheeky human. It was not your virus. It was you."

"What?" she asked, her eyes wide.

"You. You are a great distraction, Sara." He nipped her bottom lip, unsure why he was sharing this with her, but he wanted to. He liked talking to her. "When I returned to Heaven, I couldn't stop thinking about you, so I took a break, so to speak, giving my prayers to my brothers."

"You can do that? Isn't that your job?"

"It's not a job, sweetheart, it's who I am. I was created to do it."

"Created. So you weren't born?"

"No. I'm not human. Humans are born."

"So you're not human in any way, not skin and bone like me?"

He glanced down at her, realizing this conversation had gone a little too far. There were strict guidelines set by God on what humans could know about archangels and Heaven.

Basically, they couldn't.

If, and when, they interacted with humans, they took their memories afterward. It wasn't foolproof, since memories were complex and leaked into one another. Still, the confusion served its purpose.

"I can manifest into whatever image I choose. I am pure source energy, as you will be when you finish your time as a human."

"But I won't become an archangel."

"No. There are just seven of us. And you"—he tapped her nose—"are no warrior."

"What would I be then?"

"You would be a beautiful angel—strong, feisty, and powerful. I can see that." He grinned at her, imagining her strutting around in Heaven and having a thing or two to say about how things were run there. Michael also imagined himself chasing her into corners and stealing kisses.

Perhaps he simply had to wait for her.

More waiting.

Although that didn't mean it would happen. Not everyone became an angel.

He frowned. What the hell was wrong with him? Wait for her? Archangels weren't monogamous.

"So what about the rest of humanity? Do we all become angels?"

Michael lowered his eyes, feeling guilty. "I'm playing

with you Sara, I'm sorry. I cannot give answer to these questions."

She let out a huff of impatience, and he laughed. He was the most powerful archangel in existence, and she happily expressed her unhappiness with him. Few beings outside his brothers would act like this around him.

He was respected and feared in a healthy way.

Mostly.

"Then answer me this," she continued. "Am I really the only human you've ever had sex with?"

Michael stilled.

An icy shiver ran through him.

He wasn't ready to examine why he felt the way he did about her or what it meant, let alone talk to her about it. Yet he saw the vulnerability in her eyes. She deserved the truth. And strangely, he wanted to give it to her.

"Yes, and you will always be the only one," he said, cupping her cheek.

"That bad, huh?" she joked with a little grin.

"No, Sara. I need you to know it's because it was you."

CHAPTER TWELVE

Raphael stood in front of his Father, arms crossed.

"Well, are you going to tell him?"

"No."

"Father!"

"No. I said no, and given how I am God, one would think I would actually get some respect around here."

Raphael rolled his eyes.

"Hear me out. Michael may be all-powerful, etcetera, etcetera, but you should have seen him with her. He's lost his mind."

God shrugged. "Oh, and is he the only one?"

Raphael stared blankly and didn't react. No way was he going to react. The smirk he received in return grated on his nerves. He wasn't going there.

"Good," the Deity finally said and wandered over to a large white sofa that looked somewhat like a cloud.

It was so cliché that Raphael actually cringed.

"I don't know why you all thought you were destined to be alone forever," God continued. He was, of course, referring to all seven of the archangels. "Your soulmates are waiting for you to meet them. Or recognize them. Like all my children, you have free will to do as you please." He cleared his throat. "With some of you exercising that free will more than others."

"I think you're referring to Gabriel more so than me," he responded with faux dignity.

God raised an eyebrow at him.

"Anyway..." Raphael cleared his throat.

"It's not to say that your mates are all human, but in Michael's case, the answer is emphatically a yes."

Cryptic bastard, as always.

"Alright, I'll let Michael decode that shit. So what you're saying is we can't interfere?"

God nodded.

"At all?"

He shook his head.

"A nudge?"

"Leave him be, Raphael. Your time will come soon enough." He glanced down into the glass he was drinking from and smirked.

"Um, what?"

God grinned.

Raphael glanced around, looking for a door to escape. The thing was, God didn't exactly have a house or an office. When you were summoned, he created a unique environment every time. You could be in a church, a library, a beach, on a moon, or in a quaint garden. They never really knew, and always prepared for the unexpected.

The cloud couch was definitely hashtag random, though.

It wasn't really a door he needed to find because he could just flash out. Except he couldn't. One didn't do that to the creator of...well, everything.

"You came here for a reason, Raphael. What is it?"

Taking a slow breath, he found his most charming demeanor.

Fuck, here we go.

"So, we're all sharing Michael's prayers right now, and as you know, I'm working overtime on this pandemic." He saw God's eyes narrowing but carried on. "So I wonder, given the circumstances, if we could discuss our little rule for a moment. You know, to help."

God turned furious.

"Get out!"

"Father, let me explain," he entreated, getting to his feet. "The humans, they're dividing as a species torn apart from misinformation and corruption, not to mention that millions are dying. Let us intervene and help them."

God stood and pointed at him.

"Free. Will! There is no other rule. It will never change. Do you hear me?" The walls shook around them as his voice boomed through the heavens.

Raphael sighed.

It was just his luck to draw the short straw. The other archangels would have felt God's response and known how he had fared.

It had been a long shot.

"Humans have survived every challenge they've created, Raphael. As soon as we interfere, the lesson is gone, and the universe will tip out of balance."

God's voice had lowered to deliver the speech Raphael had heard a million times.

Literally.

"And if they all die? What if humans become extinct?"

"Then it is their choice."

Raphael didn't miss the flicker of sadness in God's eyes.

"You're right to be concerned, my son, but it remains their choice."

CHAPTER THIRTEEN

"So what happened?" Michael asked, proud of his little human. Well, not his. She was kind of his. He'd claimed her on a level he didn't understand, but he couldn't keep her.

Soon she would realize he would leave again, but for now, they were in a bubble he never wanted to burst. Because once it did, he was facing the rest of his life without her, which would be an eternity.

Literally.

Michael's chest clenched, and he forced his focus back to their conversation. Sara was telling him how she'd sued her previous employers, and damn, he was impressed with her self-preservation and strength.

"Well, I told them I wouldn't accept their behavior toward me." She shrugged. "I'd put up with months of bullying, and aside from the fact it's a breach of employment laws, I just simply couldn't allow people to treat me like that. I deserve much better."

Michael pulled her closer, laying his lips over hers. "I'm so proud of you."

He knew her history, but hearing her tell it with such passion was a completely different experience from scanning her memories. It was more intimate, and it connected him to her in a way he'd never felt. It was different with his brothers. They were warriors; they were family.

Over the next few hours, they talked and pleasured each other, and Michael had never felt such pure bliss. Eventually, Sara's stomach grumbled, reminding him she was human and needed to eat.

Michael wasn't sure what was more exciting, her delight when he manifested food at her request, or watching her lips as she moaned while she ate his delicious creations.

"Seafood linguine." She clapped her hands. "My favorite."

"That's five favorites now." He smirked, and she playfully punched his arm.

"Ouch. Are you made of concrete?" Sara shook her hand.

He grinned and cleared the dishes with a flash of his hands. Sara stretched lazily across the bed, and he considered flipping her over and entering her from behind. Again.

He ran his hand over his cock.

"I'm going to shower. Will you stay while I do?"

"If you let me shower with you."

"Yes," she purred and then danced naked into the bathroom, calling out, "Did I tell you how much I'm loving isolation now?"

Michael knew he shouldn't linger much longer, but he couldn't seem to leave her.

The water flowed down Sara's back from three different showerheads. Despite the whirlwind of the past few days, she was still in a heightened state of gratitude for her beautiful home.

Michael had gotten every little detail perfectly, including the balcony off the main bedroom where a set of white wicker chairs and a small table sat so she could have her breakfast—or a cocktail—and gaze across the ocean.

The multimillion-dollar beachfront property had set her up for life, as she'd wished for, providing the ultimate financial security. Her bank account was also flowing with all the cash she'd ever need.

For the first time in her life, she could relax and not worry. Her body was feeling extremely relaxed after being made love to by a gorgeous man for hours.

Sara sighed and tipped her head under the water. She knew it was a one-off thing.

Michael stepped into the shower, wrapped his beautiful enormous body around her, and she melted into him. When he touched her, nothing in the world seemed to matter. She felt safe, protected, and adored.

"Michael?"

"Mm-hmm?" he hummed, face buried in her wet hair, nibbling her earlobe.

She turned into him, and his lips found hers lazily. Sara wanted to stay like this and kiss him for eternity.

"Ask your question." His voice was deep and husky.

She ran her hands over his broad shoulders, the water flowing easily over his golden skin. "Hey, I thought archangels had wings?"

He didn't answer immediately. His blue eyes held hers in a piercing hold. She shivered. "Yes, we do."

Confused, she ran her hands over his back. "Then why can't I see or feel them?"

"Because I'm not showing them to you."

"Would you?"

He shook his head and kissed her nose. "No."

Reaching for the body wash, Michael soaped up the sponge and started washing them both. When she tried to argue further, he ran the shower sponge between her legs, nudging them apart. She sucked in a short breath and forgot her question.

Afterward, as Sara tugged on jeans and a sweater, she heard the roar of the fireplace in her bedroom. The nights were getting cooler as they nudged closer to fall, and she smiled at his thoughtfulness.

She walked into his arms and laid her head against his chest. "Thank you."

"It is nothing," he murmured into her hair and kissed her head.

"So now can you show me your wings?"

"No, I cannot."

"Can't or won't?"

"Won't. Both."

She sighed and frowned as the damn sexy archangel patted her bottom and walked off. "I'll meet you downstairs."

Something was up with him. He'd begun to retreat from her.

She knew then he was going to leave soon.

Her emotions rose to the surface. She knew she would never see him again, and suddenly, she felt her heart begin to break one tiny bit at a time.

One day, a human man would turn up in her life, and this would all feel like a dream. It was her time to love and be loved. Yet, her heart was betraying her with an archangel.

She hadn't meant to start falling in love.

When she'd read out the attributes for her perfect man, she'd done so from memory. For years, people had told her to write a list of what she wanted in love. At this point, Sara wondered if she'd made more of those than grocery lists.

So as she had spoken the words and felt an energy run through her body, she had felt Michael moving closer. She'd recognized the similarities, even though she barely knew him. It was a knowing she couldn't explain.

Throwing caution to the wind, she'd let her body take over, and when he'd touched her, she'd lost all control.

She didn't regret it. She had made her decision, and now it was time to be grateful for the most magical and delicious sexual experience she'd ever had, and let him go.

Somehow.

Downstairs, another fire was crackling in the living room. Michael was stretched out in front of it, treating Tilly to an angelic tummy rub. Sara joined them, lying out next to him.

"What a lucky girl." She tickled the cat under the chin and her purr intensified.

"Do you need petting too?" Michael asked, kissing her neck. Her body immediately tingled, wetness pooling in her panties.

God, he had only finished making love to her just minutes ago. She was insatiable for him.

"And then you'll leave?"

Michael closed his eyes and turned into the roaring fire. "I will return."

"Why?" she asked quietly.

He turned to her, the fire in his own eyes boring into her. "Do you not want me to?" He looked angry.

"You said this was all you could offer," she replied.

Michael pulled her up against him and ran his hand up under her sweater. She'd taken to not wearing a bra during lockdown and hadn't thought to put one on tonight. His thumb and fingers tweaked her nipple.

"You are so reactive to my touch, little human. How could I stay away from you?"

"So this is just sex."

His eyes narrowed at her, and he frowned. She couldn't tell if he was annoyed with her or himself. Instead of answering, he opened her jeans and reached in, slipping a finger inside her panties.

"Michael," she moaned.

She gasped as his finger touched a sensitive spot. He looked down at her, eyes dark and sultry. Sara knew if she let this continue, she'd lose herself in him again, then he'd be gone, and she'd be left with a million questions.

"Michael, stop. What do you mean you'll come back?"

"I'll return. When I can," he simply said, as if that was okay.

It wasn't. She couldn't sit around waiting and desiring him. She would go crazy.

"No. We can't do that. What if it's weeks or months from now and I've met someone? I don't think—"

Michael suddenly sat up, leaning over her. "What?" he asked, anger very evident now.

"Well, I can't just wait for—"

"You want to take another lover after what we just shared? Already? Now?"

Sara reached out to him tentatively and placed a hand on his chest. It would be wise, she realized, to remember this was an enormously powerful being. Sexy as he may be, he was not human, nor would he think like one. She could sense his possessiveness, and while it was terrifying, it was also a little awesome.

"One day. Not today. You know I want a forever love." Sara looked at him, hoping to reach his compassion and understanding.

Of course she wanted that love to be him after what they had just shared, but she knew it was impossible. They both did.

She lowered her eyes.

Michael took her chin. "Sara, I do not want another man touching you. I forbid it," he declared, voice commanding.

Forbid it?

No.

Having a powerful and gorgeous archangel ravish your body was one thing. Having him trying to control her was a completely different one.

"You can't forbid it. Let me up. Stop." She pushed against his chest, but he didn't move an inch. His eyes swirled like an angry ocean as the air shifted around them. "Michael!"

"You are mine, Sara. I will have no other man touching you." Michael stood and lifted her to her feet.

"You're scaring me," she cried out.

Michael stared at her for a long moment as if in a

trance, and then shook his head.

"I'm sorry," he apologized, pulling her against him. "God, I'm sorry."

He released her and held her gaze intensely. "Do you not want me, Sara?"

"Yes, but..."

"I cannot share you."

Her eyes lowered.

"I don't want you to leave," she said.

"I do not want to leave."

She looked up at him, and he began to remove her clothes. He nudged her against the arm of the sofa, forcing her to sit down, and found her sensitive spot. They never looked away as he worked it, his eyes swirling like a stormy ocean. His own clothes disappeared as he took his cock in hand, stroking it.

"Say it, Sara. Say you're mine."

She was no longer afraid. She knew he was struggling with his emotions just as she was. The connection and attraction between them was overwhelming.

Still, he was being selfish.

Sara moaned, her mind losing ground.

He leaned down and took a nipple in his mouth as his fingers continued working through her folds, his other hand stroking himself. Her body pulsed with the need for him to be inside her.

Finally, Michael pressed against her entrance, one hand in her hair.

"Tell me."

She shook her head. She couldn't; it would destroy her. She looked away from him as he roared and pushed into her. He lifted her as if she were nothing more than a cushion and placed her on the sofa. Gripping her hips, he began thrusting in deep.

There was nothing gentle in his lovemaking. This was absolute possession, and they both knew it.

He grabbed her chin and claimed her lips harshly. As he began to spill inside her, he held her eyes, veins pulsing along his neck.

She blinked, and a tear slid out.

CHAPTER FOURTEEN

As his breathing normalized and he felt Sara wriggle under him, he sat up.

"Are you okay?

God, what was wrong with him? Michael wanted to possess this beautiful female even though he knew he couldn't, never mind free will.

Sorry, Father.

And yet, as he apologized, he knew he wouldn't leave without her understanding she now belonged to him. No other male would touch her, or Michael would...

What? What would you do? Kill an innocent human? Shit.

"You can't ask that of me, Michael." Sara glared at him after catching her breath.

"Have I not pleasured you enough?"

"You know you have. But I will not sit around waiting for you." Sara found her clothes and began dressing. "What do you plan to do? Leave me here with a dildo and return when you want sex? Is that your plan?"

No. He had no plan. But suddenly, he wanted to fuck her with a dildo.

A lot.

He watched as she ran her eyes over his body. She'd been tracing her fingers over his tribal tattoos and muscles all day, and he wanted her to touch him again.

"Sara," he started with quiet authority. "I don't know what this is. I'm confused. I do not attach to females." He stepped closer and saw the emotion thick in her eyes. "I know it is a lot to ask, but I need you to give me some time."

Sara looked away, a tear sliding down her cheek. Michael pulled her into his arms.

"Please."

She sniffed against his chest. "I won't wait for you forever. And Michael"—she looked up at him—"I reserve the right to change my mind at any time."

"Sara," he warned softly, his jaw tight.

"No. That's all I can offer. You know this isn't going to end with us living happily ever after. I will die, and you will live forever."

Michael's entire body tensed, and he gripped her chin. "Sara, you're mine. I can't explain it; this has never happened before, and I'm old, really fucking old. I need to understand what this all means, and it's going to take some time."

She shook her head at him. "What are you saying? Don't archangels have girlfriends?"

"Well, no."

Never.

They were the ultimate playboys. No archangel had ever desired to be in a monogamous relationship. They felt no romantic feelings, aside from desire, and he'd always thought it was because they had been created, not born, so they felt no need to procreate to continue the species.

They had each other for companionship, and while his six brothers drove him crazy, he loved their stupid faces.

"Oh," Sara said. "Well then, what is this?"

"I don't have the answers for you today, Sara, but I know I am not walking away from you."

Sara shivered.

Michael picked her up and sat in a nearby armchair, placing her on his lap and wrapping her in a cashmere throw blanket.

With his arms tight around her, she laid her head on his shoulder, and he dropped his own on hers. "I just need some time."

They watched the sun sink low into the sky until darkness settled around them.

Michael gently ran a hand over her hair. "I must go."

"I know."

"I will be back, beautiful Sara."

He'd wanted to give her everything, and he had. Except for the love she deeply desired. He felt selfish, but not enough to walk away.

He didn't know when he'd be back, but he would.

One day.

"Thank you," she whispered. "Thank you for everything. Even if you never return."

He stood, picking her up and placing her back on the chair, then pointed his finger at the fire to give it a boost. Crouching in front of her, he took her face in his hands and kissed her deeply.

"My beautiful human, this is not goodbye."

The tears in her eyes were the last thing he saw before he flashed away.

CHAPTER FIFTEEN

Sara pulled the zipper up on her jacket and closed the gate behind her as she stepped down onto the sand. The good thing about living at the beach during a pandemic was being allowed to walk on it. Unless you were a local, you couldn't.

Damn lockdown rules.

She wondered about her old house. What did her neighbors think about her disappearance? A simple question with a complex answer, she imagined. But as the saying went, she wouldn't look a gift horse in the mouth. And even if she'd love to, it had been three long days since Michael had left her. Aside from her new home and a much-improved financial situation, it all felt like a strange dream.

An unbelievably delicious sexual dream.

Desire had wracked her body in his absence, and she had an incessant need to be in his arms. Even knowing it was impossible, Sara needed him so much it ached. This wasn't some schoolgirl crush. It was like she needed him on a level she'd never felt before.

Was it because he was an archangel?

She'd said she would wait for him, but even as she'd made the promise, she knew it would be difficult. Not because she desired him and only him, but because every moment he was not with her, she was grieving.

Bedtime arrived, and she curled up with one of her romance books. She fancied the supernatural romance genre, and letting out a little laugh, realized she was now living it.

Opening her book, she delved into the world of bear

shifters. The two main characters were obviously attracted to each other despite knocking heads for a few chapters. Their bickering inevitably turned into an erotic sex scene as the heroine gave herself to the rugged, powerful alpha male.

Clenching her pussy, she tried not to think of her archangel, but failed. Soon she was wet, the ache inside her impossible to ignore. Sara let the book drop beside her and reached down under the sheets.

Closing her eyes, she imagined Michael spreading her legs and licking her core with his talented tongue, all while pushing his fingers inside her over and over again.

She moaned and rubbed her sensitive nub. Arching at the vision she saw of his face between her legs, his eyes holding hers, she reached beside the bed and pulled a dildo out of her drawer. Though it was cold, she imagined it was his hard cock and quickly pushed it inside her wet and ready pussy.

She gasped and then turned it on.

"Oh my God, yes, Michael," she cried out.

Afterward, she turned into her pillow, letting a little tear fall.

This is ridiculous. It was just sex.

She knew it was a lie even as she thought it, but the fact was that he was an immortal archangel and she was a grown woman. She needed to forget him and get on with her life.

She hiccupped and let out one small word that would change everything.

"Sorry."

It was better to let him go.

CHAPTER SIXTEEN

Michael looked out at the angelic faces staring back at him. Well, they were angels, but not all that angelic looking if you compared them to the human vision of them; at least not the male angels.

These angels were warriors.

Warriors of God's army, of which he was the leader.

Each year, Michael gave a speech at the graduation ceremony, and today was that day. He stood on stage in an auditorium filled with over a thousand newly qualified angel warriors. Offstage to his left stood Raphael and Stefano, one of their senior warriors.

It had been a long day, and he'd just finished his inspirational speech. They were all looking a little stunned, so he might have gone a bit heavy on them, but damn it, these angels would be responsible for protecting the realm, which included humans.

Like Sara.

Christ.

He needed to get ahold of himself.

"Go forth, warriors. Protect the immortal realm and all of God's children."

"Thank you, Archangel Michael. Does anyone have any questions for the Supreme?" Stefano asked, stepping up onto the stage.

Michael folded his scroll, expecting none, as usual.

"Lord Michael. I have a question," Severial spoke up from the front row.

Michael looked up and over at him. He knew who the angel was, which was never good for a young warrior. The angel had been recognized as a troublemaker during his training.

"Go ahead."

"What would you consider is God's greatest weakness?"

Michael arched an eyebrow at the question as the room shuffled uncomfortably. Several wasn't the first angel to push boundaries, and Michael liked to encourage free-thinking, but something about the question sent a chill running through him.

"You believe God has a weakness, Several?"

The tall blond angel nodded and grinned with an arrogance which wasn't respectful toward a leader. Certainly not toward an archangel. "Of course. We all do, don't we?"

"And what would be yours?" Michael asked, spreading his legs into a warrior's pose and placing his hands on his hips, but not showing any emotion.

There. That twitch. He'd hit home, but it was quickly hidden.

Interesting.

"I see what you did there," the angel replied with a sly grin. The crowd quietly gasped at his inappropriate comment to the Supreme Archangel. Michael's irritation increased, but he kept his blank stare.

The angel was a fool to think he could play this power game with him.

"But seriously, as the Lord Protector and head of our army, surely you must see the wisdom in sharing his weakness so we can best protect him."

Michael wandered across the podium, handing his scroll to one of the awaiting cherubs, taking his time in answering.

"Fake news," he finally said.

"What?" the warrior asked, confused.

"Fake news, Several. That's his weakness."

Michael looked out across the audience, his legs spread wide again, and crossed his arms. He looked every bit the enormous and intimidating Supreme Archangel of Heaven he was.

"Who here believes they are here to protect God?" His voice boomed loudly around the hall.

More than a few fidgeted in their seats. A couple of hands went up, then a few more.

"And who believes they are here to protect humans?"

The room was filled with arms pointing at the roof.

Several sent him a dark look.

"And you, Several, who do you protect?"

"God, of course."

Michael's eyes darkened. "Then you believe him weak and paid little attention in your lessons."

To his credit, the warrior pushed his shoulders back and held his stare before finally looking away.

"Mark my words, angels. You may now be warriors under my lead, but our Lord has no need for protection. He has no weakness. Only perhaps that you believe he has one."

He glanced at all the faces one by one.

"You protect Heaven, the realm, and God's children. You have been trained to be loyal and obedient. Go forth and protect all those in our stead from any and all enemies."

Looking back at Several, the warrior eventually bowed his head and followed the others out of the room.

Michael watched him until he was out of sight.

"Bit dramatic, brother." Raphael grinned as he pushed off the pillar.

"Monitor him. Something's off."

Raphael nodded as they fell into step together. "Sure, but fake news? Really?"

He smirked. "I heard Sara talking about it. Seemed like

a good analogy."

"Riiiight, Sara. I think our boy's in lurve."

"Drop it," he growled.

"Yeah, nah. I don't think so. I've waited an eternity for this."

"Waited for what? What do you think this is?" Michael snapped. He had stopped walking and was glaring at his brother.

"Nothing. Jeez, just that you've got yourself a girlfriend." Raph held up his hands, backing off, still grinning.

Michael stalked after his brother, grinding out his words. "I don't have a girl, Raphael. She's a human. I'm a damn archangel. We don't have girlfriends."

Raphael tilted his head. "Or do we?"

When Michael continued to glare at him, Raphael shrugged. "How about we go out for a big fly? You need to relax, bro. When was the last time you hit the sky?"

He'd been keeping himself busy to distract himself from thoughts of Sara. Thankfully, he'd stayed connected to humanity, but his brain was all tied up in knots, as was his body. His need was a giant ache he couldn't budge, and it was doing nothing for his mood.

"Fuck, I'm sorry," he said, stepping away.

"Jophiel and Gabe will return soon. Let's head out after."

He nodded. "Fine. Get some eyes on that fucking Severial. I want to know where he goes and who he's talking to."

"I'm not your bitch, Michael," he heard Raphael call out from behind him, and he grinned.

He knew his brother was already on it, but he hadn't been able to stop himself. Every one of his senior warriors would be watching the young angel after his display of insubordination.

Michael walked into his chambers and dropped his jacket onto the chaise longue when he heard her voice.

He stilled.

"Oh God…"

What the hell? Her voice was dim, like a distant echo, but he knew it was Sara. He expanded his energy out, sensing she was not in pain nor fear…suddenly, he felt it. Pleasure.

He roared, the walls shaking and crumbling around him. Paintings fell off the wall, and a vase crashed.

Was she with a man?

Michael walked to the wall and smashed his hand through it. Fury poured off him as his mind imagined all kinds of scenarios. Other men wrapped around her, holding her, touching her, kissing her, inside her.

He howled.

Being separated from her was tearing him apart. Surely something was wrong with him.

Father!

She'd reached him again across the heavens. How was she doing that?

His doors burst open.

"Get out!" he boomed, turning to face two of his brothers who stood armed with their swords, ready for battle. They looked around, and of course, found nothing.

"What the hell. Are you chasing ghosts?"

"You try my patience, Gabriel. Get out." He stalked toward him, plucking his own famous sword of light from the air.

"Put your damn swords away!" Raphael demanded in a voice he rarely used with anyone, let alone him. Unfortunately, he was too riled with fury to respond.

"You dare tell me what to do?" Michael roared and felt himself begin to glow.

"Michael, tone it the fuck down or you-know-who'll intervene," Gabe said, lowering his sword.

Michael grunted. He dared God to show his face. He'd been seeking answers for days and had heard nothing.

"Do us all a favor and go see your damn human," Raphael ordered sternly.

He looked at both Raphael and Gabriel. They weren't his enemies. The true enemy was in his head—or in Sara's bed. The latter he would kill.

"I think she's with a man."

He released his sword and it disappeared. The pain in his chest was unbearable.

"I need to get out of here."

He needed to fly. Raphael was right. He'd grounded himself to stay busy and distracted, hoping God would shine some light, but he'd done the one thing he'd promised Sara he wouldn't do. Stay away.

His huge wings burst from him, the room glowing from their bright, divine white light. Few could look upon them with the ease his brothers did, as he did with theirs.

"Don't jump to any conclusions, Michael. Human women are complex, as is love," Gabriel advised.

"And you know this how, brother?" He stepped outside, his wings itching to take flight. "Archangels don't fall in love, so how would you know?"

"Don't we?" Raphael asked for the second time today.

"What do you know?" He spun around.

His brother shrugged, and he growled in response. Raphael was the eternal playboy. The guy fell in love every fifteen seconds, for fifteen seconds.

"Get out of my chambers. I'm heading to Earth. I'll be back in a few days; I have to end this and get my head back in the game," Michael growled. "In my absence, I expect you to keep an eye on that angel, Raphael. I'm not kidding around. My hackles are up."

As his brother crossed his arms and frowned, Michael rose into the sky.

Then he was gone.

CHAPTER SEVENTEEN

Sara tossed and turned in her sleep. She'd thrown off the covers and then pulled them back over her at least three times. Suddenly, she sat up and caught her breath.

What had woken her? Had she had a nightmare?

She rubbed her head, trying to remember.

Cold air bit into her chest as she noticed the front of her cotton shirt was drenched. Night sweats? That was unlike her.

Moonlight poured into the bedroom, landing along the polished wooden floors. She'd left the blinds open, and the chilly air was now seeping through the glass. Climbing out of bed, Sara ripped off her wet shirt and threw it in the washing basket, then she closed the blinds.

Flashes of her dream began to return.

Michael. Again.

She sighed. Getting over him was going to take some time. His screams and howls had sounded so real. Nearly as real as the touch of his hands on her body.

Sara pulled open a drawer and grabbed her favorite blue cotton tee. It was long and covered her bottom. She let out a little laugh at the NAMASTAY ASLEEP printed across the front. Such a stupid joke, but there it was, the only thing able to crack a smile on her face today.

The clock told her it was now 2:00 a.m. She flopped back on the bed and snuggled under the covers. It wasn't like she had to go to work tomorrow, so she relaxed and let sleep return.

A noise on the balcony caught her attention. She turned to the now closed blinds and stared, grateful she had pulled them shut.

"Sara."

She let out a scream and leaped back against the headboard.

"Sorry, I was trying not to scare you. I see I failed."

"Michael?" She clasped a hand at her throat as her heart thundered. "Fuck!"

"Again, I'm sorry." He held out a hand.

"What are you doing here?"

"I heard you."

"Heard me?"

He nodded, and a look of displeasure crossed his face. "You cried out. In ecstasy."

"Oh."

She knew exactly what he was talking about and blushed. How had he heard her? Was he monitoring her?

"Were you alone? I need to know," he demanded, his voice low.

A storm of emotions raced through her, the first being fury. How could he think she could have sex with someone else so soon after they'd been together? She was also embarrassed. He had pleasured her more times than she'd thought physically possible, and in only a few days, she already needed to pleasure herself. What would he think?

She sighed.

"Yes."

She watched as he breathed out and visibly relaxed. "Good. Okay, that's good."

As he relaxed, she let her fury rise.

"It's not good. Do you think I'm the kind of girl who would let another man in her bed so soon?"

"No."

"Then why did you ask?" When he just stared at her, she continued, "For all I know, you have goddesses or angels or whatever lined up at your door. Do I need to ask who you've had in your bed?"

Michael's face turned red. "Do not accuse me of things you know nothing of."

"Which isn't a no!"

He stalked to the side of the bed and leaned over her, hands on either side of the headboard.

"Stop." Taking a long breath, he seemed to be grasping for control. "I've been obsessing over you every single damn minute since I left."

Silently she high-fived herself, then remembered she'd decided not to do this with him again. It was wrong. He was an archangel, and it would only hurt each time he left.

"See, you expect my loyalty, but wouldn't give me yours." Michael held her stare. "I imagined you with another man, and goddamn it, I pulled a sword on Gabriel and Raphael."

Sara gasped. "The archangel Raphael?"

"Yes."

"Wow." Her face was lined with awe.

"Wow?" He narrowed his eyes at her. "You know who I am, right?"

She smiled, and he shook his head.

He sat back on the bed. "Yeah, the most powerful archangel, and you're a danger to me. God, Sara, I want to kill anyone who would dare touch you."

Her mouth fell open.

"Fuck. I exist to protect humans, not harm them."

She sighed.

"I know you wouldn't harm anyone, Michael. And if it's any consolation, if you were human, I would be yours exclusively."

Sara knew she shouldn't give her heart away so easily, but he looked so pained.

Michael stared at her for a moment before standing and walking to the French doors. He opened the blinds and gazed out across the water.

"I came here to end this. I should leave."

"Fine, go," she said, her heart aching. "But don't come back again, Michael. Ever."

He whipped around.

"Do you know how many women pray for my touch, for my love? I've never once desired a human until you. And all you do is push me away."

"I'm not saying I don't want you, Michael. I do. God, my body aches when you're not near me. Hell, it aches when you are near me."

He stalked to the bed and took her face in his hands.

"Then explain it to me, Sara, because I do not understand."

"I'm protecting myself. I want things you can't give me. I want forever. Love, marriage, children."

"Human things."

"Yes."

"Tell me what things, Sara," he demanded.

"Well, like going on a date."

"I can take you on a date. Wherever you want to go. Paris. Egypt. Dubai. Right now. Let's go."

She shook her head and let out a little laugh. He didn't get it. Of course he didn't; he wasn't human. He answered prayers and made dreams come true, but Archangel Michael could never be a human.

She didn't want him to be human, she truly didn't, but he needed to understand why she was pushing him away.

"I want flowers..."

A moment later, the room filled with dozens of vases of white roses. The scent filled the air, and she sneezed around a laugh.

"What else, Sara? What else can I give you? Anything."

She frowned. It was time to get serious and touch on the things he could never provide her with.

"I want to make love, travel, and create memories. I

want to move in together and talk till midnight. Plan and make a family. Have babies. Decorate."

"I got you a house, didn't I?"

"Michael, stop it. You know you can't be here every night. I want to lie in your arms each night, not lie awake wondering when you'll appear."

Michael pulled her flush under him. "Little human, I dream of this too. I do. And I never have in all my existence."

His words melted her defenses a little, and when he laid his lips on hers, she melted some more. Soon he was inside her, and the now familiar feeling of being whole and complete was hers once more. A bold statement coming from an independent woman, she realized as she clung to him like her next breath depended on it.

Michael pulled the covers over them.

"Sleep, my beauty. I'll be here when you wake up. I promise."

Closing her eyes, Sara pretended to sleep. Her body might have been sated, but her mind wasn't. She had too much experience in life and love to lie to herself. It was going to hurt when this incredible being left, and he would. And afterward, it wasn't like she could ring Lisa and be like, "Oh, hey, I've got a broken heart. I've been seeing a cute guy, kind of a long-distance thing. Lives in a place called Heaven, you might have heard of it. Please console my dumb ass."

She could already hear Lisa's response.

"Sara, we need to invest in a nice resort holiday for you. They'll provide you with a lovely white jacket with little straps and daily therapy sessions."

"Go to sleep, sweetheart," Michael whispered, and her mind began to quiet. Damn archangel and his magic powers. Before she drifted off, she promised herself that when he left this time, she'd tell him not to return.

It was the only way she'd survive.

CHAPTER EIGHTEEN

Michael gazed down at his beautiful human as she lay sleeping in his arms. He hated manipulating her like that, but he could sense her mind spiraling.

Sprawled across him naked, her hair wild from their lovemaking, she looked blissfully satisfied. Yet the little frown on her forehead told him she had the same thoughts running through her head as he did.

How was this possible? His brothers had never told him how wonderful being with a human could be. Was this what he'd been missing?

Or was Sara different?

Perhaps with Sara being his first, he'd reacted powerfully. Humans were a special gift in their unending universe, and he had had no idea it could be like this. Which posed the question, how did his brothers spend only one or two nights with their humans before leaving?

He did not want to leave.

And that was a new feeling, one he'd never thought possible. Michael loved humans. He was the Lord Protector, after all. He had been created to protect them. What he felt for Sara, though, was different. This was something new and unknown to him.

His fingers ran over her arm mindlessly, and she sighed gently. His heart clenched.

Yes, she was special.

He tucked his arm under his head and stared up at the ceiling, thinking. There had to be a connection between his dreams and these unusual feelings. The Oracle had told him of her arrival and that she would be important, but had given no more details.

Nothing new about that. She was as vague as God at times.

And he still didn't know why her energy field shone so brightly.

He shook his head slightly. There was a connection here. He just didn't know what. Yet.

He looked down at her.

"What am I missing?" he whispered into the bedroom.

About time you asked, son.

Father?

Keep asking questions.

Who is she?

She is yours.

Mine?

Archangels didn't have a mine. Despite his strong desire for her, he knew he couldn't keep her. Sara wanted a man who could love her her entire life. Someone to build a life and family with. He couldn't give her that.

And yet, he couldn't let her be with another man even if his life depended on it. And now God was saying she was his.

What are you talking about? I am an archangel.

The silence was deafening.

He should have known God would not explain further. It was the way he was. Often, the archangels were left to translate his messages on their own, and this was yet another one of those times.

She couldn't be his. Could she?

He looked down at her again and ran his hand over her golden hair.

God was mistaken.

Okay, so the creator was never wrong. But Michael still wasn't jumping to any conclusions.

All he knew was he had felt the strong urge to claim her the moment their bodies had joined. He was protective by nature, but he'd never felt such possessiveness. The desire to flash her to his chambers in Heaven and keep her safe and all to himself was a powerful, overwhelming sensation.

But he couldn't. Literally.

Any mortal he attempted to take into Heaven would be killed. A soul, once it left a human body, could enter, but he wasn't damn well killing her so they could be together. That was all kinds of messed up.

So what in the heavens did God mean when he said she was his?

Who is this woman?

With her ability to reach him in Heaven and her larger than normal energy field in the forefront of his mind, Michael decided to delve deeper inside her to get some answers.

He closed his eyes, releasing some of his energy. While on Earth, archangels contained their full power lest it destroy everything around them. Michael was a supernova compared to the beings on this planet.

Carefully, he let out a thread of energy and reached for Sara's soul as she lay in his arms. At first, he discovered the beautiful, swirling gold energy common in humans. Sara's twirled happily, dancing around, feeling youthful and playful.

He smiled.

He attempted to connect with her energy and discovered solid resistance. He swirled around it, dancing and twisting until finally, after many minutes, he found a gap and quickly darted inside.

What he found surprised him. Instead of the gold, calm center common in humans, he encountered an intense white energy common with celestial beings.

He was suddenly pushed out with substantial force.

His eyes burst open.

"What the hell?"

Sara snuggled in closer, the moonlight draping over her shoulders as if everything was as it should be.

But it wasn't.

Whatever was inside of her should not be there.

Father!

Deafening silence.

Michael's eyes darted around the dark room as he considered his next steps. Whatever was inside Sara appeared to be protecting, not harming her, so for now, he just pulled her tighter into his arms while looking through his memories for anything that could help.

He knew one thing; he was going to need backup.

CHAPTER NINETEEN

"I know you did magic and everything, but it's so strange that not one of my neighbors has asked me why I suddenly just appeared. I even put a photo on Facebook, and nobody has said anything about my new million-dollar view. It's as if the entire world thinks this is normal."

"They do," Michael mumbled.

Sara poured cat biscuits into Tilly's bowl.

"I mean, I know you created it, but even so, it's weird, right?"

Pouring almond milk into her cereal, she sat on the stool next to Michael at the kitchen counter. She loved the view overlooking the ocean from this spot.

Glancing up at him, she munched on a spoonful, smiling. "Are you sure you don't want anything more than a glass of water? Maybe a coffee or something?"

He shook his head and continued sitting there, looking hot as hell in a pair of blue jeans and a gray knit sweater.

"You know, you're pretty fashionable for an angel."

"Archangel."

She arched an eyebrow at him.

"I am the Supreme Archangel."

"And not a morning person, I see."

He stood and placed his glass in the sink, then turned, leaning against it.

"What's wrong?"

"I need to return to Heaven, Sara. I don't know when I will be back," he said with a touch of regret in his voice.

Sara dropped her spoon. She swallowed what felt like a lump of wet concrete. "Okay."

She took a deep breath, feeling nauseous, and pep talked herself. Just let him go and then throw up. You'll be fine. You'll be fine. You'll be fine.

Michael narrowed his eyes at her. "Have you ever met another celestial being prior to me?"

You what now?

"No. Why?"

"Do you have any idea how you could speak to me directly? Did you know you were?"

Her forehead creased in irritation. "Why do I feel like you are accusing me of something? Don't people pray to you all the time? Hell, I didn't even know you were real until a few days ago."

Michael let out a big sigh and walked around the counter, taking her face in his hands.

"I'm not accusing you of anything, Sara. I'm just trying to understand how you were able to reach me personally. No one who isn't an archangel has ever done that. No one. Ever."

She shrugged. "I mean, I was pretty mad," she said with a cheeky smile. She dropped it when he frowned again. "Aaaand this is not a joking matter."

"No."

"Am I in trouble?"

He dropped his hands and sighed. "No, but I am going to need your help figuring out how you did it."

"I don't understand."

"Neither do I, and that's a problem."

CHAPTER TWENTY

Michael stared down at Sara. She looked confused. His instincts told him she didn't know what was inside her, and he trusted them.

What he didn't want to do was say goodbye.

Despite her feelings for him, Michael had picked up on Sara's thoughts—okay, he'd gone digging—about sending him away forever when they said goodbye.

He couldn't allow that.

So he did a really shitty thing. He kissed her harshly on the lips and flashed away. He winced as he felt her pain and tears, and berated himself for it all day.

And the next, and the next, and the next.

Days turned into weeks.

Michael tried to stay busy but found himself torn between needing to touch her, hold her, taste her, and fighting the belief she could be his.

That he could even feel her was weird. Beautifully weird, but he shouldn't be able to. How were they so connected?

If she fell in love, would he feel her love and pleasure with another man during the length of her life? She's mine. He growled before he could stop himself.

God had refused him an audience yet again, leaving him alone in researching Sara's situation. Whatever was inside her needed to be removed, and in the absence of God's insight, he only had one other option available to him.

Letting out a loud groan, he departed for Olympus to visit the Oracle.

Michael flew over the ancient city, taking in the lush green foliage and the great structures. He landed on the cobbled footpath that led through the main village and started making his way to her home.

He felt the irritating presence before she spoke.

"Well, well, well, look who has lowered his standards and graced us with his presence." Artemis, the huntress goddess, sidled up to him, her flowing white gown threaded with gold trim barely covering her breasts. Knowing her, she'd rearranged the dress as soon as she'd seen him. "Have you finally realized I'm the only woman able to please you, darling?"

Michael cursed the day he'd copulated with Apollo's twin. She'd never let him forget it. Not because it was memorable, but because of her obsession with him ever since.

"Artemis. Not today, please. I'm here on business."

She narrowed her eyes at him. "What kind of business? I haven't seen any of your rascal angels getting up to mischief recently."

Since the battle between the archangels and the Olympic gods, the seven brothers rarely spent time on the gods' plane. Unsurprising, given how the gods had tried to breach Heaven's gates and enter. They had failed and always would, but that didn't mean Michael was going to sit down for a glass of ambrosia with the fuckers.

On occasion, one of their warrior angels would create trouble with a young goddess—generally the undressed kind of trouble—and one of the archangels would fly over to resolve it, but otherwise, they kept their distance from one another.

Zeus saw himself as equal to God, but he was not. Not by a long shot.

Still, if you asked any of his meddling brats, they all denied God his status as their creator.

If it had been his choice, Michael would have eliminated them all, but it was not. That was God's choice, and he loved all his creations—including the idiots, apparently.

Today, Michael had no patience for their egos and games. He needed answers to help Sara so he could get back to her. Or, if this was some kind of witchery, disconnect from her so he could leave her to live her life.

Just the thought darkened his mood.

"Let it go and be on your way."

"Oh, come on, Michael." She stepped into his personal space, and he snapped.

"I said go!" Michael let out a small blast of power, and her dark hair blew off her face as her body flew backward. Whipping out a hand, he stopped her before she crashed against a marble pillar. Not that she would have been hurt or killed, being immortal, but there was no point causing a scene.

Or at least a bigger scene.

"Jeez, what is wrong with you?" she sneered at him once she got her balance. Whipping her hair over her shoulder, she flashed away, but not before giving him the finger.

Michael ran a hand through his hair and continued on his way. He really didn't need to attract any attention while he was here. Not that anyone would be surprised at their less than friendly interaction. His disinterest and her obsession were common knowledge, if only because she never shut up about it.

Arriving, he entered the building at the bottom of the hill. Sitting on a throne in a large, empty room was an old woman. Sun streamed through the large windows in wide, dusty rays. As he neared, she changed into a beautiful young lady.

"Stop that, old woman."

"Am I?" She grinned cheekily.

"It matters not. I have no time for Olympian games today."

Her smile faded, and she glared at him. "Take that back."

"My apologies. I forget you are not originally from this place. It has been a long time."

The Oracle was one of the only few saved when Floris had been destroyed by a comet. The beautiful planet had been stunning, with two red moons, lush forests, mountains, and oceans.

The Florisians, renowned for being foreseers, had been a significant loss across the universe. That Zeus had been the one to save the five remaining females was interesting. They all lived on Earth except for the Oracle. Why she stayed on Olympus was something she had never revealed.

Michael knew Zeus used her for his own gains; however, he never stopped her from sharing her gifts with others. Michael doubted the Olympian god would have the power.

An elder even those many eons ago, the Oracle was powerful. And he had his suspicions she had a link directly with God, something very few beings in existence had.

She lowered her head in acceptance of his apology. "So. Your human has been born."

"Yes." Michael waved his hand, and a chair appeared. He sat down in front of her, throwing his ankle over his knee.

The Oracle narrowed her eyes at him. "Do not use your magic in here, archangel."

"Then provide more seating." He shrugged.

"More seating gives the impression I want company." She raised an eyebrow.

He let out a sharp laugh and saw the shadows of a smile hit her lips. The Florisians had been a social and vibrant race. It saddened him to see her like this.

Her eyes glazed. "Do not pity me, archangel. Ask what you came here to ask."

He held her eyes for a long moment, and then he nodded. "The human. Who is she? What is she?"

"The one from your dreams."

It wasn't a question, but he nodded all the same. The Oracle shook her head back and forth as magic started to swirl around her. Her dark eyes turned white, and her head began nodding rapidly. She finally stopped and stared at him blankly.

She spoke. "She is not what you think."

"And?"

"She hides a secret. A great gift. You must protect her and return what doesn't belong to her. Only then…"

"What is she?"

The Oracle shook her head. "It's not safe to discuss such matters here, archangel…"

"Goddamn it, tell me what she is!"

"She is yours, archangel. That is all you need to know. You will find the way to free her, but it will take great faith from both of you."

He groaned. "How?"

"By loving her."

"Love? No, I…"

He stopped himself. Did he love her? He loved all beings. He was the Archangel Michael. But that wasn't what the old woman was saying, and he knew it.

"The longer you question it and hold back, the more danger she will be in." The Oracle began shaking violently. "She will be hunted, Michael. You must go and protect her."

Michael stood suddenly.

"What?" he growled. "Who hunts her?" It was unlike her to give such a warning. Like God with his cryptic messages, the Oracle was known for sharing only small amounts of information.

"I cannot see who, only that you will fight a battle for her. Only then can you two be together."

He would fight a thousand battles to protect her, but it wouldn't change the fact of who they each were. A mortal and an immortal. He was the Archangel Michael. She wanted a husband, a picket fence, and a baby stroller.

"Together? She is a mortal. I am…"

"The answers will come. You must go now."

He nodded.

"Thank you. Be well, Oracle."

She bowed her head, closing her eyes.

Michael flashed the chair away and marched out of the building. Outside, he'd taken only a few steps when he heard a voice that made his skin crawl.

"Michael."

He turned slowly.

"Ares," he greeted darkly.

"Why are you on Olympus?"

"Worried?" He raised an eyebrow, taunting the god of war.

Ares glowered back at him.

"Don't start anything you're not willing to finish, Ares. I have no patience for your little god games today." Michael realized he was poking the bear, but if there was going to be an altercation, he wanted it over quickly. He needed to get back to Sara.

The god lifted his hand, and a fireball began forming in his palm. "I care not for your patience, little angel."

Arch-bloody-angel to you, motherfucker.

Zeus suddenly appeared beside his son and snuffed out the fireball with a wave of his hand. Ignoring the glare from Ares, he turned to Michael.

"Archangel Michael, to what do we owe this pleasure?" The sneer in his voice was clear.

"Zeus," he replied coldly. Michael never explained himself to the Olympians, and he would not start today.

Knowing Sara was in potential danger had his usual lack of patience wearing very thin. "Rein in your son. I'm not staying." He crossed his enormous arms and smirked. "Unless I see another fireball, then I could find the time."

Okay, so he had a few moments to poke the bear some more. It had been a long time, and he wasn't one to miss an opportunity to piss off an Olympian or two.

"Is that a human I smell on you?" Ares sniffed.

Michael stilled. Gods couldn't smell other species. That he mentioned such a thing immediately sent a chill down his spine.

"What did you say, you piece of shit?" He took a step forward just as Zeus flashed his son away. The father of the gods was nothing if not intuitive. "Smart move, god."

"As is your decision to leave, Supreme," Zeus replied, crossing his huge arms across his bare chest.

"Keep him away from the humans, Zeus. I've warned you before," he said, pointing at the guy.

"You have no authority over us, archangel. I tolerate your kind on my planet, but that is it."

Michael barked out a laugh.

"How long will you remain in denial over God's existence, Zeus? This entire universe is mine to protect, and that includes Olympus." He waved his arms. "But by all means, please try to stop me."

Make my day.

Although perhaps not today, he had to get to Sara. But one day he would delight in going face-to-face with Zeus.

The father of the gods' eyes flashed with fury. "Be careful what you wish for, archangel."

He snorted.

"You are lucky I have other, more pressing plans. Until next time."

Michael left before he changed his mind.

CHAPTER TWENTY-ONE

Sara wandered through the mall with a big smile. She didn't care that she looked like an idiot because she wasn't alone.

Lockdown was over, and everyone was out shopping, lining up in drive-throughs to get their favorite takeout, and catching up with loved ones. It was such a relief after being stuck inside for so long.

Winter was coming, and people were stocking up on warmer clothing, bedding, and other key items they hadn't been able to purchase when the shops were shut. Many could not trade for months, nor deliver.

A dose of retail therapy was just what she needed after spending weeks in tears. Michael had left without a word of goodbye. Just kissed her and vanished.

She had been hurt, angry, and then just plain sad as she grieved the loss of him from her life. He'd robbed her of the opportunity to say goodbye. Sure, she had been planning to ask him not to return, but planning it and doing it were two different things. Plus, closure was important. All she'd been left with were unsaid words and the desire to both yell at him and run into his arms.

Sara had gone over it in her head a thousand times, wondering if she would have had the courage to ask him not to return had he not left. A moot point, of course, but one she had strangely enjoyed debating with herself.

Yes, she was a strong woman, so of course she would have.

No, Michael was her weakness.

Sara was exhausted after the roller coaster of emotions she'd ridden over the past few weeks. She needed some fun with her friends, and now that they could socialize in groups, Lisa had organized a dinner party this weekend.

As she walked past the shops, she took in the changes. Lines on the floor reminded people to keep a six-foot distance when queuing, and Perspex separated retailers from shoppers to stop the spread of the virus. Shoppers wore masks and tried not to look at each other.

It brought tears to her eyes. People wanted to hug, touch, and shake hands. It was an unusual time in human history they'd never forget.

Shaking herself out of her funk, she dug into her handbag for her phone.

Where's my list? Okay. Next, David Jones.

The Australian-owned department store was right at the other end of the mall. Sara tugged her handbag further onto her shoulder and made her way down there, swinging her shopping bags happily.

"Sara."

Stumbling over her own feet at the sound of his voice, she felt large hands grab her, halting her fall.

She looked up. "Michael?"

Despite all her grief, she turned and let him pull her into his arms. She melted into his large, warm body and sighed.

Damn traitorous body.

"Hello, sweetheart," he breathed into her hair.

Then it all came rushing back to her. "You just left. How could you?" she cried.

"I was a coward. I'm here to ask your forgiveness."

She lifted her head and looked at him. He gazed down at her, looking somber. His hand landed on her cheek, and she gazed into his beautiful bright blue eyes.

God, he was so gorgeous.

She noticed the people around them. Both men and

women were staring at him unashamedly in much the same way as she was.

Michael was an exceptionally large man, and while she'd been aware of that when they had been alone, now with others around to compare him with, it was far more obvious.

And not just his size, but also his presence. Wearing normal old jeans and a blue shirt—which looked damn hot—there was something powerful and magical about him that words couldn't describe.

Still. He'd left her. Despite his apology, she knew he'd do it again, and she wouldn't survive going through that over and over again.

"What kind of archangel hurts a human?"

He went to speak, but fish mouthed for a moment before just nodding. "You are right."

"What do you want?"

"Your forgiveness."

"Well, I'm shopping," she said as if it wasn't obvious.

He glanced around and then sent a small smile down at her. "You cannot forgive and shop at the same time?"

Now the staring was getting annoying. People were closing in on them as if he were a damn celebrity. Noticing her discomfort, Michael lifted his finger, and suddenly everyone just carried on with their day as if he weren't there.

"What did you do?" she asked, narrowing her eyes and looking around.

"My energy is highly attractive to humans. You distracted me and I forgot to rein it in."

"Oh. Crap. Is that why I was attracted to you?"

"Was?" Michael inquired with a tilt of his head.

She frowned. "Fine. Am."

Damn archangel. Why couldn't she just lie to him and pretend he was just a one-night stand she wasn't interested in like any old guy. Or archangel.

"No. This is different, Sara. Much different." He lifted

her hand and kissed it.

Dammit. Damn him.

"But the fact remains that I am an archangel and need to be careful of my energy levels around you. You distract me."

"So you can't relax around me and be yourself?"

"I am being myself. However, I would fry your brain and everyone around you if I were to lose control."

Sara's mouth fell open.

"How often do you lose control?"

"Never."

She blinked.

"Do not concern yourself with all that, Sara. We are here to protect humans, not harm them."

He cupped her cheek again, and his blue eyes held hers. "So, am I forgiven?"

"No."

"Then how can I earn your forgiveness? Let me take you on a date. Like a human."

Say no. Say no.

As she felt her defenses fall away while having an internal argument with herself, Sara drew in a long breath. Truly, how was a woman supposed to say no when a six foot five god of a man stood in front of her looking like something out of a magazine? He oozed sex as he looked at her as if she were the latest luxury yacht.

She was no saint. But she wasn't an idiot, either.

"Well, I'm shopping, so you'll need to wait until I'm finished."

"Really?"

She turned and walked toward the store, calling over her shoulder, "Yes, really."

Grinning, she felt him catch up to her, take her bags out of her hand, and walk beside her.

An hour later, Michael loaded their shopping into the

trunk of the car while Sara climbed into the driver's seat. She unzipped her white puffer jacket and pulled the faux fur hood off.

"You look cute in this." Michael smiled, lifting the hood back over her head. "How about we go skiing in Switzerland?"

"No. God no." She shook her head. "I want sunshine, beaches, tropical islands. No snow. No cold anything, except ice creams or cocktails."

"The Bahamas, then."

Sara tilted her head at him. "So wait. We can go anywhere in the world? How?"

"Sure. World, universe, wherever. I was just on Olympus, so yeah."

"Olympus is real?!" she cried out.

Michael ran his hand over his face. "I'm so bad at this. Yes, it is. Everything is real. Well, except vampires. That's just weird."

She stared at him blankly.

"Okay, let's skip that conversation," Michael said, squeezing her leg. "You like Hawaii, right? Want to go there?"

"I love Hawaii," she replied, fully aware he'd used the tropical island as a distraction. And succeeded. "But that doesn't explain how."

"One step at a time. Just say yes."

"Yes," she said, then held up a hand. "Except I have rules. This time, you have to say goodbye when you leave. And we say goodbye for the last time, okay? I can't keep doing this."

Suddenly, the world around her wobbled. Her brain spun as the parking lot was replaced by her garage.

"Jesus!" She gripped the steering wheel to find some stable foundation.

"You are home."

She turned and raised an eyebrow, all you're kidding

me, right? He gave her a small, cheeky smile, then he cupped her face and kissed her, deep and slow, full of unspoken promises. When his lips left hers, she sighed.

"I'm not leaving you, Sara. Not this time."

His kisses felt different from the last time they were together. Like when you knew the guy liked you for more than just your boobs.

"What does that mean?"

"It has hurt me also to stay away from you. I shouldn't feel like this. I'm an archangel. It's confusing. All I know right now is that I cannot leave you. I will not leave you."

Energy rushed through her body. It was both thrilling and terrifying. They were the words every woman wanted to hear, but they also felt possessive and demanding.

"If I have to leave again, I will come back to you."

"Why?"

In a flash, he appeared beside her and opened the car door, helping her out. "Because I cannot stay away."

None of this made sense. There was no future for them.

Then a thought struck her.

"Wait, you're not going to be one of those fallen angels, are you? Where you lose your wings and become human. You don't have to do that for me."

Michael shook his head and let out a laugh. "No, there's no risk of that happening."

Ouch.

Okay, so he still saw this as a love affair, not a long-term thing. She'd stupidly misinterpreted his words. He would eventually leave her once he'd worked out his confused feelings. Not that she wanted him to fall, but he could've been a bit more sensitive about it.

"Oh, good. Cool. That's great," she said, sidestepping him.

"Stop."

"Don't stop me, angel," she snapped and shook him

off when he grabbed her arm.

"Talk to me."

"No, it's fine."

Fine.

"What just happened?" She shook her head stubbornly, still pulling her arm. "You want me to fall for you?" he asked, astonished. "Why?"

Sara continued to get her arm loose. "Michael, let me go." When he didn't, she sighed and turned away from him. "No, I don't want you to fall. I just thought for a moment you wanted something more serious. I'm an idiot."

"Archangels don't fall. That's a human myth," Michael explained, and she shook her head. When he let her arm go, she walked away, rubbing it, and mumbled, "Missed the point, Michael."

Upstairs, Sara found her shopping on the bed. Archangel magic. She made some rude comments under her breath and unpacked with more gusto than was needed.

She felt Michael come up behind her. He laid his hands on her hips while she hung up her new coat.

"I've never had a girlfriend before, remember?"

She froze.

That was the last thing she'd expected to hear. A small smile formed on her face.

"I've got no experience with relationships."

"Is this a relationship?"

"I think so."

"Think?"

"I don't know, Sara." He turned her in his arms. "I don't have any answers for you, which is why I've been trying to dodge this conversation, but I see now that was the wrong thing to do."

Sara chewed her bottom lip.

"I can lead archangels in battle, intimidate powerful gods, answer prayers for billions upon billions of beings around the universe, but I can't say the right thing to you.

It's very frustrating."

"You just did."

Michael gazed down at her, confused. "I did?"

She nodded. As he leaned down to kiss her, she pulled back. "You battle?"

Michael's eyes closed. "One thing at a time, little human."

"Okay."

His lips landed on hers.

CHAPTER TWENTY-TWO

Uriel winked at the young minor goddess and turned to Gabriel. "Nothing's changed in this place."

"Not even the name," Gabriel sneered over his mug of ambrosia. "Idiots."

The two bare-chested archangels sat side by side on wooden barstools at The Fat Angel, the popular drinking establishment on Olympus. It was an open garden style bar where celestial beings from across the universe came to enjoy the nectar of the gods.

A tropical breeze drifted through the large windows as Gabriel watched a group of cherubs socializing with some of the recent warrior graduates.

"Totally childish." Uriel smiled. "Directed at Michael, obviously."

Gabe laughed, then nodded to the table of angels. "No sign of Several." Uriel had lost track of the warrior angel a few days earlier, and so far, they'd been unable to find him. A rare occurrence for an archangel, and one that raised an even brighter red flag.

"Where is the little shit? He hasn't been hanging out with his peers. You think he's on Earth?"

"Why would he be?" Gabe asked. "We have to find him before Michael returns. Raphael said he's out of control over this human."

"So weird."

"Yeah. Let's go…" Gabriel watched as Uriel suddenly stiffened. The goddess Aphrodite had slid up next to his brother, rubbing her breast against his arm and purring into his neck.

"Hello, boys," she said with a thick, sexual drawl.

"No, no, no, no, no. Leave him alone, Dite. We're busy working," Gabriel growled.

"Hey, gorgeous," Uriel greeted, giving him a dark look mixed with an apology—if that was even possible.

Aphrodite was beautiful. Hell, she was a goddess. Gabriel shook his head as Uriel's eyes fell into her cleavage where tanned, plump breasts were tightly packed into a white dress that wrapped around her body secured with gold and gems most females would die for. Then he breathed in her rich scent, which was erotic even from where Gabe was standing. The guy stood zero chance.

Again.

With a dart of annoyance, she ignored him and turned to Uriel, laying a long fingernailed hand on his pec. "Uriel, darling, I've missed you."

"Ah. Yup, I've been busy. Pandemic on Earth," he answered and grabbed her hand. At least he was trying not to fall into the abyss this time.

The two of them were a complete mystery to the rest of the archangels. She had some sexual power over their brother, and if they tried to talk to him about it, he snapped their heads off. He assured them it was nothing and seemed to be able to keep away from her for periods of time, but as soon as they were together, something shifted within him.

"I heard," she said breathlessly, though Gabriel imagined she'd never run a mile in her life. "You must be so exhausted, expending all that archangel energy. Let me take care of you. I know exactly what you need."

Gabriel raised an eyebrow as the cunning female ran her hand over his shoulder and over the guy's biceps. Uriel swallowed, then looked at Gabe.

"Oh, come on, you two."

"Fine!" she said, standing back up and pouting. "But you owe me an explanation. Where have you been?"

Uriel had kept away from Olympus for the past almost two hundred years or so. Ever since the battle with the gods where they had breached the wards of Heaven, all of them had refrained from visiting Olympus unless there was a need. But Uriel had not returned.

Gabriel knew the two of them had been lovers on and off for centuries, a situation no other archangel could claim, not to the extent these two did.

They would spend days or weeks holed up in her home on Olympus. Once he was inside, and unless there was an archangel emergency or they went in to retrieve him themselves, there was no getting him out.

Gabriel had lovers. Many. And on occasion, he'd go back for seconds, but never more than that. Why, when there was such a selection of beautiful women and men to enjoy.

Had his brother been with another lover since the 1800s when they'd last visited Olympus? It was a damn good question.

Uriel adjusted his shorts and Gabe rolled his eyes.

Aphrodite stared at the two of them, then huffed and walked off. Uriel glanced at him before he called out to the goddess, following her.

"Dite, wait." Uriel grabbed the goddess's hips to halt her.

"Almost two hundred years, Uri. I've waited long enough."

He turned her around and tugged her against him. She sighed and placed a hand on his chest; shivers ran throughout his body. He both hated and loved the way his entire being reacted to this female. No one else made him feel as she did.

"I've deeply missed you, Uri. Your lips on my body,

mostly, but other parts of you as well."

His cock twitched.

"Yes, that." She smiled at him innocently.

"Stop it," he groaned.

She shrugged. "What are you doing here, Uriel?"

"I'm not here looking for relief, if that's what you think."

"But it would be with me if you were, wouldn't it?" Her eyes flickered with a threat for a split second before it disappeared.

"Careful, goddess," he growled. He was an archangel first and was only willing to be manipulated so far.

"Why would I want to share this perfection?" Aphrodite cajoled, stepping into his body further. His hands landed on her soft, round bottom as her breasts pressed into him. Yeah, fuck, he was toast.

I could get some information out of her while I'm here, brother.

Uri, don't.

I'll be okay. Just one night.

If you aren't back tomorrow, I'm bringing Raphael with me!

Fine.

His cock jumped for joy at the pleasure it knew awaited them. He pulled the goddess up his body and claimed her mouth.

"One night, and you better do that trick I like."

"For you, I'll do it twice," she said, smiling and biting his lower lip.

Fuck.

CHAPTER TWENTY-THREE

"Wow." Michael's eyes ran over Sara's figure-hugging blue sundress. She stood in front of him, shivering. "It really is possible to look both hot and cold at once."

"Funny guy. Are you going to change?"

He waved a hand and was instantly wearing a pair of board shorts and a T-shirt. Sara shook her head at him, and he grinned.

"Come." He took her hand and pulled her into his body. "Ready?" As she nodded, he wrapped her in his arms tightly. It wasn't necessary, but she was still getting used to him flashing her to different locations.

The tropical heat and delicious smells of Hawaii hit them as they stood on the sands of Waikiki Beach.

"Oh my God," Sara squealed joyfully in his ears, then she gasped. "Oh no."

"What?" Michael asked, spinning around, looking and attempting to sense the danger.

"We can't be here. They're in lockdown still. I totally forgot. We've got to go home."

The beach was empty. Aside from a few police officers and one or two random people, there was no one around. He hadn't been to Earth for a long time, but even he could sense the strange and eerie feeling around them.

But he would not miss this opportunity to impress Sara. He took her hand and pulled her down onto the beach. "You're completely safe. I have protected you from the virus. Plus, nobody can see us."

"Really?" She squinted at him in disbelief, which he

ignored, but couldn't resist a smirk.

He loved surprising her, but it was obvious she didn't believe he was capable of…well, everything, because a moment later, she waved at a police officer standing on the edge of the beach.

"Aloha. Can you see me?" The man did not react or see her. Because he couldn't.

"Wow, that's incredible."

"What would you have done if he'd seen you?" he asked with an arched brow. "The current laws here would see him arrest you for being on the beach."

"Oh, um." Sara stopped walking and chewed her lip. Then she shrugged. "I'm going to assume you'd save us."

He laughed.

They found a spot and sat down in the sand, and he watched her soul bask in the warmth and ease of the ocean around her. He kissed her nose. "You really, really love it here, huh?"

"More than just about anything. Well, except Tilly."

Michael stared out at the ocean, thinking. He was now confident Sara was human and had another soul along for the ride. Why, he didn't know. But it was rare and dangerous. And powerful. Souls didn't just hide inside humans for no reason. He needed to gain its trust and help both Sara and the soul of whatever was inside her. But he didn't want to scare her.

Reading between the lines, Michael suspected this was why God had connected him with Sara. He had been sent to protect her and this other soul. It made sense. But once he helped them, he didn't see himself wanting to leave her any less than he did now.

For now, he wanted to focus on the incredible feelings he was experiencing being with her.

"You're glowing," he said, turning to face her. He meant it in the human sense—she just had a sparkle about her as she took on the energy of the place.

"Well, we're in Hawaii. It's paradise."

Michael couldn't help but be infected by her joy. He manifested towels and they ran down to the water and swam for a few hours. He kissed her about seventy-five times, approximately, and later, as the sun began to set, they wandered along the pier and sat with their feet dangling in the water.

Michael handed her a Mai Tai.

"Whoa. You're the best date ever." She laughed, taking the tall glass dressed with the little umbrella, a straw, and a slice of coconut.

"When in Rome, right?"

"Mahalo," she said, thanking him in Hawaiian.

"Aloha."

They watched as the sky changed from pinks to orange until it eventually darkened and filled with millions of twinkling stars.

"Just so you know, I don't need to fall from grace to be with you. I'm here. That's what I meant," he said quietly, slipping an arm behind her. Sara leaned back against him.

"I shouldn't have gotten mad. That was immature. You know my background, though. I have major trust issues."

"You have my loyalty, Sara."

"I know, but I can't give you my heart. I can't fall in love and plan a life with you."

Her words ripped at his heart. He would never hurt her as others had, and yet, hadn't he already done it? Something stirred within him. A desire for her to fall in love with him. It was the most selfish feeling he'd ever felt, one mixed with the need to give Sara everything she wanted.

Confusion rippled through him. Was he in love with her? Given it was something he'd never experienced firsthand, he did not know. Men and women around the world fantasized about being in love with him, but this wasn't fantasy or lust. This was a power that felt even greater than him, if that was even possible.

"Would it be so bad if you did?"

"Yes!" she exclaimed, and he heard the emotion in her voice. "Because you'll leave, and we won't get to make memories or build a home. Or have children. We'll be in different worlds."

Michael wrapped his arms around her. "We'll figure this out."

"Don't make promises. I'm no angel expert, but I'm fairly sure I can't go up to Heaven, and I'm not ready to die."

"Hey! You are not dying. I would walk away before that happened."

"Great. See what I mean?"

Michael stared out at the ocean, pulling her closer. They were both frustrated, he understood that, but still had no answer.

"I hate seeing Hawaii so dead. Damn virus."

"This isn't the first viral pandemic in human history, nor will it be the last, sweetheart. And it will pass."

"Can you not rid the planet of it? Say, if I asked you?"

"Yes." As a smile appeared on her face, he added, "But in the microsecond between you asking and me saying yes, millions of conflicting requests have come in, countering it. I fulfill them all. As of this moment in time, the virus is still in existence. Though it's weakening."

"Free will."

"Yes." He nodded.

"Why would someone want a virus?"

"It is not our job as archangels to judge. We simply answer the prayers."

"What if someone prayed for you to kill me?"

He frowned. "We do not harm humans. But another human has free will to do so, and we cannot interfere."

"So if someone walked over and attempted to shoot me, you would allow it?"

"No…" He frowned further.

"Well?"

"It's different. You are…",

Sara stared at him, waiting. He pulled her into his arms, forcing his lips onto hers. She responded, letting him own her mouth and taste the deliciousness of her. Eventually, he had to look at her.

"I cannot answer you. But I would never allow anyone to harm you."

She sighed and leaned into him. He kissed the top of her head. "I think it's time I took you home, my beautiful little human."

"Give me just a minute more."

He nodded, and she stood for a moment breathing in the warm, tropical air and smells around her. Sara closed her eyes, and he knew she was taking in the sounds of the waves and the palm trees as the air brushed through them.

He brushed across her mind, intrusive but with good intentions, and found a desire.

Bringing her close against him, he pulled her into a romantic, passionate kiss—the kind she'd always dreamed of. She moaned against his mouth, leaning into his hard body.

He flashed them home, wrapping her in a long cardigan before the cool air of the southern hemisphere could chill her.

Sara opened her eyes and smiled.

"Thank you," she whispered. "That was the best date ever."

Tilly looked up from her sleeping spot on the cat tower and let out a soft, welcoming meow.

"It isn't over yet, sweetheart."

CHAPTER TWENTY-FOUR

The next morning, Sara woke up early and was relieved to find Michael still in bed with her. She rolled over, snuggling into his warm body while pulling her feet out from under the cat. Tilly sounded her annoyance at being disturbed, and Sara murmured something in return.

Michael sniggered.

She opened one eye. "It's not funny. How can something so little take up so much space?"

The bed shuddered, and when she opened both eyes and sat up, she saw the bed had grown at least twenty percent. She shook her head and lay back down.

"It won't help. She's like the Tardis in Doctor Who."

"Who?"

"Never mind." She laughed. "You need to watch some TV. For about twenty years."

"What I need is more of you," he said and pulled her thigh over his.

She melted into him as his morning wood easily slipped inside her. They both moaned.

"Oh God," she uttered as his thrusts sped up.

Next minute he had her on top of him, gliding her up and down his cock. She clenched her muscles around him, and he let out a guttural noise she was beginning to associate with his climax. It triggered hers, and together, they orgasmed.

She just never got enough of him, no matter how many times they had sex. And it appeared he felt the same.

Michael flipped her over, remaining inside of her.

"Good morning," he greeted, desire still rich in his expression.

"Morning." She smiled like an idiot.

God, but he was just the most gorgeous man she'd ever seen. His enormous body completely swamped hers, but all it did was make her feel feminine and protected.

"I could do this for hours, but I am trying to understand your human limits," he said, slowing moving in and out of her.

"No limit reached yet," she replied, losing the ability to think as he took her hips and deepened their connection. When his thumb crossed over her rear hole, her mind went blank. Her body pulsed and exploded.

"Yes, baby, you like that, huh?"

And then she was being flipped and put on all fours as he thrust into her again.

"Touch yourself," he ordered.

When she did, she began to cry out, feeling his cock swell inside her. He was close.

"Yes, fuck, yes. Aghh," Michael groaned, a palm on the wall above them, the other gripping her hip.

Then she was being wrapped in his arms as he laid her down on the mattress once more. He nuzzled into her neck, holding her tight. Protectively. Possessively.

"Do you sleep? I feel like you do, but do you?" she asked.

"I slumber. Rest. Our bodies have different needs than a human's."

"So you don't need to sleep?"

"No. I am pure light energy, as are you, but as a human who cannot shift back into spirit, you also require sleep, food, and water, to put it simply."

"To put it simply," she repeated, wondering what that meant.

Michael kissed her nose. "Let's save the archangel biology lesson for another day. Just know I enjoy sleeping with you, so I slumber and enjoy the feel of your body and warmth. And even Tilly's purring."

"While you're also fulfilling prayers."

"Yes."

"So answer me this, archangel. I believe I create my life. What I focus on, I draw to me. The good, the bad, and the ugly. Am I wrong?"

He smiled at her.

"No. You are not wrong."

"Why are you staring at me like that?"

"You've been studying this topic for a long time, Sara, so you knew the answer."

She smiled.

"Yes, but I wanted to be sure because every time I feel like I'm getting ahead, something comes along and derails my plans. I'm still confused about why."

Michael nodded, his expression curious as he ran the back of his hand over her cheek. "You created me being here with you."

"I really don't know how I did that," she said.

"Well. I still don't know how I heard you."

Something had been nagging at her, and she decided to ask him about it. "There's something else."

"Tell me."

"I feel this built-up energy within me sometimes. Some days it's not there; other days it's like this frustration that wants to explode out of me."

"Tell me in more detail."

"Well, that's really it. I used to think it was anger, but when I shared this with other friends, they thought I was crazy. Honestly, some days I feel like it wants to burst out of my chest and explode into the sky and zoom across the galaxy." She laughed. "I'm sorry, that sounds really silly."

Sara looked up at Michael and froze when she saw his face.

"Oh my God, what?"

CHAPTER TWENTY-FIVE

Gods, why hadn't he thought of this earlier? Michael had a feeling he knew what she was talking about, but it seemed impossible.

Absolutely impossible.

He was using a vast amount of willpower not to launch off the bed and scream to the heavens. He took a deep breath. Then another.

"Michael. What's wrong?"

She'd allowed herself to be vulnerable and share something with him, and he was just staring at her. He had good reason, though—it was a miracle if he was right.

Had God sent him to Sara? Did he know? Of course, God knew everything. For the most part.

If Michael was right, Sara was hosting something incredibly precious within her soul, hidden so deep it was imperceptible even to him and Raphael.

"Come with me, gorgeous." He climbed out of bed and took her hand when she stood next to him.

Flashing them to the living room, he waved his hand to clothe them both, grinning as he did.

"Really?" Sara looked down at the low-cut emerald-green silk gown.

"What?" At her raised eyebrow, he chuckled and changed her into a pair of jeans and a white sweater.

"Okay, here's the thing," Michael started, directing her to sit on the sofa. He kneeled in front of her, wondering where to start. He needed to figure out if he was right. "I want to try…"

Michael.

Raphael?

He turned, and the archangel was standing in the living room.

What's going on?

The angel.

That same dark feeling that had run through his body a few days ago came back.

Tell me.

"Try what?"

"Do you meditate?" he asked, trying to multitask two conversations.

What's going on? Raphael asked, taking a step closer.

I think she's carrying a special being.

A demon?

Michael shook his head. The angel Severial. Did you find him?

"Yes, sometimes. Not all that well," Sara replied, and he moved to sit beside her, glancing at Raphael.

Tell her I'm here. I want to meet my brother's girl. Raphael grinned.

No. Update me now.

He's gone rogue, and there are rumors he's been prophesied to bring about the death of an archangel princess.

Michael frowned. There's no such thing.

Raphael shrugged.

He sounds insane. Find him and lock him up. I am done playing nice.

Well, here's the thing. We cannot find him.

What do you mean you can't find him?

No angel could hide from an archangel. Not without assistance from, say, a witch.

And Michael, the gods believe your human is the princess from this prophecy.

Michael erupted and launched to his feet, flying across

the room at his brother. "What!"

"Michael?!" Sara cried out.

He froze just before reaching Raphael, who'd put his hand out, slowing him with his celestial power. Raphael wasn't powerful enough to stop him, but the act of doing so had snapped him out of it.

"What are you doing?"

You are scaring her, Michael.

"Shit. I'm sorry. Give me a minute, and I'll explain," he said, running his hand through his hair.

Ares mentioned Sara when I was on Olympus yesterday. I nearly ripped his head off but didn't have time to deal with him because the Oracle told me she was in danger.

You never go to Olympus. Not since the battle. And you went to see the Oracle? Raphael asked.

Yes. Fuck. Something bigger is going on here. Why do the gods know about her? She has a soul inside her; one you and I cannot detect, but it's there.

Then let's extract it.

Michael raised an eyebrow at him. Tried. It booted me across the room!

What?! Raphael stared at him in shock before starting across the room toward Sara.

Michael grabbed the top of his brother's arm with great strength. Stop. Do not go near her, Raphael.

Let go of me, Michael, Raphael growled at him and shook him off.

Michael may be the Supreme Archangel, but that didn't mean he could micromanage his brothers' every move.

Still. He didn't want anyone to touch Sara. No one.

Not another step, Raphael. Neither she nor the guest mean us any harm. It is a gift of which we cannot speak of while we are on Earth.

Raphael crossed his arms and smirked. Are you in love with her?

Michael sighed. Sara was staring at him in confusion, patiently waiting for him to explain. *You know that's impossible. But for some reason I feel that she is mine, and I will protect her with everything I am.*

He turned to look at Raphael.

Tell the archangels I am bringing her home.

How? You know you can't bring a human into heaven…

Let's just say I have a feeling it will be possible.

Then I will see you back home.

Michael wiped his face with his hand.

"I'm sorry." She stood and walked up to him, her hands landing on his chest. He placed a hand over hers and one around her neck, pulling her into him, kissing her. "Raphael was here."

"Raphael was here? In my house?" she squeaked.

"Yes." He frowned. "Why?"

"The Archangel Raphael. That's kind of a big deal."

He pointed at his chest. "Have we met? Supreme Archangel?"

She grinned and kissed him, and he shook his head. "Anyway, I'm going to ask Raphael and Gabriel to return and stand guard while we…"

"To my home?" Her voice was high pitched now. It was like he was inviting the Beatles, or whoever the latest boy band was.

"Yes, Sara, please calm down."

He placed his hand on her stomach and guided her back onto the couch to sit.

That's when he felt it.

The subtle pulse.

"Oh, my fucking…" He stared at Sara with complete and absolute astonishment. "What the actual fuck!"

Michael had lived forever—literally forever—and never had anything surprised him like what he had just felt.

Unable to, for the first time in his existence, contain

his true self while on Earth, his soul began to release. An almighty flash of white light exploded out of him for miles. In less than a second, he pulled it back as he caught himself. But it was too late.

Sara flew back onto the sofa and passed out.

"SHIT!"

RAPHAEL!

"What the hell, Michael?!" Raphael roared as he appeared in the room.

Michael, what the fuck?

Uriel! he called to his brother. I'll explain later. Damage control, please.

Roger that, Uriel answered.

"What happened?" Raphael asked, his eyes wide.

"I released some of my power. Fucking hell," Michael explained, his hand over his mouth.

"I know what you fucking did. Why?" Raphael glanced at Sara, not daring to step toward her. Michael knew he presumed she was dead. "Five million New Zealanders and parts of Australia are without power right now! Let's not even start on the damage to life and technology."

We've got fifteen human deaths in the immediate vicinity. Two traffic accidents. Chamuel and Zads are on the South Island. Gabe is in Australia.

Thanks, Uri, Michael said, hanging his head in shame. Shut down any news media on it.

Already done. Australia just has a few power outages. No fatalities, Gabriel reported.

Thanks, Gabriel.

"She's alive," Michael informed Raphael, kneeling and placing his hand on Sara's forehead. He pushed his healing powers through her. "Just."

Her life, energy, and heartbeat were subtle, but she'd survive.

"How?" Raphael asked with raised eyebrows.

"I believe her guest protected her. Self-preservation."

Raphael kneeled down beside Michael and started helping with her healing, placing his hand over her abdomen first. "Are you going to…holy shit!"

Michael glanced sideways at his brother and gave him a small smile. "Yes, brother. Now you know why I lost it. Be very careful with her."

"Yeah, fuck," Raphael muttered. "Fuck."

Michael watched as Raphael, the Archangel of Healing, stared wide-eyed at her. She should be dead.

"This is crazy."

They could both feel his energy signature within her. As impossible as it was, Sara was carrying his child.

The first archangel baby.

"You can sense it just as I can, Raphael."

"You need to speak to Father."

The way Raphael spoke got his attention. He turned fully toward his brother and frowned. He knew something. "He's spoken to you?"

"Yes."

"He told you about this?" Michael asked angrily.

"No, but…shit, he's going to kill me, but I think you know this already, so what the hell. She's your soulmate, Michael."

Soulmate. Archangels didn't have soulmates. "My what?"

"Yeah, a little gift from Dad. Apparently, we all have one. Eventually."

Michael stood and paced the room.

Soulmate.

Trust God to throw something like this into the mix. It would have been nice to have a family meeting about it. Maybe a BBQ and then a little announcement and heads-up, say, a thousand years ago or something.

"So, like millions of years after our creation, we are suddenly going to start meeting our soulmates?"

Raphael kept his energy flowing into Sara, aiding in her

healing, as he stood to face Michael. "Well, you have, brother. It may be a million more before the rest of us do. If we ever do. I probably won't."

Michael gazed at Sara, who looked like she was simply taking a nap. Instead, she was undergoing the most powerful and intense angel healing. Of course, with all of them here, it would be stronger, but he didn't think it was necessary. Raphael would call them if they were needed.

"This doesn't make any sense. Why a human? Am I to fall?"

Was that a thing now? Raphael's announcement had single-handedly blown his entire understanding of their existence into question.

"He didn't give that impression, but you know what he's like. Cryptic as fuck." Raph hesitated. "Would you?"

Michael looked at his brother, then down at the woman carrying his child, unable to answer. He loved this woman. He would never give her up; he knew that. But to fall? Fall from grace, from who he was, who he'd been created to be? To give up his protection of God, his brothers, humanity?

"That would be a cruel thing to ask after an eternity of service. I'm going to assume it is still human fiction."

"I agree."

Gabriel appeared in the room. Raphael must have called him. He was, after all, the archangel who watched over children.

"Hey," Gabriel said as he strode into the room. He looked at Michael, ready to enquire about his energy release, when he glanced at Sara. "What the…"

"Michael short-circuited his soulmate?"

Michael glared at Raphael. "I did not short-circuit her."

Gabriel snorted. "She does look short-circuited. That whole soulmate thing is a buzz, huh?"

"Does everyone know—"

"Oh shit," Gabriel suddenly exclaimed, looking at

Michael with pity. "Shit. Sorry, buddy."

Michael frowned.

Gabriel pointed at her stomach. "You know she's pregnant, right?"

"Yes, it's mi—"

"What on Earth!" Gabriel jumped to his feet. He turned to look at his brothers, his eyebrows at his hairline.

"...my child," Michael finished.

"Well, fuck me."

Raphael and Michael stared at their brother, nodding. And nodding. They were all in a state of shock. In a matter of minutes, he had discovered that Sara was his soulmate, that they were capable of having soulmates, and that she was pregnant with his child.

Later, as Michael sat staring at Tilly curled up on Raphael's lap, he thanked his brothers for taking turns with him to heal Sara. Predictably, they just shrugged.

Michael, we're heading back to Heaven. Everything is taken care of.

Thanks, guys, he said to Chamuel, Zadkiel, and Uriel, who had spent the last few hours cleaning up his mess.

"A baby archangel, what a blessing." Gabriel sighed. "What should we call it?"

"Let's leave the mommy and daddy to name it, shall we?" Raphael rolled his eyes.

Michael smirked. His brothers were going to be a handful for Sara to manage, and with six archangel uncles, their child would be well loved and protected. However, they couldn't forget the danger in the background.

"Can we please focus on the fact that we have a rogue warrior out there who thinks he's destined to kill my soulmate? Or worse, my child."

"Our child."

"Mine and Sara's child."

"She's all of ours," Gabriel stated firmly.

"Gabriel, you are the Archangel of Children, not the father of my child. Don't push your luck with me today." Michael sighed.

"You'll be a great uncle," Raphael placated. "But right now, Michael is right. We need to protect them both. So what do we know?"

"When was he last seen?" Michael asked, still glaring at Gabriel.

"Just after graduation, when you rode his ass. Before that, on Olympus a few weeks earlier, mingling with the usual troublemakers."

Michael snorted. "That doesn't narrow it down." But he knew who Raphael meant.

Ares.

Raphael checked Sara's progress.

"Ares knew about Sara. How?"

His brothers looked at each other and shrugged.

"Does this have anything to do with the guest you mentioned?"

"What guest?" Gabe asked.

"Later. I don't want to discuss it outside of Heaven." They all stared at him, then nodded. It was probably highly relevant, but it was far too dangerous if his suspicions were correct.

"She'll wake up soon," Raphael said. "She's strong."

"So there's no damage to the child?" Michael asked Gabe again.

"No. It's simply a life force developing into an embryo right now, so it was never at risk. You can feel its strength as well as I can, Michael." Gabriel slapped him on his shoulder in a friendly manner, all animosity gone between them. That was their way. They all forgave and let things go quickly. "Do not worry," he added with a kind smile. His brother had the most loving heart when he wasn't charming the pants off the ladies.

They all stared at Sara.

"Will you tell her?"

"Yes."

And he would. There was no reason not to, and Michael knew with her awareness, Sara was likely to feel it very quickly in any case. Running his hand through his hair, he let out a dry laugh.

"God. That day in the Great Hall when she called and the walls shook? What a metaphor for the shake-up she has brought into our lives."

"I believe this will be a great gift. A little archangel running around Heaven. Or flying." Gabe laughed.

"Call us if you need anything." Raphael stood, placing the cat gently on the chair, ignoring Michael's smirk.

"I will. Thank you."

They left him alone with his human and his growing child.

Michael sat on the floor, holding her hand for the longest time, thinking while he waited for her to wake.

Father, you should have told me.

They are your greatest gifts, Michael. Protect them with all you are, as I have my beautiful sons.

I love you.

As I love you, Michael.

Michael laid his hand over Sara's belly, feeling the warmth of their child's energy, and smiled. God was right. They were the most magical gifts he could never have imagined.

He would remember forever the moment he had felt the child's existence. He'd been so shocked and overwhelmed, unable to control his true self, that his soul had exploded open. He shook his head in grief as his heart cried for the loss of the lives around them. He sent his own prayer of forgiveness to God and felt warmth run through him as it was given.

He could never do that again. Never slip up. As the pregnancy progressed, so too would their vulnerability.

Michael would protect them with all that he was.

Sara was going to have so many more questions now, and still, he had no answers.

Except one.

He would never leave her ever again.

She was his number one priority. Sara and the child.

And he knew something else for certain now. The guest was providing her with celestial powers she wouldn't have otherwise. That meant Michael could get her to the safest place in existence.

He was taking her home.

To Heaven.

CHAPTER TWENTY-SIX

"Michael? Ow, Jesus." Sara gripped her head. She knew she shouldn't blaspheme around an archangel, but God in heavens, her head hurt.

Yeah, not a good start.

"Sara?" Michael was leaning against the sofa beside her on the floor and spun to face her. "How are you feeling?"

"Like someone has my head in a vise." She grabbed her head on either side. "What happened?"

Michael smiled at her, and she wanted to smack him.

"Did I pass out?"

The last thing she remembered, they were talking in the living room, and Michael had told her the other archangels were going to visit.

"Oh! Did Gabriel and Raphael show up?"

"Yes."

He then placed his hand on her head, and the pain eased. She twisted her head and kissed the palm of his hand. Looking at the clock on the wall, she noticed it was nearly 4:00 p.m.

"Did I sleep all day?" She quickly sat up and tried to stand, but instead crumpled to the floor in pain. Michael swept her up and carried her into the bedroom. Like, in supersonic angel speed.

"Careful, sweetheart."

"What's going on?" she groaned.

He lay down beside her and wrapped himself around her. She could feel his energy pulsing through her.

"You need to just rest some more. Stay calm, please."

"Did someone hurt me? Your brothers?"

"No. Actually…I did."

"No, you didn't. You wouldn't." She shook her head, not believing a word of it.

"Yeah. But actually, I did."

She narrowed her eyes at him.

"Something surprised me. A lot. And I lost some control of my energy."

Oh.

"That's never happened. Ever. In existence."

She didn't know what to do, so she laughed, and he frowned at her.

"This is serious."

"I know, but you have to look at it from my point of view. My life has been a train wreck. Of all the people in the universe, in all of history, I am the cause of the Archangel Michael losing control. Yup, that'd be bloody right."

His lips twitched.

"Oh, come on. Laugh. If I can laugh, you can too."

Michael shook his head. "My little human. You could have died. You should have died."

Well, when he put it like that, it wasn't funny at all.

"Then why didn't I?"

As she attempted to wriggle loose of his suffocating embrace, Michael laid a hand on her belly. The warmth was delicious. Suddenly, she felt an ache within. Oh, great. Talk about bad timing.

"Damn it. I must be getting my period. I'm crampy." She cringed. "Sorry, TMI."

He smiled at her.

Of course, he probably heard all the girly stuff from women praying all the time for things like a cure for painful periods or getting pregnant.

A very warm sensation began under Michael's hand, and she looked down. "What are you doing?"

Was he healing her? She'd had painful periods forever,

and if he could heal her of it right now, she would grant any wish he desired.

"Nothing." He grinned.

Her stomach began to glow.

Like, actually fucking glowing.

"Stop fooling around. Tell me what you're doing. Are you healing me? Because honestly, that would be a-ma-zing."

"I'm honestly not. It's not me." He smiled.

Excuse me? It's not him?

"Then what the hell is happening to my body right now?" she squealed.

Her stomach continued to glow.

Michael took her chin in his hand, and his bright blue eyes filled with—were those tears? "That, my sweetheart, is our child."

Our. Fucking. What. Now?

Sara stared at him blankly for a long moment, then stared down at her stomach.

"No."

"Yes."

"No."

"Yes."

She stared some more.

"We've created a baby, Sara." He lifted her head and kissed her. "An archangel baby."

Sara wriggled away from him and stood, wobbling. She held out her hand when he moved to help her. "No. No. No. No. No."

His face fell. "I thought you'd be happy. Why aren't you happy?"

Sara stared around the room, looking for an anchor. Some sense of normality. She went into the bathroom and used the toilet, not because she needed to but because her brain needed to do something normal. Washing her hands, she stared at herself in the mirror.

"You look sane; you really do," she muttered to herself. "No archangels, no babies, no, no, no, no, no."

She returned to the bedroom, and Michael was still lying on the bed, legs stretched out, waiting for her. Damn, why did she have to notice he was so big and sexy.

Sara began pacing.

"I can't be pregnant, Michael. You're an archangel. I'm a human."

He nodded patiently.

"I'll probably die giving birth or something."

"No, you won't," he said, frowning at her.

"What will I do with a flying baby?" She threw her hands up in the air. "I'll lose it and then get in trouble with God."

He burst out laughing, then failed in his attempt to cover it. She glared at him as he responded, "A genuine concern. We'll work out how to deal with that when the time comes."

She flopped on the bed.

"I don't wish to disrespect your"—she waved her hands in reference to all of him—"superior godliness or whatever, but there has to be a mistake. Perhaps your energy leaked and got inside my belly."

Michael tried to hide his laughter yet again, but this time completely failed, and burst out laughing. Sara couldn't help but smile a little herself. It all sounded ridiculous to her too. But not any less crazy than her being pregnant. To an arch-bloody-angel!

Clearing his throat, Michael answered, "Okay, so first off, I'm not a god. Gods are really annoying. Not God, God. He's…well, yeah, he's annoying in his own unique way, but we're getting off track."

He moved to sit in front of her, a leg tucked under him. She laid a hand on his large thigh and ran it up his leg. He grabbed it. "Oh no, you don't. Stay focused."

He didn't sound all that convincing, and Sara reckoned

if she could just distract him for a moment, she could make all of this go away. Trying to move her hand further up his leg proved impossible, so she looked up at him and sighed. "Fine. Carry on."

"I don't leak energy, and okay, yes, I exploded earlier, but energy doesn't leak. Everything is energy. You're energy. You know this."

Sara flopped back on the bed, hand over her face, ignoring the science lesson. "I can't have a baby, Michael. I can't have an angel baby."

"Archangel baby."

She spluttered. "Details!"

"Well, no…"

She sat up and grabbed him. "Michael, you need to hear me. I can't have a baby with you and live down here alone and have a flying baby or whatever it will be."

"Okay, calm down."

"Calm d—are you kidding me right now?" she yelled.

"Sorry, wrong thing to say." He leaned back, holding his hands in the air. "Go crazy."

I'll give you damn crazy.

"What if you take it away from me because I'm human? Because I can't teach it archangel things?"

Sara stared at his calm, stoic face and shook her head. This just couldn't be happening. They hadn't even worked out how things would be between them, let alone having a baby together. She just couldn't deal with this news.

Perhaps he was wrong.

"Look, I'm just not pregnant."

"Yes. You. Are," he stated emphatically, pulling her into his arms. "And I'd really like it if you could be a little happy about it."

She wrapped her arms around him, recognizing she was in a state of shock. Nuzzling into his neck, she sighed. He smelled so delicious. Like vanilla and whisky, if that was even a possibility.

"Sara, we've created the most magical baby in the universe. We did this. You and I." He pulled her back, and as she gazed into his eyes, she saw they were filled with pride and joy. Cupping her face, he added, "Our love."

She went dead still, and heat rushed through her. "You love me?" she whispered.

"Oh, I love you, sweetheart. I've loved you from the moment I saw you."

He slammed his lips down on hers, and she let herself be swept away. Lifting his head, he looked down at her in question, and she smiled. Then her clothes fell away.

Now this she could get on board with. She'd deal with the rest of the madness later. Michael prepared her body and then pushed inside her. They fit together like two pieces of a puzzle, she realized as he glided in and out.

"I love you, little human. God, how I love you."

"I love you too," Sara said, taking in his sparkling blue eyes full of the emotion he spoke of. "Damn it all, I do."

He lifted her ass up off the bed and dove deeper, taking complete possession of her.

"You are truly mine, Sara. Forever."

And while those words filled her heart with a joy she had never felt in her life, she had to wonder if he had felt this way before discovering she was pregnant.

And if her fears of him taking the child after it was born were grounded in fact.

CHAPTER TWENTY-SEVEN

Ares leaned against the bar, legs spread, sipping his ambrosia. He'd built The Fat Angel nearly a thousand years ago, and it was still thriving.

Nymph servers attended the gods, goddesses, and guests from other realms wearing barely more than what their mommas gave them. Not that they had mothers, but whatever.

There were also a handful of angel warriors who had ventured further afield to celebrate graduation. Ugh. It was like spring break in the cosmos. He sneered.

"And?" he asked one of those angels who currently sat beside him.

The little shit may have been prophesied to have a hand in this game of his which had been unfolding for hundreds of years, but as a god, Ares had seen prophecies play out vastly different from their interpretation, so he had a healthy dose of skepticism when it came to this particular warrior.

Plus, he hated angels. All of them, no matter what was between their legs or who they were predicted to kill.

A female archangel? How ridiculous.

They didn't exist.

When they'd first heard the prophecy by the Oracle, Ares had declared her insane. Then Zeus had sneered at him—he had a soft spot for the old hag—rendering his exclamation void. Zeus had also ordered for the prophecy to be kept a secret from those in Heaven.

The Oracle had proclaimed that a rogue angel in the

year of the Earth, 2020, would murder a princess archangel. So when the Oracle had identified Severial as the angel by his specific tattoos, Ares had kept the young warrior in his sights. Nurtured him, so to speak.

On the male's wrist were three tears as if falling down a cheek. You couldn't get more specific than that. When asked why he had gotten the tattoos, the angel hadn't been able to answer—he'd just liked them.

So fine. Perhaps there was some truth to it. But what interested Ares more was the second part of the prophecy. The return of a long extinct creature, one with immense power capable of mass destruction or great creation, and this being a fork in the road of power in the universe.

He had told no one about the magical creature he'd been plotting to capture for hundreds of years, but he knew if there was a chance to eliminate that arrogant fuck, Archangel Michael, once and for all, this was it.

It had been his greatest desire for thousands of years.

When he'd trapped the creature's soul inside the human woman, he had cursed her. Only suicide would free to creature, allowing Ares to take possession and be master over it and its power.

Yet here they were, over a hundred and seventy years later, and he was still waiting. Connected to the human soul, the creature transferred in the womb to the next female in line. Child after child, adult after adult, he had waited, watching as they suffered in their pitiful cursed lives from heartbreak, disease, career failure, rape, relationship struggles, poverty, and yet, these stupid humans continued to live.

He'd become extremely hopeful with Sara. No husband, no children, her career a failure, and now, a pandemic. He was sure she would hang a rope any day now.

She was beautiful, there was no doubt about it. Men desired her, but thanks to his curse, the only ones who pursued her were rats. Ares had considered making her his lover, but frankly, he couldn't be bothered with humans and their incessant blabbering. This one in particular had a sound mind and voiced her opinion strongly. He'd likely backhand her and kill her within a day, and he couldn't do that. Murdered souls went straight to Heaven. Suicide souls recycled. And he needed it to recycle so he could grab it and take possession in those few moments while it waited for a new vessel on Earth.

"Michael is on Earth with her. He's been there for days."

Ares looked up. "What?"

Did the archangel know about the soul trapped within this human? There was no way he could.

"With Sara?"

"Yes, sir."

Michael rarely went to Earth, and that he'd visited so frequently was being noticed by many around the realm.

"They appear to be…"

"To be?" Ares dropped his glass on the counter and stood up to his full height. Dressed in typical Olympian garb which left his strong, muscular chest bare, he placed his hands on his hips and glared at the angel. "Speak, angel, or get out of my sight."

"In a relationship."

He cringed. And three, two, one…

"What the fuck?" The female screech sounded like nails down a blackboard. Artemis had been sitting behind him, listening to every word. "That cheating—"

"Get over it, sister. It was one damn night nearly two hundred years ago," he snapped and rolled his eyes. They were all sick of her going on about the archangel. That he hated the guy didn't help.

"It was only one hundred and seventy-seven years ago, thank you very much. Plus, he told me archangels didn't have relationships. Now he's in one, and with a mere human?"

I don't have time for this.

"Keep your beak out of my business, Artemis. I mean it." He grabbed Severial and walked out of The Fat Angel.

"I have another job for you," he whispered. "Go find the warlock, Harold Rivers. He lives in Phoenix, Arizona. Take him to Auckland and wait for me there. Monitor the archangel and human, and report anything odd to me immediately."

Several glared at him. "Remember, Ares, I'm the one prophesied to kill his human."

Egotistical angels. They drove him mad.

Lowering his voice to a low, threatening growl, he leaned in. "Don't be so sure you know how this will play out, young angel. Assumptions will get you killed."

Or his hand would, if the little shit wasn't lucky.

"Are you threatening me, god?"

"What exactly do you think you're going to get out of this, warrior?" Ares crossed his arms and narrowed his eyes. He was thousands of years older than this mouthy winged shit, and twice his size.

"God will finally see how powerful I am and make me an archangel. I was born to be great. He will see." Severial puffed out his chest.

Ares rolled his eyes. "Okay, tiger, whatever gets you through the day."

"God does not respect weakness. When he sees I am superior, he will be proud."

"When was the last time you talked to God?" Ares asked. Everyone knew the gods of Olympus did not believe in this heavenly God of theirs. The twitch in the young angel's eyes gave him his answer. Never. Ares shook his head. "Just go do as I ask."

Ares would deal with him after he had procured the creature. For now, he had to speak to Artemis before she messed this up for him.

CHAPTER TWENTY-EIGHT

"You love me," Sara said as she kissed one of his pecs.

He smiled as she continued over his chest and licked one of his nipples. Michael never tired of her. Not her touch, not talking to her, and not gazing at her. "I do. Every little inch of you."

"So this baby thing. It's real?" she asked again.

By the tone of her voice, Michael knew she was hoping he would tell her he'd only been joking. But he wasn't. This was no joke at all. Michael realized she'd had a lot of changes in her life since they'd met. Not normal changes, either. She'd learned that supernatural beings existed, had become an extremely rich woman, fallen in love with an archangel, and now, she was pregnant with an immortal baby. Pregnant to a being she had no idea if she would see again.

"Very real, sweetheart."

Her fears that he'd take the child were reasonable. He had no plans or desire to do so, but the reality was, if he couldn't find a way to make Sara immortal, then she wouldn't be able to take care of an archangel baby.

"Okay."

Over the next few days, Michael stayed on Earth monitoring the baby, who had now implanted into Sara's uterus as an embryo, making it a true pregnancy.

When he told her he wasn't leaving their side, she simply nodded. Something was off. But he knew he had to show her, not tell her, to win her trust.

She had called Lisa to say she couldn't attend her dinner party, and while on-screen, had introduced her to Michael. Her narrowed eyes had given away her distrust, which he respected. He was pleased Sara had such a loyal, loving friend.

"So you've merged your bubbles?" Lisa had asked, nodding slowly when Sara had said yes.

Michael had had to remind himself of the lockdown rules in Sara's country. They weren't allowed to go into one another's homes.

"She's just worried you'll hurt me. Moving in together is a big step," Sara explained when he mentioned it, placing a hand on her stomach. "If only she knew about this wee thing."

He was pleased she had now accepted its existence, but she was still not glowing with the joy of a soon to be mother.

"I know you'd like to tell your friend."

"Kind of. But there would be a lot of explaining to do if I did, so it's easier this way," Sara said, frowning. "Do you think the baby will change me?"

"It's already changed both of us," he replied, watching her walk into the kitchen.

"No, I mean...will it make me magical or immortal...or something?"

Michael glanced out the window. He did not know how this would affect her body, but he was certain of one thing. "No. It will not make you an immortal."

But he was near certain she now needed to be. He wanted her up in Heaven with him, safe with their child so they could live out their life together. He was optimistic God would gift her with immortality, because Michael did not have the power to do so.

"How would you feel about becoming immortal, Sara?"

Sara climbed onto his lap, looping her arms around his

neck, and kissed him. "It would mean being with you forever, so I guess it would be amazing. If you'd have me."

He smiled, running his fingers through her hair. "Try getting rid of me, gorgeous."

That got him the smile he'd been missing the past few days. He tugged her in closer and kissed her deeply.

"Leaving you and our child in thirty or forty years is unthinkable," she added when he released her lips. It was unthinkable for him also, and he would not let that happen.

No damn way.

"But I wouldn't be human anymore, would I?"

"No."

Michael watched as the idea of giving up her humanity sunk in. He left her to those thoughts, knowing it would take some time to process. In the meantime, he had to get her that damn immortality, and the first step would be taking her home to Heaven. For that to happen, he needed to have an important conversation with her.

"Sara, when you reached me in Heaven, it was a surprise to me and the other archangels."

When she just stared at him, he continued, "One night, when you were sleeping, I reached out to your soul energetically, and I got kicked, physically, to the other side of the room."

"Well, good on me. You shouldn't just go having private conversations with my soul when I'm not awake."

He smirked at her sassy comment. He loved seeing her sparkle again.

"You don't understand. No one has the power to do that."

"So let me get this straight. My higher self kicked your higher self's butt?" she asked, grinning wider.

He let out a laugh.

"Yes." His smile faded. "But, sweetheart, here's the thing." Sara's grin also disappeared, and finally, he had her attention. "The soul with the power to boot me out is not yours."

Michael waited and let that sink in.

"Wha…?"

"There's no need to be afraid. If there was, I would have acted immediately.

"What?" She stood up and stared down at him in horror. "Something is living inside me?"

"Yes, but it's not dangerous, and it's been there your whole life, I would guess. And it's one of Heaven's most precious creatures."

He understood the shock and horror of what he was telling her. Michael reached out his hand, but she ignored it.

"There is nothing to be concerned about; it's very protective of you, and it's immensely powerful. That is the energy you've felt your whole life."

Sara began to pace.

"Oh no, no, no, fucking no. First you turn up and tell me all this Heaven stuff is real. Then I get pregnant by a bloody archangel. Now I have some alien inside me!"

"Oh, baby, come here." Michael stood up and wrapped his arms around her as she began to shake. He pushed relaxing energy through her and felt her calm down.

"Stop it," she mumbled, and he shushed her. "Trust me to fall in love with an angel and have some magic thing stuck in me."

"Archangel," he mumbled through gritted teeth.

"What?"

"Nothing," he said, rubbing her back. "The good news is, I can remove it."

"You can?"

"Yes, but not here. I am taking you home. To Heaven."

And it was about then she blacked out.

CHAPTER TWENTY-NINE

Michael leaned against the bathroom doorway, watching her. "You don't need anything. Like, anything."

Sara finished brushing her teeth and shook her head at him.

"Men. You guys have no idea. How long will we be gone?"

"I don't know," he answered, wanting to remind her he was not a man. "A few days, maybe."

"Then we need to take Tilly with us. I can't leave her alone or put her in a cattery because of lockdown. And no one can leave their bubble to look after her. She would starve."

Michael turned to look at the cat curled up on the bed and groaned. "Give me a minute."

He walked out of the room and paced in a circle. He knew Sara would not leave the cat alone, and she was right. They could be gone longer, and it would starve. He really didn't want to do this, but there was no other choice.

Father.

The answer is no.

I am brining something of great value home with me.

Still no.

I'm bringing Sara into Heaven, and I need to bring the cat. I know it's a breach of the rules, but Father, I promise it will be worth it when you discover what we have.

No.

Then I am staying down here, and you won't get to meet your first and perhaps only grandchild.

Thunder clapped above the house in a loud boom. Sara came running out. "Oh my God, did you hear that? There are clear skies out there."

He nodded.

Fine, but the cat stays in your chambers, and no one sees it.

Done. We will see you soon.

And Michael. No more threats.

Yeah, that had been a low blow on his part, but desperate times called for desperate measures. Plus, it wasn't like He couldn't see all, anyway.

He had needed God's protection of the feline. Taking anything mortal into Heaven had permanent consequences. One fundamentally died.

Michael may have never had a girlfriend before, but he knew if he killed Sara's cat, he'd likely never see her smile again.

Plus, he secretly liked Tilly.

"Finish packing, sweetheart. Tilly is coming with us."

"Thank you!" She planted a kiss on his lips and disappeared into her bedroom again.

An hour later, Sara had a suitcase full of clothes, toiletries, cat food, cat beds, bowls, and toys.

"Should we just take the entire house?"

"Can you do that?" she asked, then shook her head. "Of course you can."

Leaning against the doorway, Michael crossed his arms and smiled as Sara walked up to him and ran her hands over them, squeezing. "Your arms are the size of my thighs. Bigger, maybe."

He dipped his head down and whispered, "Stop procrastinating. If you don't get the cat, I will drag you into the bedroom, and we can compare sizes while my arms are wrapped around your thighs, young lady."

Her breathlessness was the perfect response. If he

weren't so eager to get her safely into Heaven, he would have followed through on his threat.

Opening his arms, she fell into him, her body flush against his, and he called the cat himself. "Tilly!"

The cat rubbed up against his leg a second later, meowing, and Sara gave him the same look she always gave him when the cat did as he asked. Disbelief.

Sometimes Michael wondered if she forgot who and what he was. Well, that was about to change. They were moments away from being in Heaven. He tucked the cat inside Sara's jacket and kissed her nose.

"Ready?"

When she nodded, he reached out to the other archangels.

Brothers.

Once he heard them all respond, he continued.

I am returning to my chambers. With Sara. Please knock before coming in from now on.

Gross, we promise not to walk in on anything.

Isn't she human?

Chamuel hadn't been keeping up with the gossip, obviously.

I'll explain everything when I get her settled. Just. Don't, I repeat, don't come into my chambers unless I'm there.

Why?

Just. do it. Please.

Ahh, the old bow chicka wow wow

Michael rolled his eyes at Uriel's remark.

He wasn't worried about them walking in during sexy times, as Raphael called it. They could do that at any point while he was on Earth. He was worried about Tilly getting loose in Heaven. God would get mad, and Sara would lose her mind.

He picked up the suitcase and pulled her into his chest.

"Close your eyes, sweetheart. Tilly, hold on to your

momma tight."

Michael took a deep breath. He was taking an enormous risk. God had gifted Tilly with temporary immortality for her stay, but not Sara. He hadn't asked. Why? Because he was banking on the celestial creature inside Sara to protect her.

He was 99 percent confident, 1 percent petrified.

Fuck.

He sent out his own prayer, released his huge white wings of light, and wrapped them around Sara and Tilly.

He held her tight against him and flashed them into Heaven.

CHAPTER THIRTY

Heart racing, Michael scanned Sara, the baby, and Tilly. All of them were fine. Like him, they had raised heart rates which calmed as he pushed relaxing energy over them.

"Babe," a voice squeaked against his chest

"Oh, sorry," he said as he released them.

Sara stepped back and looked around in awe. Heaven was a magnificent place, and seeing it through her eyes was a new experience for him.

She walked around, holding the cat tightly to her chest with her mouth gaping open. She was such a protective mom already. It made him smile, but it was also very sexy.

They were in his chambers, which were the size of a five-bedroom house on Earth. The room had high ceilings, pillars made of white stone, and floor-to-ceiling windows with drapes in off-white tones. A set of doors opened to an enormous courtyard with lush, tropical gardens, a water feature, and roaming wildlife. Birds sang, squirrels darted around, and a tiger sat lazily in the sun.

Oh shit.

Sara froze. "Oh my God, there's a tiger…wait, where'd it go?"

"All sorted. I just moved some of the animals to another section."

Sara continued to stare at him.

"You can put her down. Tilly will be safe." He looked at the cat. "Tilly, stay close by and don't eat any birds or hurt any butterflies."

She meowed at him.

Sara raised an eyebrow and placed the cat on the ground. It began to examine its surroundings with the curiosity of all felines.

Michael took the suitcase into the bedroom where his enormous four-poster bed sat in the middle of the room. It was draped in white organza and clothed in crisp white cotton sheets with at least half a dozen pillows. Sara ran her hand along the back of the chaise longue and then peeked her head out the French doors that led out to the same courtyard.

"What a romantic-looking bedroom for a bachelor."

"I may have decorated it to please you." He smiled, pleased with himself for having such foresight into what pleased a female. "Here's the bathroom."

Michael grinned as she made joyful noises as she saw the huge shower, deep claw-foot bath, double vanity, and the views out across the gardens.

"It's just stunning, Michael. I love this place."

He grabbed her as she threw herself into his arms. "I can change anything you want."

"Do I have a wardrobe?"

What an oversight. His little human loved her clothes, and everything related to them. "Show me what you'd like."

She looked confused. "Like on my phone? I won't get reception here, will I?"

He laughed. "No. Close your eyes and imagine what you'd like. I'll see it."

"Best boyfriend ever."

He saw the walk-in wardrobe with shelves and mirrors, racks of clothing, shoes, hats, scarves, jewelry, and more. In the middle, she'd imagined a cushioned seat. Taking her hand, he walked out of the bathroom and back into the bedroom. A new door had appeared.

"Your new wardrobe, milady."

Sara squealed and ran to open the door. "Oh my God.

Look at all the clothing and…" She turned back and glanced at him. "Thank you."

"Anything you desire is yours; you know that."

"I know, but I like it when you surprise me."

He wrapped an arm around her lower back and pulled her up against him. "I love having you here. In my home."

Sara smiled. "It's not how I expected Heaven to look, honestly. Then again, I've never given it much thought."

"I'll take you for a tour, but first I need to meet with my brothers. Unpack and get Tilly settled, then I will return." He kissed her passionately before he left.

"When can we meet her?" Uriel asked.

Gabriel kicked him.

"What? She's our new sister. Who thought we'd ever get a sister? I'm excited."

Michael sat in Raphael's living room with all the archangels. He felt so content having his mate in Heaven. He felt different, calmer. More whole.

But there was also a sense of comfort knowing she was safely tucked away in his chambers where no one could reach her. It was in his nature to protect, and he knew enough about mated couples to know the male became incredibly dominant of his female. Fortunately, his human had a powerful mind to ensure he didn't go overboard.

But yeah, it was still a risk. So tempting to lock that damn door and throw away the key.

Still, he was here for a reason. While he awaited an audience with God, he needed to update his brothers.

He couldn't share anything about the guest with them yet—God needed to know first—so today, he needed them to understand how important she was to him, and that she was his family now. Plus, not all of them knew about the baby yet.

They also needed to discuss the rogue angel.

"She is my mate. I'm sure Raphael has told you all

about Father's announcement we are all to have one?"

A mix of pale faces nodded at him.

If it hadn't happened to him first, he imagined himself reacting the same way. It was not natural at all for them to be monogamous. And they all loved…well, fornicating.

"It doesn't mean we all will," Raphael interjected hopefully, and Michael tried to hold back his grin. He failed.

"Ah, brother. I know it feels like a fate worse than letting the gods of Olympus rule Heaven, but love is a beautiful thing."

Groans filled the room.

He laughed.

"There's something else you need to know. Gabe and Raph know because I called on their help." Looking around the room, he dropped the bomb. "Sara is pregnant." Then added, "With my child."

Jophiel, Uriel, Zadkiel and Chamuel stared at him like he was mad, and he didn't blame them. Archangels couldn't and didn't procreate.

Until now.

That their leader, their big brother, was making such an impossible claim was madness. If he hadn't been in the situation himself, he'd be looking at them the same way. In fact, he'd had moments of shaking his head to himself this past week, but many more of them were spent gazing at Sara in absolute astonishment and gratitude.

He continued. "Hence the incredible surprise and my loss of control for that split second."

"Michael, you know that's not possible," Zadkiel said, glancing at Gabriel and Raphael with a pleading look. "Come on, you guys, you said nothing?"

Zadkiel was the most practical and serious among them. As the Archangel of Benevolence and Forgiveness, he had great kindness about him, and Michael saw the archangel was struggling not to judge him. Goodness knew they'd all seen the gods, goddesses, humans, and beasts lose their sanity over love and passion throughout their long lives.

"It's true, brother," Raph informed him.

"I'm sure there's a good explanation," Chamuel added, always the peacekeeper between them. "Perhaps—"

"I believe it is only with our true soulmate that we can procreate," he interrupted, wanting to move the conversation along. He had no proof of this—their child may be the only one. They were all learning the rules of this new era they were stepping into.

"I don't mean to cast doubt, bro, but…er, could it be a human's child?" Jophiel asked tentatively.

"Oh boy," Gabe said, jumping to his feet in front of Jophiel and holding up his hand in his defense. Then he frowned. "Hey, why aren't you blowing something up?"

Michael laughed.

"Hey, I can defend myself, dude!"

"Sit down, Gabriel. I am far too happy to be fighting today. That child is mine, and my woman loves me. I'm blessed beyond words."

A glow emanated from him, and his brothers watched him in awe. As he cast his eyes over the archangels sitting around him, he tried to put into words how he felt.

They all loved God, and they all loved each other with unbreakable loyalty. They also loved all the beings they watched over around the realms. They were blessed with absolute, pure, eternal love from God, their Father.

They were no strangers to love.

This was different.

To be adored, loved, and desired intimately and completely by one being who you felt the same way about on a soul level so unconditionally was the most magical feeling he'd ever experienced.

"It's Michael's child. I felt his energy signature. It's…well, it's remarkable."

He looked at Uriel after Gabriel spoke. "Uri, you're

quiet."

He was worried about his brother after hearing he'd spent a night with Aphrodite. He had returned without being summoned, which was unusual, though it had been over one hundred and seventy years since he had last seen the goddess.

And as Raphael had warned him, Uriel was quieter.

"I am happy for you, Michael, truly." His brother smiled at him. "I'm just sorry I wasn't able to gain more intel while on Olympus."

The tension in the air thickened.

Michael leaned back in the high-backed chair. "I spoke to the Oracle on Olympus, and she told me Sara was in danger. I didn't know what that meant at the time, but I'm beginning to understand."

Gabe leaned against the fireplace, arms crossed. "No one will harm her or the child, Michael, here or anywhere. She is one of the family now."

Everyone nodded and murmured similar statements.

"Remember, she's still human, so this is a temporary visit and I'll need to return to Earth quickly."

"You can't stay down there forever," Zadkiel said, pointing out the obvious.

Michael stood up and sighed. "One step at a time, brother. One step at a time."

Michael.

He smiled.

"Daddy dearest is calling. I'll bring her to meet you all after."

"Good luck." Raph grinned.

Michael gave him the bird as he walked out, smiling at their laughter in his wake.

CHAPTER THIRTY-ONE

Sara felt like she was in a movie.

Michael's home was huge and luxurious. The luscious contemporary vibe was totally her style. It was filled with stylish yet comfortable furniture and what appeared to be dozens and dozens of cushions, mirrors, large paintings, statues, jugs, and other décor. The mix of modern and ancient was a delight.

In short, she loved it.

Tilly had curled up on the thick comforter on the bed after a short adventure in the garden.

After pouring herself a large glass of water, Sara had returned to the wardrobe to play. Finding a white lacy balconette bra and matching panties set, she dressed in a white cotton dress with cap sleeves. The square neckline and tight bodice accentuated her breasts and waistline, then fell in layers down to her calves. Adding a pair of sandals, she sat down at the dresser and added some lip gloss.

Michael walked in and leaned against the doorframe, his huge build taking up the entire space. She stared at him in the mirror, neither of them saying anything.

She smiled.

Some days the heat that sizzled between them felt normal, and other days it took her breath away. She stood and walked into his arms.

"Shit. You look so damn beautiful."

Oh.

It wasn't like Michael never complimented her. He did. Daily. But the way he had looked at her and spoken so breathlessly took her own breath away. This man loved and adored her.

She let that sink in.

"Thank you."

"I love you, Sara."

"I love you too," she whispered back.

His lips lowered to hers, softly, then more firmly. Then more firmly. He pulled her hard against his body as his tongue plunged inside. She groaned at the intensity of his desire for her.

Too soon, he released her, and they stood gazing into each other's eyes.

"You ready to meet my Father?" he asked eventually.

Her mouth fell open.

You what?

"I'm sorry, what?"

"You have nothing to fear. He's…" Michael tilted his head. "Well, he's God."

Sara stepped out of his arms. "Yes, but generally, one doesn't meet him until they die. Wait, I'm not dead, right?"

Smiling, he shook his head.

"No, but we shouldn't keep him waiting any longer so that remains the status quo." He laughed, but her horrified expression made his smile disappear. "Sorry, insider joke. He won't harm you. I promise."

"Michael!" she growled, slapping his arm.

"Come on, beautiful." Michael threw an arm around her and led her out of his chambers and down a polished marble path.

Eventually, they came to an open space which reminded her of a tropical resort. Large palm trees were scattered around a big lawn, with pathways weaving through it. There were half a dozen park benches and trees with oversized plumeria-looking flowers bursting through the abundance of green leaves.

Animals and birds flittered around, giving it a

springlike feel which matched the clear blue sky. It was sunny, but she could see no sun. Not a cloud to be seen. So much for heavenly clouds.

Up ahead, Sara saw buildings which looked like they were made from marble and clay.

Around them were a range of beings. Some looked human, dressed in modern clothing, and others wore outfits she didn't understand. A group of what appeared to be the warriors Michael had spoken about crossed in front of them and lowered their heads at him.

"My lord," they all said, and she glanced up at him.

He gave them a slight nod in return and instinctually placed a protective hand on the base of her spine as they kept walking. Sara's body tingled at his touch and the power he exuded. He glanced down at her and smirked.

Powerful and he knows it.

They crossed over a path and turned a corner. Coming directly toward them was a group of five beautiful young women with long, flowing hair in all different shades. They were dressed in sheer draped clothes with delicate chains acting as a belt, their nipples visible and in some cases threatening to completely expose themselves. One of them had a string of flowers around her head in a crown-like fashion.

Sara noticed they all had an aura which seemed to glow, and they weren't walking; they were skipping like happy little girls. But what stood out most was the extremely powerful sexual energy pouring off them.

When they spotted Michael, it was like one of the Jonas brothers had arrived in town. They launched from their spot, and with no regard to her, danced up to him.

"Lord Michael." They giggled.

"Will we see you at Eden's Bar later?" one of them asked as the rest of them twirled in a circle around them like there was music playing.

"Hello, my lord," a demure, purring voice said. A dark-haired woman stood a step away while the fairylike girls continued dancing. She was extremely beautiful, but seemed aloof. She didn't look at Sara, simply held Michael's stare in defiance.

And yet, Sara saw a vulnerability within it.

Michael slowed down to accommodate the angels, but Sara hadn't missed the tension that was suddenly in him.

"Regina," he responded, nodding at her coolly as he always did nowadays.

Shit.

He didn't need this right now.

Queen of the angels, Regina, his former lover. She was demanding in and out of the bedroom—not that they'd always used a bed—and though he'd not shared pleasure with her for a long time, the female constantly tested the boundaries of power with him. She was rebellious and manipulative.

When he chose one of the other angels, she would storm into his chambers in a fit of rage and jealousy. Every time, he'd respond the same way, "I will enjoy any female I want, Regina. Remember who you're speaking to. Leave my presence before I lose my patience."

Eventually, his patience had run its course when one afternoon at Eden's Bar, a pretty little angel had glanced away from his wink. He hadn't been offended—like all beings, they had free will. It had, however, raised his suspicions. Rarely was he rejected.

Michael's instincts had roared to life. He'd watched as the female glanced at Regina nervously, and it had been all the confirmation he needed. The queen had warned all her angels away, claiming him as her own.

Standing up from the barstool where he sat with Raphael, he had stalked over to her. Putting his hand around the queen's throat, he had lowered his face to hers and quietly but deeply growled a warning, "You have twenty-four hours to correct the rumor that we're in a relationship or I will do so in a way I'm sure your ego will not appreciate. Do not mess with me, queen. This is your one and only warning."

She had never even blinked at him. Brushing her dark hair off her face, she had held his angry gaze with heavy-lidded eyes and let her lips fall slightly apart.

The thing was, her arrogant confidence turned him on. A lot. And she knew it.

He could have flashed them to his chambers, pushed her over the back of the sofa, entered her swiftly, and fucked her till he was dry, enjoying every damn moment. Until afterward.

Michael had held her stare for a long moment, letting her know her sexual play would not work this time, before he had returned to his barstool.

"About fucking time," Raphael had said, his powerful archangel hearing allowing him to hear the dark, quiet conversation.

Glancing down now, Michael noticed Sara's discomfort at the current tension. He would not allow Regina to upset his mate. Taking her hand, he pulled her into his side and laid his hand on her lower back.

"Angels, I want you to meet Sara." He smiled down proudly at her. "She is my life mate."

They gasped happily, clapping as they continued bouncing around them.

"Does she sing?" one of them asked.

"Or dance?"

There were giggles as he shrugged and raised an eyebrow at Sara.

"Um, sometimes." She laughed at the excited angels.

Michael watched as her smiled faded when she looked at Regina. Sara was strong, Michael reminded himself. She would need help and support learning the ropes in Heaven, but she was not an idiot. Still, he would ensure Regina knew her boundaries and any consequences if she made his mate unhappy.

Sara was now, mortal or otherwise, a senior member in Heaven. He expected all its citizens to respect her.

"You have to come to Eden's Bar and do karaoke with us," Selena, one of his favorite angels, said, bouncing up to Sara and taking her hands.

The queen cleared her throat elegantly. "Ladies, let us leave Lord Michael and his friend to their day."

Bitch.

He wasn't biting.

"I'll bring her along one day, I promise." He smiled at Selena, appreciating her kindness despite the queen's behavior. "Now, off you all go."

Regina glanced at Sara's abdomen and then back at him, sneering judgmentally.

Really, Michael? A human? A pregnant human?

Keep your thoughts to yourself, witch. You know nothing.

Regina had been a witch when she was human. She had kept her abilities but been banned from using them in Heaven. However, in hindsight, it didn't surprise him that she could sense a female's pregnancy. But she did not have the same ability to sense his energy signature in the child as the archangels did.

He was happy to let her think what she liked. Unfortunately, that meant she would spread gossip, but he had bigger issues to deal with.

Once he got Sara into Heaven permanently, then he'd make everything official. One step at a time, he reminded himself.

Shaking off his irritation now that Regina was gone, he grabbed Sara's hand and continued on their path.

What a fool he was.

He glanced down at her in question when she wouldn't budge.

Pulling her hand out of his, she crossed her arms. "So, how many of them have you slept with?"

Oh crap.

"The question really, sweetheart, is how many of them am I in love with," he said, placing a hand on her cheek.

"The fuck it is!" she exclaimed, pushing his hand away.

Worth a shot.

He knew how illogical humans could be about monogamy. Sara would never understand the way Immortals lived.

"This is something we need to discuss, Sara. I am eons old. As old as time. Yes, I've had lovers—many—but I've never been in love."

She glanced away, her emotions swirling in her eyes. He could manipulate her to let it go, but he wouldn't do that.

"Our lives are different, my love. I know you cannot understand it right now, but can I ask that you try to accept this and trust me?"

She chewed her lip.

"Hey"—he took her chin—"I meant what I said. The important thing is I've never been in love with anyone else. Ever. I've never been exclusive or chosen one female. Until you. You're my soulmate, end of the damn story."

Sara nodded.

"Carnal pleasure is just a way of life when you're an archangel. You'll see this with my brothers, but never me. I am yours."

"Forever?" she asked, eyes full of unshed tears.

"For eternity." Michael took her face in his hands and pressed his lips against hers.

"So who is she?" Sara asked as they walked, his arm around her.

"Regina, queen of the angels. You should know," he said, giving her a sideways glance, "she was a regular lover for a while, but not for a long time now."

"I don't like her."

He grinned. "No. I don't imagine you would."

Michael wasn't worried. He would ensure the queen shifted her attitude when Sara and the baby moved into Heaven. Sara would hold a position of power and influence that would intimidate the queen and protect his mate.

He thought back to that fateful time when he'd met Regina, the night after sleeping with the goddess Artemis. Both of them had wanted to claim him as his, despite his constant reminder that it was not his nature.

They would both be green with envy over Sara, and he would need to be conscious of protecting her from it.

Why none of his brothers suffered from the same issues with their lovers, he didn't understand.

"Because you're the Supreme Archangel," Zadkiel had told him once. "It makes sense. Their desire for power is reflected in their desire for you."

He'd replied with a grin and a glance down at his abs, "So it's not all of this?"

"Unlikely." Zadkiel had grinned.

Michael opened a set of doors and waved Sara inside.

"This is the Great Hall," Michael announced, smiling. "Where I first heard you screaming at me."

"Oh." He saw the reality hit her. "You heard me in here?"

He nodded repeatedly as she stared at him with awe. "Yes. Loud and clear."

"Oh my," she gasped when a cherub flew in through the window.

"Cherub. There are a lot of them around. You'll get used to them. Don't leave any treats unmanned; they'll steal them."

"They will?" she asked incredulously, and he nodded seriously. Because he wasn't joking.

Sara looked around at the enormous hall with the highest ceiling she'd ever seen. On the floor were beautiful, intricately designed tiles in gentle blues, whites, and grays. There was no furniture, just pillars and large windows all wide open.

"Is he here?" she whispered.

"He's everywhere." Michael winked at her, grabbing her hand.

"Okay, that's just creepy."

She felt the air shift and Michael's hand tighten on hers.

"Don't scare her, Michael."

She turned and faced God.

God.

Her legs suddenly buckled under her. Michael came to her rescue, holding her around the waist. Heat flowed through her body at being in the presence of the Creator, and while she had never been religious, she was still totally aware of the enormity of the situation. She was standing in front of God.

She hadn't prepared for this.

Should she thank him? Ask him for things? Speak on behalf of humanity?

Think, think.

World peace. End of famines. End of the virus. Save all the animals. A thinner waistline…

Crap.

"It's okay, sweetheart."

Sara felt calm wash over her. She was about to smile at Michael in thanks when it struck her. It may have been God.

Good grief, she was just standing here staring at him.

"Oh my God."

Oh shit.

Heat filled her face as her hands flew to her mouth.

A smile appeared on God's face.

"It's okay. I'm not offended by the use of my name as much as your religious folk would have you think."

She tried to respond. She really did.

All that came out was a squeak.

The man in front of her was old. Large, like Michael, but older. Power poured off him like she imagined it would when you met a world leader or someone with great personal power, but a millionfold.

He was dressed in what looked like awfully expensive black suit pants and a sky-blue shirt. No shoes. No robe or long beard. He had a short beard, though, and his hair was short in that distinguished salt-and-pepper look wealthy men had. But what she noticed most were his eyes. He had the brightest and wisest hazel-green eyes she had ever seen.

If he had been human, she would have described him as a kind and successful-looking grandfather who was still fit and in good health.

One who would see right through your bullshit.

He smiled at her, then looked at Michael.

"Let's find a seat or two so you don't have to continue holding her up, shall we?"

The surrounding room blurred until Sara found herself in a new place. A study surrounded by walls lined with scrolls and books. A fire crackled in the fireplace, with two leather couches facing one another in front of it.

Michael led her to one of them, laying his arm along the back behind her. Sara inched closer to him.

God sat opposite them, tipped his head at her, blinked, and then the coffee table between them filled with fruit, freshly baked apple muffins, and jugs of lemon water. All of them her favorite.

She smiled nervously and continued to stare.

Because. God.

"Dear child, you are our first mortal visitor in Heaven." He waved his hand out in front of him. "Well, and your cat."

Her mouth fell open. She did not know.

"Thank you. I didn't want her to die." She felt tears form in her eyes irrationally.

"The love you have in your heart for Earth's animals has always been acknowledged, Sara." God gave her a knowing smile.

Tears began pouring down her face.

Sara hadn't believed in God—at least, not in the traditional way many used to manipulate and control—yet on some level, she'd always believed in something. An entity or universal force, perhaps.

Yet here she was, sitting in front of the creator of everything. Having afternoon tea.

Michael rubbed her shoulder.

"It's beautiful to see you with your soulmate, Michael."

Michael kissed her on her cheek. "I am beyond blessed, Father."

"And soon, you yourself will be a parent. Both of you."

Sara nodded, wiping her tears while trying to smile. Her heart was pounding in her chest, her body flushed with emotions, leaving her incapable of forming a sentence. She simply sat there, holding onto Michael's knee, aware she was staring like a deer in the headlights at the Deity.

Sara wondered how many people would give anything to be in her shoes right now. Roughly seven billion, at a guess. Yet she just stared.

"It will be a blessing to us all," God continued. "However, there are lessons for you both before the child arrives."

Wait a minute. What lessons?

Sara glanced at Michael and back at God, wondering how she'd made it all the way into Heaven and was still being told she had personal growth to do.

It was a firm no from her—no more damn lessons.

Michael tensed beside her, and she looked up at him.

"First things first. Father, we have a special delivery for you."

"Oh?"

"Yes. Have you not wondered how I was able to bring

Sara into Heaven without your protection?"

God looked over at her and winked. "No, my boy. I gave it freely. Although temporarily."

Michael raised his eyebrow. "You did?"

"Yes."

"Wait. Temporarily? What do you mean, temporarily? Sara's my soulmate and belongs in Heaven with me."

God shrugged. "Free will, Michael. The rules don't change just because of who she is to you. Now tell me about the special delivery."

"Of course she chooses to be in Heaven with me. Please, Father. Will it now."

"Does she?" God asked with a raised brow.

Sara suddenly froze while the two males stared at her. "Umm…"

"Tell him," Michael urged, squeezing her hand.

"I…ugh."

Of course she wanted to be with Michael, but put on the spot, she didn't know what to say. Giving up her humanity required some thought. She had to think about this.

God gave her a soft smile, and a feeling of calm washed through her. "Give her time, son. Now what is this surprise? I am curious. One doesn't surprise me often. Or ever."

Michael stared down at with a touch of hurt in his eyes.

"I'm sorry," she whispered.

He shook his head and squeezed her hand.

"Sara has a soul piggybacking on hers. I…well, Father, you should feel for yourself."

God tilted his head in growing curiosity and stood. Stepping around the coffee table, he walked over and laid his hand on her head.

Sara had never sat so still in her life. Not even the time Mrs. Wright had threatened her and six-year-old Sally Berkley with detention when they wouldn't stop playing wiggly worms.

She felt warmth ripple through her body, and then God gasped.

"Good heavens!"

Michael smiled. "I'm right, aren't I? It is my honor to return it to you, Father."

Sara finally found her voice. Michael had refused to tell her anything until they were safely in Heaven. "Would you please tell me what it is?!"

"Sweetheart, I strongly suspect you carry within you the most magical of God's creatures." He smiled, his eyes full of tears of love. "One that has been lost to us for an exceptionally long time. That's when I knew I had to get you into Heaven as soon as possible."

"You made the right decision, my son. What a gift," the creator agreed, then cupping her chin, he simply said, "Sleep, my child."

A bright light flashed around her, and she passed out.

CHAPTER THIRTY-TWO

God held up his hand when Michael leaped to his feet.

"She's fine, Michael."

They watched as light emerged from Sara's chest until it completely exited and hovered above them. Beautiful, glorious, and magical. The golden light exploded in a ray of sparkles, as if doing so for the first time in a while.

Michael guessed it actually was.

"Hello, dear one. You've been missing for a long, long time." God beamed, holding his arms apart in the air in a welcoming gesture.

Michael laid a hand on Sara's stomach, taking comfort in the gentle heartbeat within.

They were both fine.

Looking back, he gazed in absolute wonder as the golden energy took form into its natural shape for the first time in nearly two hundred years, its wings proudly sprouting from its back.

His face broke out into an enormous smile. "Hello, Pegasus. Welcome back to Heaven, beautiful one."

It had been more than one hundred and seventy years since one of their kind had been seen in Heaven. There had never been a great abundance of them, as they were not highly sexual creatures and their gestation period was one hundred years.

Pegasus held significant power, second only to an archangel. However, they had a vulnerability. If someone claimed ownership over them, they became its master and could channel the power for themselves. In the wrong hands, they were a weapon, which was why no one outside of Heaven knew about it.

Pegasus rarely ventured far. When the Great War had broken out between the gods, Michael had sent them and his angel warriors out to ensure humans and several other species in the realm were not harmed.

The war had raged for ten years before the Olympians had won.

While the Pegasus were powerful, they were not agile, and the Titans had taken exception to Heaven's interference. Many Pegasus had been killed. It had been a surprise, and one Michael had deeply regretted.

At the end of the Great War, it was thought they were extinct.

"Your Grace. My lord," it said quietly and lowered its head in respect. "I am Aria. I am sorry I've been absent. I was in danger, weakened, and unable to get back to Heaven."

God laid a hand on the creature, even though it was still not in a completely manifested form, and released his own white energy to help energize it. Michael could feel the unconditional love and nurturing essence, and smiled as Aria stretched out her neck, shaking her golden mane.

"Tell me your story, child of mine."

"Exhausted, I entered a human's body after being hunted by an Olympian. I was weakened, and my shield failing. I had no choice."

Aria bowed her head in shame.

"Why would one of the Olympians hunt you?" Michael asked, confused.

"They know," God answered, low and dark. Not a question, but a knowing. The Pegasus nodded as she began manifesting into a material form.

Diamond tears fell down the white fur of her face. "Yes, my lord. At least this god knows."

Michael's body went taut, and he stood, taking a moment to gently lay Sara down. "Who was it?" he asked, his body pumping and ready for battle.

God held up his hand to halt him, giving him a look of impatience. Like Father, like son. "Finish your story, Aria."

"I have been the cause of great pain to her bloodline." Aria looked down at Sara with absolute love and hung her head in shame. "The god Ares cursed them, hoping one of them would commit suicide so it would expulse me from their body. Then, as you know, he could be my master."

Michael cursed.

"Yet each of these strong women struggled and lived on despite the challenges. I was passed from soul to soul at the birth of each firstborn daughter. So very strong."

Michael frowned. "For nearly two hundred years?"

"Yes."

God ran another hand over the Pegasus, and a white haze covered her. Her wings fluttered and tail lifted as her body regenerated further.

She let out a little neigh in gratitude.

"You're so glorious," Michael admired, taking a moment to appreciate the rare and unique beauty that was in front of him. Even archangels could be wowed occasionally, and this was certainly a moment he would remember.

Pegasus were the most unconditionally loving creatures. To know that one had been imprisoned for so long was absolutely heartbreaking.

"You saved me, Lord Michael. You saved me, and you saved Sara. I'm so happy she is now free to live her life."

"Did you know it was me?" he asked curiously, remembering the day her energy had booted him across the room.

"Not at first. I've been shut down so long, and I wasn't expecting you." Aria's eyelashes fluttered shyly. "I apologize."

Michael shook his head. "No need. You did the right thing protecting yourself."

"As Sara fell in love with you and her heart reached out to yours, I could recognize you. Then the baby came, and I knew for sure."

Michael stared down at his beloved human. "You saved her. When I exposed her to my light. I am forever grateful to you."

Aria bowed her head. "I owe her far more."

"What will happen now, Father? She's just a human again."

"She was always human, Michael."

He narrowed his eyes at God. "You know what I mean."

"She's your soulmate. There's no great mystery."

Was the guy kidding him right now?

"And?" he pressed.

"She's the mother of the next archangel. Oh, and pro tip, don't tell her the sex of the baby. It won't go down well."

He arched his eyebrow at God while he crossed his arms, big muscular arms that usually had a big impact when he wanted things to go his way. In this instance, they made absolutely zero difference.

"Awesome, thanks for the tip, Dad. My point is, she can't remain here as a human or raise an archangel on Earth."

God shrugged. He damn well shrugged.

"Father!"

"The decision is hers, Michael. Honor her free will, which I know you will. You have the power to grant her immortality."

"I do not."

"Son, you are the Supreme Archangel Michael."

"I don't have the powers to make someone immortal. You know that."

"Don't you?"

"Oh no, no, no. Don't you get cryptic on me now,

please," Michael pleaded.

God sighed at his eldest son and turned to the Pegasus. "Go rest, little one. I will finish up with Michael and then visit with you. Your healing will take time."

Aria lowered her head in gratitude.

"Thank you, Your Grace." Aria glanced at Sara with eyes of love. "Please tell her I said thank you, and I look forward to meeting your child soon."

"I will," Michael agreed gently, reigning in his frustration for the moment. When Aria left, Michael glared at his Father for a long, stubborn moment.

"Thank you, son. What a magnificent gift to have a Pegasus back in Heaven."

He nodded once more, breathing out the last remains of his patience.

"You're welcome. Now, Father, tell me, if you won't gift Sara with immortality, how do I do it? You know that's not within my power."

God sat down with a sigh.

"Listen, Michael. Humans marry, and the beasts mate. Commitment given freely bonds two beings together, no matter how they choose to do it." He crossed his legs. "That's all that's required. If she chooses you—body, mind, and soul— then she will in turn share your immortality."

Michael narrowed his eyes. Things were never just that simple.

"However, here's the caveat."

And there it is.

He frowned.

"You cannot tell her. The commitment has to be given freely."

"She won't. Sara doesn't believe we can be together, so there's no way she's going to give herself completely." He groaned. "Not after all the pain she has suffered because of this curse by the gods."

"I'm sorry, but that changes nothing. She must choose it for herself. You know my one and only rule."

Yeah, yeah. Free fucking will.

Standing, he began pacing around the room. He had been counting on God's gratitude in returning the Pegasus and his need to protect his grandchild. That was the thing about expectations—they created nothing except disappointment.

His mate was still a mortal. His child and Sara were both vulnerable.

"She will need time to recover. I will grant her five days in Heaven, and then you must return her to Earth. Have faith in her love for you."

Michael groaned, lowering his head into his hands.

"At least tell me you'll grant the damn cat immortality if I can do this. She deserves that much after her bloodline kept the last Pegasus safe for generations."

God smiled. "Very well. Tilly likes it here and will always choose her human. I think I'd be fighting both you and Raphael if I didn't. He's taken quite a liking to the feline."

Yeah, that was weird.

CHAPTER THIRTY-THREE

Sara opened her eyes slowly, blinking as Michael came into focus. He was standing with his arms stretched above him, holding onto the doorframe in their bedroom, the upper half of his warrior body bare and beautiful.

She ran her eyes over the mystical tattoos she'd become so familiar with over the past few weeks. How many hours had she now spent running her fingers over those markings? Not enough.

She needed to stretch, but knew as soon as she did, it would interrupt this rare moment. It wasn't often she got to observe her powerful archangel in such a private, thoughtful pose.

That he loved and adored her the way he did was still amazing to her. The way he protected her and their growing child completed her in ways she never knew could exist. He was worth every second of loneliness and heartbreak she'd endured.

As he stared out into the lush, tropical garden, Sara knew her beloved was worried about something, and it likely had to do with her.

"Michael," she whispered.

He whipped around and stalked to her bedside, full of power and energy. "You're awake."

He sat on the edge of the bed and lifted her hand to his mouth.

"What happened?"

She recalled being with God, the food, the fireplace,

and the feeling of Michael beside her, warm and solid. Then nothing. It was as if she'd dreamed it all and woken up.

"He put you to sleep so he could release the guest's energy from your body. You've been healing from the extraction." He gazed down at her, the worry still on his face. "How do you feel?"

She moved to sit up, but Michael lifted her like she was as light as one of the pillows behind her. Smiling, she grabbed his forearms and sighed at how damn sexy he was.

"I feel fine."

As Michael relaxed, she suddenly had a thought. "Wait, does that mean I only have one soul now?"

He nodded. So that was why he had a look of strain and worry lining his face.

"I'm not immortal?"

His jaw tensed.

"Not yet. But you will be. I'm going to work this out." He took her face in his hand and kissed her hard. "Trust me. Can you do that?"

Trust him? Of course. She loved him.

Yet this wasn't just about her heart anymore. She was pregnant with his child. An angelic child. Memories of the conversation before she blacked out returned.

"So, free will. I get it. But it's pretty crap God won't gift the mother of his grandchild immortality. I mean, who does that?"

Tears formed in her eyes as Michael pushed her hair off her face. "Do you love me, Sara?"

"Of course I do."

"Then keep doing that," he said firmly, nodding. "I know humans hate hearing these words, but please have faith. In us, in our love, and in me."

Faith? Was he kidding right now?

Here she was, in Heaven, with God and the most powerful archangel in existence, and they'd both said they couldn't grant her an eternal life. So who could? Who should she now have faith in? She couldn't get any closer to the source of all the answers in the universe if she tried.

Faith?

No way.

Swallowing down all the four-lettered words on the tip of her tongue, she nodded. She wanted to believe in him, she really did.

"Fine. But as I said the other day, if you leave me or try to take this child away from me, I will raise hellfire across the Earth and all of God's precious children."

Mother-fucking-fucker.

She was furious, and by the look on Michael's face—the one he was trying to hide from her—he was just as mad.

Which worried her even more.

She was trying to hold it together, but all the emotions suddenly rose up from her chest, and she burst into tears. Michael cursed and pulled her into his arms, letting her cry for what felt like hours.

"It's okay, baby, I promise. We'll work this out," he whispered over and over.

Eventually, she hiccupped and took some long, deep breaths. "So what was it? Inside me?"

Moving to stretch out beside her on the bed, Michael pulled her against him and folded one of his huge biceps under his head. "A Pegasus, Sara. The most beautiful sight. We thought them all extinct."

Michael shared the story of the war, how it'd hidden in her bloodline for almost two hundred years, and how the gods had cursed them.

"Holy shit. I can't believe my whole life has been a struggle because of a curse."

"I'll be taking revenge for your family, don't you w—"

Sara cried out as Michael cursed and ran a hand through his dark hair. It wasn't often he forgot his power around her. "Sorry, I didn't mean to scare you, but dammit, knowing those gods have been near you, watching you, makes me furious."

"They were watching me?"

Michael pulled her under his body, planting a kiss on her lips. Protective. Possessive.

"No one will harm you, Sara. I swear it. There will be consequences for this."

"I don't want you to get hurt. Don't get me wrong, I'm furious as hell, but it's over now, and you are impor—"

"My little human, I will not be harmed. I am God's greatest warrior, my love."

"Don't suppose the Pegasus can grant immortality, can she?"

She let out a big sigh when he shook his head.

"Man, God's loyalty program sucks. No reward whatsoever for keeping a magical being safe for centuries."

Michael nodded in agreement.

Later, Michael held Sara's hand and led her along the paved streets of Heaven to Gabriel's chambers.

We're on our way, brothers.

"Are you sure I look okay?"

"You're too beautiful. I don't want their eyes all over you," he said, looking down and shaking his head. A long black cloak suddenly draped her body.

Laughing, she began trying to untangle herself. "You're crazy! Get it off me."

"Oh, alright." He grinned.

The cloak disappeared, exposing the blush-pink chiffon dress she wore over a white bodysuit. The long sheer fabric split to midthigh on each side, revealing far too much skin in Michael's opinion. A pendant hung between her breasts, directing the eye to areas he did not want his brothers looking at.

They stopped outside a door. Tucking his hand gently

into her hair, which was pinned up in loose curls, Michael leaned down and kissed her. "Ready?"

He knocked on the door while Sara tightened her grip on his hand, and he tucked it around his arm.

My girl.

"Welcome!" Raphael opened the door dramatically, and Michael rolled his eyes.

They stepped into the spacious living room, which was decorated differently from his own. Gabe's house was more Victorian in style, with dramatic arched windows, moody drapes, and the era furniture. With the large windows, it still remained an open, bright space, but it had more of a masculine feel to it than Michael's.

"My brothers. Meet my soulmate, Sara."

She lifted a hand and squeaked, "Hi."

Meeting all seven of God's archangels was no mean feat for anyone, let alone a mere human. They all understood that. His eyes roamed the room and took in his enormously powerful brothers, trying to see what she saw.

Yeah, intimidating.

Larger than human men, they were in fact the largest and most powerful angels in the universe. Each of them wielded their own set of abilities gifted to them by God, along with a spectacular set of wings.

"It is my honor to meet you, Sara," Gabe greeted and kissed her hand. "Messenger of God and Archangel of Children and Fertility at your service."

Michael rolled his eyes at his charming brother, or so Gabriel liked to think.

An inch or two shorter than Michael and nearly as broad, ladies loved him. His olive skin, blond hair, and silver eyes drew them in.

"Forget him. I'm the Archangel Raphael, and the pleasure is all mine." When he flashed his pearly whites and the double dimples which got him into so much trouble appeared, Michael wanted to bust the guy's chops right there and then.

"H-hi! So nice to meet you," Sara replied, blushing.

He ignored Raphael's smirk and glistening eyes, because the show was all for him, and he wasn't going to bite.

Or at least try very hard not to.

Raphael had recently taken to socializing with the elite on Earth and was usually dressed in Saville Row suits or other high-priced attire. He couldn't argue his brother had style in spades, but he was also a powerful warrior under all the layers. He was the closest in build and height to Michael, and could always be relied on to be a cheeky ass.

Why Sara reacted the way she did to Raphael was still a puzzle. Grunting, he pushed past his former best friend and introduced her to the others.

"Sara, this is Uriel. He's the Archangel of Wisdom. Except when it comes to his love life."

Everyone sniggered. Uriel shot him a glance which he had trouble understanding. Annoyance, yes, but something else too.

Lean and muscular, with short blond hair, Uriel was the shorter of them all—but by no means short—with eyes the color of the ocean. When not brooding over one particular goddess, Uri was a playful and creative archangel, often reciting poetry and flirting with angels.

Weren't they all?

Well, not him anymore.

"Hi, Sara, nice to meet you."

She lifted a shy hand.

"Chamuel—or Cham, as we call him—is the Archangel of Pure, Loving Relationships. A true gentleman."

Said archangel coughed. "Oh, come on, don't spoil my reputation," he joked, pushing off the wall. He took Sara's hand in his and with a kindness Michael expected from the archangel, said, "It's a pleasure to meet my brother's mate. Welcome to Heaven, Sara."

"Thank you," she replied, and as Michael had expected,

she was mesmerized by his piercing electric-blue eyes.

While Chamuel might be a peacekeeping romantic, as a warrior, he was fast. Extremely fast.

Michael took her hand and turned her to meet Zadkiel.

"Archangel of Benevolence, nice to meet you." Zadkiel bowed his head to her.

"If you want to know anything about our history, he's your archangel."

Zads had that professor look perfected; dark, cropped hair, clean shaven, and smartly dressed. Like all of them, he was muscular, but he had a more athletic body compared to Michael, Gabe, and Raphael. At six foot three, he held his own with his brothers despite his quieter personality.

"I want to know everything."

"All in good time." He smiled. "And please, call me Zadkiel."

A few of them let out a laugh, knowing how much he hated his eons-old nickname.

"Last but not least, the Archangel of Divine Beauty, Jophiel," Michael introduced.

The muscular, green-eyed beauty was an enigma to women…and men. Michael likened him to those human surfers who were free spirits, so in love with life that people loved being around them even if they were unaware of it. He even had sun-kissed, light-brown curls, but his tall, bulky frame wouldn't bode well on a longboard.

"Hey, what's up? You liking it here in Heaven so far?"

Sara sat down next to Michael on the sofa when he gave her a nudge at the hip. She crossed her legs, and her dress floated open around her legs.

Michael groaned.

Uriel smirked.

Eyes of sunshine.

"It's not at all how I imagined," she answered.

They all nodded knowingly. They'd heard it for

thousands of years. Chamuel handed her a glass of something bubbly, and Sara held up a hand. "Oh, thank you, but, ah, I can't."

"They know about the baby, Sara."

"It's ambrosia, not alcohol. You'll love it, trust me," Cham said.

She took a sip and her face lit up like New Year's Eve.

"That's the most delicious thing I've ever had in my life."

Michael loved watching her learn about his home and look so happy. One day soon, he wanted her and the baby to remain here permanently. He hoped she did, too.

"Welcome to the family, Sara. I know this is probably overwhelming for you," Zadkiel said.

"It is, but you are all being so nice. I guess it's your job, being archangels and everything."

"Not really. Raphael is a jerk most of the time," Gabriel quipped. One arm punch later and the two were tumbling on the ground. Michael rolled his eyes and grinned at her.

"It's not our job to be nice; they just know if they aren't, I'll beat the shit out of them."

A round of pffts sounded out, and he almost glowed watching Sara giggle. When they all calmed down, she took another sip of her drink, and her smile faded.

He tensed.

"I hope I can return one day and truly be a part of your family."

Michael's heart nearly tore in two.

The situation for both of them was in the air, and the pressure intense with their growing child in her womb. For the first time in his existence, he truly felt powerless. Sara held all the cards but didn't know it.

He had figured out why God had said he couldn't tell her about how to achieve immortality. Telling her would interfere, and they couldn't do that. And if she knew, it would make it nearly impossible for her to choose freely, knowing she had to.

Michael frowned. No, he wasn't powerless. He just needed to work on building their trust and deepen their love and commitment. How he was going to do that was the challenge. It wasn't like he was an expert in relationships. At all.

"You will. I promise, sweetheart." He kissed her forehead.

"And is Tilly enjoying Heaven?" Raph inquired.

"You know Tilly?" she asked, astonished.

"Raphael was with me when you blacked out. He gave Tilly some treats, and now the cat loves him."

"Hey! I can't help it if pussies just like me." Raphael grinned.

"Gross."

"Photo or it never happened."

"You're the pussy."

"And you wonder why there were statues made of me and not you, bro," Gabriel said, shaking his head in good humor.

Sara laughed, choking on her ambrosia. Dealing with these six idiots was like being in a circus some days, but this was his life, and he loved it.

They each had a very important role in protecting the mortals in the realm, but when they got together like this, they were just a bunch of brothers. Large, powerful, boisterous brothers, for sure.

Things often got out of hand when they got too playful, but Michael had warned them that with a human—his pregnant human—in the room, they were to behave. He knew they all felt very protective of the new archangel baby already, so would take his warning seriously.

It would take Sara a while to get to know them well and feel comfortable, but this was a good start.

He smiled.

For the archangels, things were going to be different,

having a new member of the family. A female. A soulmate. And they were all eventually going to have one. He hoped his brothers would find theirs soon.

Life in Heaven had now changed, he realized as he watched his brothers interact with the woman he loved.

Jophiel asked about her meeting with their Father.

"Yes, this morning. Boy, what an experience. He's so…what?"

Joph looked over at Michael in question.

Sara had spent three days recovering. Distracted by their conversation when she had woken up, he'd forgotten to mention it. She also hadn't asked. He didn't think she'd appreciate his male logic, so he kept his thoughts to himself.

More importantly, God had given her five days, so the clock was ticking. He had two days left with her in Heaven before he had to take her back to Earth.

"You were asleep for three days, sweetheart. I apologize. I should have told."

"I was?" Her eyes were wide. "Crap. Well, I guess we got a bit sidetracked when I woke up."

Raph held out a hand. "TMI. TMI. Please, no gross details about my brother's love life or I'll barf."

Michael gave his idiot brother a shake of his head, and a few of the others laughed. They'd all seen it all, including each other. That's what happened when you were immortal.

"Raphael, what my beautiful human means is that we were discussing something of great importance."

"They don't' know?" she asked, looking up at him.

"No."

"What don't we know?" Uri inquired, leaning forward.

"The soul inside Sara, and all the women in her bloodline for the past one hundred and seventy years, was…a Pegasus."

A moment of silence, then he grinned as the room

exploded.

Three of the archangels launched to their feet.

"Impossible!"

"They're extinct."

"You have to be shitting me?"

"What?! How?!"

Eventually, after a lot of shaking their heads and questions, they all sat down.

"You've certainly brought some color into our lives, Sara," Chamuel said.

"When we return to Earth, we'll need to protect her," Michael stated fiercely. "Ares was responsible and has been patiently waiting for its release. Through childbirth, the Pegasus passed from generation to generation, trapped because of Ares's curse."

Michael felt Sara tense beside him and then squeak out a, "What?"

"Dude, you have to tell your partner first."

Michael sneered at Raphael. "And you know this how, husband of who?"

"He's right," she snapped.

"See?"

Michael sighed and ran his hand through his hair.

"Fine. I apologize. The curse trapped Aria, not allowing her to return to Heaven. Through pregnancy, she was passed on from female to female. The gods waited in the hope that her spirit would be released in the only way it could be. For one of you to, well, end your life."

"Suicide?"

"Yes."

He saw her eyes dart to the floor, knowing she had started on that path just before calling him. Didn't she realize that by shouting and asking for help, she had shown true inner strength? Damn, this human of his didn't give herself enough credit.

"Fool them for choosing such strong women,"

Raphael stated, and Michael sent him a grateful look.

"What were they hoping to gain?"

"Yeah, what's the end goal?" Zadkiel asked.

Michael held up a hand as the questions started to flow.

"Me, apparently. The Pegasus, Aria, believes Ares wanted her powers to overpower me." Michael let that bombshell sink in.

"The fuck?" Raphael said.

"So he believes that by destroying you he can take control of Heaven?" Zadkiel asked again.

"No offense, Michael, but there are six more of us," Chamuel added.

"Hey, I'm not saying the fucker is smart. I'm just repeating what Aria told us. "

Sara placed a hand on her belly. "Oh God. So it might have passed to our baby if we hadn't discovered it."

Michael shook his head and placed his hand over hers, not at all concerned. "No. I would always have discovered her, and I did. Aria was protecting you. She loves you."

"So that's why Several believes he is predestined to k—" Gabe froze.

"Predestined for what?"

Oh shit. Sorry, Michael.

Michael shook his head, knowing it couldn't be helped. He needed to tell her everything. But first, she needed to understand how protected she was.

Taking her hand, he clasped it in his. "Look around you, sweetheart. Seven of the most powerful warriors in existence are with you. No one is getting near you or our child."

"But it's not inside me anymore. Just tell them that."

"Ares doesn't know that, and at this point, I believe it is best we do not share what we know with the Olympians."

When she went to respond, he continued. "One of our angels has gone rogue. He believes he is predestined to kill an archangel princess, which doesn't exist, but it's likely they will think it is you when they learn of you. Which they probably have by now."

So far, their investigations had showed proof of meetings between Severial and Ares going back decades.

"You plan to make me and your child bait? Absolutely no way!" Sara exclaimed as she tried to stand. Michael grabbed her.

"Sweetheart, stop."

The tension in the room rose as her fear hit them all. He felt them all react, their energy flowing to his mate in waves of protectiveness that nearly brought tears to his eyes. She must have felt it too, because she tensed and looked up at all of them.

"You have my word he'll never get near you," Gabe promised, standing away from the wall, legs apart in warrior pose. "Whether that princess is you or the child."

Next, Raphael stood and pulled his blade out of its sheath, a powerful green light glowing. "I swear on my sword to protect you both, Sara, mate of Michael."

"And I," Uriel added, joining him.

Michael's heart ached as, one by one, they all stood and pledged themselves to their protection. Then they all bowed their heads, something no archangel did. He couldn't speak, but he definitely swallowed.

Loudly.

When he nodded at them, they returned to their seats and leaning places.

It was a moment he would never forget.

Sara wiped the traitorous tear from her cheek and thanked the archangels. She was overwhelmed by the powerful declaration she could feel through her whole being.

One look at Michael told her everything she needed to know; these males loved each other. They may be strong, masculine warriors of God, and good grief, they were enormous, but they were also full of love, loyalty, and affection for one another.

It was sexy as hell.

She didn't feel disloyal to Michael for acknowledging it—though she wasn't stupid enough to announce it out loud. These archangels were sex on legs, all of them unique in their own way. Yet, while she appreciated their tall, broad frames, long, solid limbs, ridiculous cheekbones, and incredible eyes, it was Michael alone who got her pulse racing. But it was more than that now. They were connected on a soul level she'd never thought possible.

And now she was carrying his child.

An incredible impossibility, and yet, here they were.

It had changed everything for them both the moment they had found out they were having a baby. She was going to be a mother.

It raised far more questions than they had had before and also created a need in her she would never have considered. She needed immortality. If her child was going to live forever, then so would she. Or at least for as long as she could. And her gift? She could spend her life with the man—male—she loved. Because she really loved this archangel.

Learning she had been cursed, along with all her female relatives, explained how her life simply had never gone to plan. Was it possible for her to have the love and family she'd always dreamed of?

This rogue warrior scared her, but Sara felt protected by the seven archangels. She had to trust them.

Soon, they sat alone with Gabriel—the other archangels having taken their leave.

"Tell us what you know about archangel pregnancies," Michael requested.

Gabriel held his fingers in a steeple. "Hmm, let's see."

After letting out a range of murmurs and other strange sounds, he leaned back and put an ankle over his knee. "Based on the long history of zero archangel pregnancies in all of time, that would be…a big, fat nothing. Good one, Michael."

Sara giggled.

"Alright, smart-ass," Michael grumbled. "Let me reword my question. What do we know about angel-human pregnancies? Or anything we can reference?"

"Nephilim. Let me look." A book appeared in Gabriel's lap, and he started flicking through it.

"Is that what our baby is?" Sara asked. "A Nephilim?"

"No," Gabe answered, glancing up quickly. "Archangels are not angels. We were created; angels are enlightened humans…among other things."

Sara quietly watched him until Michael turned her chin in his direction and winked at her. He smiled as her heartbeat increased in response.

"Want to go on a heavenly date tomorrow?" he whispered.

"A date in Heaven. What would it entail?"

"Whatever you desire."

"Dinner on a fluffy cloud?"

"If you want." He smirked when her mouth dropped open.

"Oh my God. Is that really a thing up here?"

"What makes you think we're up?" He laughed.

Her mouth dropped open again, and she slapped his arm.

"Stop teasing her, Michael." Gabriel tsked, then placed the large book on the table in front of him.

Michael laughed and kissed her on the lips.

"Later then, gorgeous."

"Okay, you lovebirds, I need to do more research. I would have expected a nine-month gestation based on you being human. However, it appears to be progressing faster, and that could be because it's a celestial being." He gestured at her belly. "You shouldn't be that visible at only four or five weeks."

Sara looked down at her little bump. "So this isn't a pandemic baby? It's actually our baby?"

"I'm sorry, a what?" Gabe squinted.

"Human pandemic joke. Banana bread…" Sara shook her head. "Anyway, never mind…so this is actually my baby bump?"

"Yes. I'm going to guess the child will grow fast now and then slow cook at the end."

"It's not a roast chicken, Gabriel," Michael muttered.

"For nine months?" she asked, ignoring him.

"Yes. Because you're mortal."

Hello, elephant in the room.

"Yeah. I am."

Michael squeezed her leg. "Thanks, Gabe."

"Well, alrighty then. I'll let you know what else I learn. In the meantime, Sara, just follow all the usual human guidelines for pregnancy." He smiled a little evil smile. "Michael, perhaps you could read a few human daddy books."

Sara let out a little laugh.

"Our child is going to be an archangel, Gabriel. As the Supreme, I'm fairly sure I know everything there is to know."

Sara rolled her eyes. "He always like this?"

Gabe nodded and nodded. "Yup. Welcome to the family."

She laughed.

His advice was excellent. She needed to learn and do some reading. She made a mental note to get Michael some pregnancy books to read as well. Whether or not he read them would be another story.

What to Expect When You're Expecting manifested on her lap, and she laughed.

"Thanks, Gabriel."

"Please, call me Gabe."

"Let's go," Michael said, holding his hand out to her, and they left.

Back in Michael's chambers, they found Tilly outside in the garden playing with a couple of squirrels. Sara sat down on the grass, watching the cat push their chestnuts around, irritating the poor creatures. Clearly, she was having far more fun than the squirrels.

"Welcome to my world, squirrels." Sara laughed, recalling all the things she had found under her sofa after she vacuumed. Hair ties, crystals, lip glosses, even nail files would disappear and resurface on housework day.

Nearby, a peacock stretched out its beautiful feathers and butterflies danced between the flowers. Bees did their busy job while colorful birds played in a nearby birdbath.

She lay back in the grass and placed her hand on her belly. She had honestly thought it was weight gain, but now that she was focused on it, she connected with the child growing inside her.

Michael sat down beside her and stretched out his beautiful body. She loved his dark jeans and black shirt which stretched taut across his chest. Sara took in those menacing blue eyes and reminded herself that he may be her lover, but he was also a warrior.

With her, he was gentle yet masculine. He carried himself with an air of power. And yet, when his hands were on her, they were greedy and delicious. His alpha nature was, despite her own independent nature, a damn turn-on.

"My brothers love you, Sara," Michael affirmed, running his hand over her hair.

"You nearly cried when they said that. I saw you."

"Archangels don't cry." He tickled her, pulling her under his body as she giggled.

"Yet," she teased.

"You plan to make me cry, sweetheart?"

"No, but the day our child arrives, I'm willing to bet those gorgeous cheeks of yours won't stay dry."

He gazed into her eyes for a long moment before lowering his lips to hers.

This child was going to have one very protective daddy and six ridiculously involved uncles. She imagined their future, living in Heaven, and wondered if she truly could give up her life on Earth.

As Michael moved down her body and lifted her skirts, she knew life without him would be one of suffering after loving him.

"Open wide for me, Sara," he indicated, pushing her legs apart. He'd been a gentle lover since they'd discovered her pregnancy, but it had been more intimate, more intense.

As his mouth covered her pink flesh, she cried out.

"So sensitive," he murmured, running his tongue fast over her nub, creating more noise from the back of her throat.

Michael lifted her hips and gained more access to her core. His expert tongue lapped away as a thumb teased her rear. Before long, she was crying out and creaming on his lips.

"So delicious, sweetheart."

And then he was inside her, long, hard, and thrusting with such ownership and determination, she could no longer think.

He collapsed over her, pulling her into his arms. "My Sara. My mate."

As she caught her breath and glanced around at the heavenly landscape, she let herself feel happy and forget all their worries for just a little moment.

She was certainly happier than the squirrels, that's for sure.

CHAPTER THIRTY-FOUR

Michael eyed the book lying on the side table and glanced down at Sara. She was napping after he'd given her two delicious orgasms.

And they were delicious, he knew, because he'd tasted them.

She was glowing. Beautiful and naked as she lay in his arms, he could see the slight bump of her abdomen. He had had no idea it could feel this way. He wanted to scream his pride across the heavens while locking her in his chambers.

Michael was not naive to women's bodies or childbirth. He'd answered billions of prayers in his existence. This child of theirs, though, was unique. The first of its kind. There may in time be others if his brothers found their mates, but until then, this little being would be the firstborn archangel in history. Or half archangel; they wouldn't know until its birth.

Michael flashed the book into his hands and flicked through it. None of it was new to him, but as he visualized Sara in each of the illustrated scenarios, his perception shifted to one of protective mate.

She could die.

The child could die.

One piece of sushi, and it was all over.

By the time Sara woke up, he had a list. A long list.

"Hey, sexy," she murmured sleepily and stretched out lazily. Michael sat up and patted the book.

"Hey! So. I've read the book Gabe gave you, and I've put together some thoughts on how we—well, you—can get through this."

Sara glanced at him for a moment, then yawned.

She'd need to take this seriously. He'd explain as he went through the list.

"So, I have a list of things you can and can't eat. Exercises and stretches. I'll show you which ones..."

Sara sat up and began to get off the bed.

Was she not interested?

He handed her a glass of water. "First, you need to increase your liquid intake. No more ambrosia, that was silly of me. My bad."

He flicked to a page in the book and tapped it.

"We'll be cutting out sugar unless it's natural—oh, and the wheat on your planet that's sprayed with poison is absolutely not going anywhere near our child. Organic vegetables and fruits. Yoga daily. Yeah, I think yoga. Or Pilates. What's your preference?"

Sara wrapped a yellow silk caftan around her, tucking it into her cleavage, then walked out of the bedroom.

He followed.

He was overwhelming, he knew, so he offered her his patience.

"It's a lot, I get it. But look, we'll do meditation to calm your busy mind. I can help with that. No running. Do you run? Walking only, I think. You don't run. I've not seen you run." He glanced at her as she stood in the middle of the room staring at him.

"Do you? Well, we can swim if you'd like instead. Or both. Actually, I'm not sure about the chemicals in the pool...what?"

Sara placed her hands on her hips and glared at him.

Oh God, maybe she does run?

"Okay, so you run. I just haven't seen it, that's all." He shrugged and flipped a page, holding it up for her to see.

"Supplements. We'll have to review what you're taking. Ignore the seafood warnings; I'll make sure you have fresh toxin-free fish from the cleanest oceans whenever you want. But fuck, no sushi."

Sara turned and walked over to the sofa, sitting down and crossing her arms. She looked more focused.

Excellent.

"We need to get you a doctor. Actually, I'm not sure if that's a good idea. I wonder if its wings will grow in the womb. Eh"—he waved his hand in the air—"we can just wipe the doctor's memory if they show up. I'll be with you, of course. Plus," he added, pushing his luck. "Water birth?"

"You done?"

He nodded.

"Nice one, Gabriel. You have created a monster."

He raised an eyebrow.

"You're not the first nor the last father in history to lose his marbles when the responsibility of bringing a child into the world sinks in."

He wasn't losing his marbles. The child was one of the immortal realm, not just her current world. It was his job, literally, to protect her and the child, and nothing would sway him from that.

When he began to speak, she held up her hand to stop him. And for some damn reason, he let her.

No one else had that power over him.

"Right now, I just need some food and to save those poor squirrels from Tilly. Can you magic up a pregnancy-approved meal for me, please, my sexy?"

Alright, she is forgiven.

He shook his head. "Maybe I'm going a little overboard." He ignored her smirk and handed her a plate of freshly sliced fruit. "Eat. I'll go sort out the squirrels."

CHAPTER THIRTY-FIVE

The next evening Michael had his plan together to build Sara's trust, which he hoped would lead to her choosing her immortality.

First, he was taking her on a special date, one he hoped would speak to her humanity and set a foundation for their life together as eternal beings.

Confident now that she'd been granted full protection from God, Michael also had a little surprise for her.

"Are you ready to go?"

"Depends. Is our date on a cloud?"

"I'm hoping this might be a little more exciting for you." He grinned and took a few steps back, releasing his enormous white wings of light. A quiet swishing sounded as they stretched out to their full length.

Sara's eyes flew open as she gasped loudly.

Michael glanced to either side, grinning with pride at his wings of light spanning at least six feet each. The vibrant appendages were made of energy just like the rest of him, and he could manipulate how solid—or not—they were.

"Oh my God. Gosh. God. Shit. Must stop saying that," Sara said, flabbergasted by the sight. "Michael. You are magnificent."

She walked toward him and reached out her hand. It slid through as if they didn't exist.

"Oh," she said, looking disappointed.

He gave her a little smile. "Try again." He curled one wing around her, nudging her into his arms, and planted a kiss on her lips.

"Wait, how did you do that?" she asked, ignoring his kiss and running her hand over his wing affectionately.

It felt more delicious than he'd ever thought possible. Archangels didn't let anyone touch their wings. Sure, they bumped against each other at times or occasionally received damage in battle, but never did they allow someone to, well, pat them.

"Like any other body part, I can control its solidity."

"Creepy."

"Come on. It's time to fly." He laughed, then in one unexpected swoop, he lifted her unsuspecting body into his arms and flew into the sky.

"Michael!" Sara squealed, her eyes squeezed shut as he rose higher.

"Open your eyes, sweetheart. I promise I have quite a lot of flying hours under my belt, so I won't drop you." He couldn't remember having this much fun. His laughter swept across the heavenly skies, and he didn't care who saw or heard them.

Finally, Sara untucked her head, and as she gripped Michael's arm, she gazed below her.

Unusual white mountains surrounded Central City, the major city in Heaven, and Michael pointed out the archangels' homes, the Great Hall, and the beautiful gardens they had walked through earlier.

"That's the training school." Michael pointed out a large campus area with buildings, lawns, and tall walls that looked like they were for rappelling.

A few minutes later, he set them down on a white sandy beach that stretched for miles. Soft waves lapped against the shore, and birds flew overhead in the gentle breeze.

A blanket and picnic basket full of pregnancy-approved delights appeared, along with a handful of large cushions.

"You're getting good at this date stuff," Sara said, reaching up to kiss him.

Proving her right, he draped a cotton throw over her shoulders and returned her kiss.

"Who knew Heaven has beaches!" She laughed, wandering down to the water's edge. She dipped her toe in and smiled at the tepid water.

So perfect.

"Heaven has whatever you want. Mostly," Michael said, joining her at the water's edge. She tilted her head to ask what he meant when she heard voices. Further down the beach, two angels had just walked out of the water. They spotted her in return and waved. Sara gave them a little wave in return.

"Are they the same angels we met the other day?"

"No, but everyone knows who you are."

"Everyone?" she asked, her eyes widening.

Heaven was a big place. As Michael had taken her from place to place, showing her around his home, she had been surprised by the number of people. She used the term people loosely because many had wings. And then there were the cherubs. She was unsure how she felt about those creatures. They never talked to her, always busy with whatever job they actually did, flying here and there. She likened them to large butterflies who darted back and forth. Big, round, chubby butterflies.

She was going to work on that analogy and send out an apology to the butterflies.

"Yes. You're my mate, Sara. It's a big deal. Bigger than if I were Raphael, by the way."

Sara let out a little laugh, ignoring the jealous comment. Michael knew she loved him, and only him.

One thing that had become very clear during her time in Heaven was the adoration and respect the citizens showed Michael. He was seen as the leader in this realm, as the archangels referred to it, much like a royal or politician.

"I know you are the Supreme Archangel, but are you in charge?

Michael plunged his hands into his short pockets and looked down at her. "Yes, in a way. God is the creator of all things. He created the seven of us to protect Heaven and all the realms. We each have our strengths, and mine is leadership. Any organized group needs a leader to be effective."

She nodded, piecing it all together.

"So that's it. You told someone I'm your mate, then they told two people, and so on…and it's a done deal?"

Michael tilted his head and frowned. "I don't understand."

"Don't worry."

Sara looked out across the water and let out a sigh. In the grand scheme of important things going on in her world, this wasn't important; she felt silly, but she couldn't help but feel a little deflated. Here she was, the mate of an archangel—the first in existence—and no one was going to even make her a banner?

Or throw them a party?

Carve their initials into a tree?

And if they did, would it be on Earth or in Heaven? Because once she left, she may never return.

CHAPTER THIRTY-SIX

Michael watched the emotions on Sara's face and dropped his face to smile. Not that he enjoyed seeing her upset, but it gave him the confidence he was on the right track.

He had no intention of living without her, and would do everything and anything to make sure she became immortal and returned to Heaven to have his baby.

Time to put his plan into place.

"What would you like to happen?" he asked.

Sara shook her head as she stared out across the water, refusing to look his way. He felt her anguish.

"It's fine. Ignore me."

"It's not fine, Sara."

She looked at him then, a splinter of hope in her eyes that he understood. And he did. He was hoping like hell her feelings were powerful enough to make her drop her fears and open up to him on all the levels required.

How he was supposed to make her immortal at that point, he had no idea, but that was where faith came in. He had to trust God.

"Perhaps we need to make things more official?"

Sara looked at him in confusion, her eyes narrowing slightly. "What do you mean?"

Please let me get this right.

He took her hand, kissed it, and then dropped onto one knee, something he'd never done before another living being. The sun was setting, and with a wave of his hand, hundreds of candles lit up around them.

Sara's hand flew to her mouth, her eyes wide with surprise.

"But…"

He shook his head, a smile on his lips. "Let me do this."

She nodded.

"Before we met, I dreamed of you. Over and over for nearly two hundred years. It has been painful waiting for you. I didn't know these feelings were possible, and yet, in my most private moments, I knew you were mine."

"You did?"

"I will fly across the universe declaring my love if that is your wish, Sara."

She shook her head. "No. I don't need you to do that."

"No?"

"Well, maybe just Earth."

He grinned, standing up, and took her face in his hands.

"I love you so damn much, sweetheart. Would you please do me the great honor of becoming my eternal mate?"

In his hand, a white gold, five-carat square diamond surrounded with brilliant baguettes appeared. Sara gasped, staring at it, until she finally looked up into his eyes.

"Is this what you want?"

Insert record needle scratching noise.

He frowned. "Of course. I want to spend my entire existence with you."

"I know, but is this what you want? Putting a ring on my finger? A ceremony? These are human things."

He pulled her down onto the sand. "I'm confused. I thought this would make you happy."

"It does, but what kind of mate would I be if I didn't care about what you wanted?"

Michael gave her a small smile. Of course she would consider him. They were both making it up as they went, and she was both a romantic and practical woman. And she loved him. No way would his Sara let him do this without making sure it was truly what he wanted.

The truth was, he hadn't stopped to think about what he wanted. All day he'd been focused on how to achieve immortality for her, how to keep their baby safe, and how a new tradition would set a path for his brothers when they found their mates.

Was this what he wanted?

Yes.

Because humans were not the only beings in the realm who held ceremonies to acknowledge significant moments. Becoming his mate, or any of the archangels', was a momentous moment in time. It also honored Sara and her human roots and presented her officially to the realm as a member of the archangel family.

Yes, he was also hoping that as part of the process, she would relax, open, and trust, triggering her immortality.

If it didn't, he would find another way.

"I want to put this ring on your finger and stand before God, declaring our commitment to one another, sweetheart. Please say yes. Even an archangel needs an answer."

"Yes," she let out tearfully as he pushed the ring onto her finger.

She threw her arms around him, and he landed on his back as her lips stole his. As they grinned at each other like idiots, Michael flipped her and laid her gently on the sand. "I love you, Sara Jacobson. Today, tomorrow, for eternity."

Sara gasped as stars started shooting above them in the sky. "Did you do that?"

He grinned.

"Let's go home."

Instead of flying, he flashed them back to his chambers, where they made love for hours.

CHAPTER THIRTY-SEVEN

Sara glanced at her enormous diamond for the seven hundred and fiftieth time that day and nearly tripped as she walked into Eden's Bar beside Michael.

"You alright?" He laughed, steadying her.

She nodded, grinning. Again. Although her smile was fading at the thought of leaving this magical place; it was her final night in Heaven. Even as she thought about it, she realized how crazy it sounded. That and being engaged to an archangel.

Michael had organized a night out and promised her music and dancing. Glancing down at her growing bump, she wasn't sure if she felt like shaking up their celestial baby.

Suddenly, she heard the beat of the drums and looked up. In front of her was a large stage full of…archangels.

More drumbeats.

Is that "Goodbye Stranger" by Supertramp?

Her mouth gaping, she watched as Gabriel, Jophiel, Uriel, Zadkiel, Raphael, and Chamuel became a rock band.

"Holy shit!" she exclaimed.

Dressed in leather pants and open shirts which did nothing to hide their solid mass of muscles, they burst into song as angels and other creatures cheered in the crowd.

Michael leaned into her hair. "Surprise."

She melted into his chest and began moving to the music.

God, they were incredible.

He pulled her against him, and she began running her hands up his chest while he gripped her hips and sang to her. He was the sexiest male she'd ever seen—a big call when she glanced to the stage—but they were no competition.

She turned and rubbed her bottom against him, feeling his breath against her neck. As the song ended, he spun her around and plunged his tongue into her mouth. She groaned, knowing they wouldn't be here long tonight.

When she regained ownership of her lips, she turned and applauded the band.

Raphael leaped off the stage.

"Congratulations, you two!" he said as an angel dived for him. He swooped her into his arms, leaning her all the way back, and placed an abrupt kiss on her lips. Then he winked at the crowd, which was going crazy at his antics.

Gabriel followed but ignored the female attention until one dark-haired angel caught his eye. He ran his hand over her hair as he walked past her, giving her a one hundred decibel smile, which promised more than Sara wanted to translate.

The angel seemed happy with that response and danced off.

The other brothers joined them.

"We're going to have a ceremony," Michael announced, placing an arm around her. "Once we've dealt with the danger to my mate and child."

A round of nods agreed this would be the safest thing to do. She ignored the fact he hadn't consulted her on timing. He was, after all, a powerful being and used to doing things his way.

That would change.

"And you can all either follow in our tradition or create your own when your time comes," Michael finished.

Around her, the archangels muttered, shuffled their feet, and scratched their necks. She glanced at Michael in question and found he was smirking.

"What did I miss?"

"They're scared of falling in love."

Raphael snorted. "Ex-fucking-cuse me? Says the guy who crumbled how many walls refusing to believe this gorgeous creature was his mate?"

Michael's chest rumbled, and she laughed. "There's nothing to fear. I can't wait to meet whoever you all fall in love with."

Sara laughed more as they stared back at her like she had five heads.

"Enough about us," Jophiel interjected as a tray of ambrosia appeared. "To the happy couple."

"To your eternal happiness. Welcome to the family, Sara."

She forced herself to soak up this moment and take it all in. Six archangel brothers-in-law. It was going to take some getting used to.

Raphael grinned and winked at her. She narrowed her eyes at him. Could they all read her mind? Uriel smiled.

Okay, this was not good.

She put a picture of dog poo in her mind and grinned as Raphael spat out his drink and started coughing.

"Smart girl." Zadkiel grinned.

She frowned at them all. "Do that again, and next time, I'll visualize your brother's private parts."

"His cock."

She let the image pop into her mind.

"Okay, no more, we promise." Gabriel held up his hands as they all laughed.

"Idiots," Michael said, shaking his head.

"So, how about we show this little lady what our big brother is capable of?" Raphael clapped his hands together.

Michael grinned. "Let's do it." He planted a kiss on her lips as they all whooped around her and jumped back on stage.

"Knockin' on Heaven's Door." Guns N' Roses.

Of course it was.

Michael winked at her as he began singing.

And God, he was good. No, not good. He was incredible. Her body went all tingly and warm in her private places as she watched him stand wide legged and dominate the stage.

His powerful voice belted out across the room, and she felt her panties get wet. Michael glanced at her, his eyes blazing, and she knew he'd heard her thoughts.

He gripped the microphone and belted out the last of the chorus. As the final chords were playing, Sara sat down at a nearby table. Around her, angels danced and totally fangirled over the archangel band.

Watching her mate rock out to the end of the song, she reached out for some nuts on the table in front of her when suddenly, out of the blue, a cherub swooped down and took the bowl right out of her hands.

"Shit!" By the time her hand flew to her chest, Chamuel had already reached out his hand, and the cherub was frozen in the air.

Her mouth flew open. Michael had told her Cham was fast, but this was something else. As the nuts fell from its chubby hands, Cham released the creature, and it flew off.

First Michael and close behind him Chamuel leaped off the stage.

Michael pulled her to her feet. "You okay? They're bloody menaces."

"What happened?" Uriel asked.

"Cherub stole her nuts," Cham replied.

She let out a laugh at the absurdity of it. "They are kind of creepy. But that was some trick."

"I know, right? I'm fast."

Michael shook his head. "Fucking cherubs."

"I'm fine." She glanced at her protective male. "I don't mean to be a party pooper, but I need to lie down. This baby is growing fast, and it's exhausting."

After saying their goodbyes, Michael flashed them home.

Later in bed, Sara twisted her beautiful ring around on her finger and let out a big sigh. Tilly was curled on top of her feet—nothing changed, even in Heaven, with that cat—and Michael was running his hand over her stomach.

"The bump is growing."

"I'll need to go to a doctor when we return to Earth."

Michael rolled closer to her and continued rubbing her stomach. The baby glowed at his touch, as it always did.

"You're such a cute daddy already."

"I have much to learn," he admitted humbly.

"We both do."

She was well aware they'd just spent an incredible few days in a protective love bubble—and heck, they deserved it. But now, it was time to go home and face reality.

She'd fallen in love with an archangel.

She'd fallen pregnant to an archangel.

She was still mortal.

CHAPTER THIRTY-EIGHT

Several slammed his fist down on the kitchen counter.

"Where is she?"

He'd been watching the human for years and knew all her habits and movements. She wasn't at the gym, her local shops, the café she frequented, or staying with her whining friends.

After he'd returned from collecting the warlock for Ares, he'd been unable to find Sara. Not a scent. It was like she'd vanished off the planet, which was impossible. Even her death would have left a trace.

The woman has disappeared.

Ares was going to be furious.

But fuck Ares. Several was furious with himself—it was him, after all, who had been named in the prophecy. She was his destiny, and not in the bow-chicka-wow-wow way.

The thought grossed him out. Ugh, humans. He just couldn't. That was one thing he had in common with Archangel Michael, or at least had. They didn't shag humans.

Over the past week, masquerading as everything from her lawn guy to a concerned friend, he'd asked neighbors and former colleagues where she was.

Lisa, her bestie, who had all but fucked him with her eyes, had told him she was with her boyfriend in Hawaii. Taking a moment, he ran his eyes over the slim brunette. Damn, if he were going to trial a human lover, Several thought this one might be worth it.

"Hawaii, you say?"

"Yes. Lucky, huh? Even in this pandemic. I wish she'd Facebook or something, though. So rude to just unplug like this. I mean…"

As the human had waffled on about social media and other human crap, Several had decided the sex wouldn't be worth it. Taking one last look at the tight top that stretched over her ample breasts, he had shaken his head and wiped her memory.

The human was not in Hawaii. They had checked.

"Check the hospitals and morgues one more time, then head back to the hotel," he instructed the warlock.

"Doesn't Ares have other minor gods watching over her?" Harold asked.

"Just do as I ask, human."

The warlock had a good point, though. The god of war had his own minor gods watching her, or so he understood. Did the egotistical male know where she was?

In hindsight, the presence of the archangels had been light on Earth the past week or so, which was unusual. Had Michael lost interest in his human toy? Because obviously that's all she was.

Wait. Or was she?

For what had felt like an eternity, Several had tried to decode the prophecy. An archangel princess? They didn't exist. Yes, there were female angels, but not female archangels; not that there couldn't be one if God created her, since they couldn't be born.

Or could they? As a divine being, he'd learned to never say never. Heaven's gossip train had been ripe with talk that Michael had finally copulated with a human.

Still, the archangels didn't mate or reproduce; they were the male whores of the universe, especially fucking Gabriel. And now there was to be a princess! God, he hated them all, righteous sons of bitches.

Looking around at the mess he'd made inside Sara's

house, he considered tidying it up before leaving, but what did it matter. When Sara returned, she'd simply call the police, who'd find no fingerprints or DNA. Besides, he quietly liked the idea of rattling her.

Sighing loudly, he reviewed everything he knew. Something wasn't right. What was he missing? Dammit all, he thought as he flashed to Olympus. It was time to speak to the god of war.

Walking into The Fat Angel—stupid fucking name—he took a seat next to Ares and waited while motioning to the nymph bartender for a pint.

"Finally gave up, did you?" the large god growled without looking at him.

So he knew something.

"Where is she?" he asked in response, giving the god the same disrespect of not looking at him.

"With Michael." Ares sneered. "In fucking Heaven."

Severial choked on his drink and sat coughing while he processed that unimaginable piece of information.

"She's what?!"

CHAPTER THIRTY-NINE

"I'm going to have some explaining to do when we get home. Look how big my belly is!"

Michael stared at the round bump and knew what his mate was getting at. Her friends would calculate the bump size and assume Michael wasn't the father. To be so far along, she would have had to become pregnant well before she had met him.

"Won't she be more interested in our Hawaiian holiday?" he asked. Before they had left for Heaven, Sara had sent a text message to her friend Lisa to say they were headed to Hawaii to visit his unwell father now that travel had opened up.

"Oh no. Me being pregnant is much bigger news. However, she will be wondering why I didn't message her and why I haven't posted any holiday photos on social media. Totally unlike me."

The term patience of a saint was currently being tested. He stood leaning against the doorframe while Sara raced back and forth between her suitcase and the walk-in closet.

Tilly sat on top of the headboard, watching as if her mistress were all kinds of crazy.

Me too, kitty.

"Right. Social media," Michael acknowledged, shaking his head at how his life had changed.

Maybe I should go stab Raphael with my sword or something masculine like that?

"I should leave this here. It's winter. Wait. Is it winter? Yes, it's still winter in Auckland, so it'll be too cold to wear," Sara mumbled and hung the dress back up. She turned to him. "You could always bring it back in the summer for me, right?"

He nodded.

"Okay, good. I'll make a pile of summer stuff, and then you'll know which ones I'm referring to. Middle shelf, okay?"

Michael left her to it.

Twice, he'd reminded her that he was an archangel and could literally manifest anything she wanted. At any time.

Forever.

But she simply nodded and carried on with her sorting and packing.

Raph.

Yo!

We're leaving soon. I think.

She still packing?

Yes, my God. Yes!

Think she's stalling?

Damn it. Of course she was. How stupid of him not to realize. He walked back into the bedroom and leaned against the doorframe once more.

"Hey, sweetheart." He waited until she looked at him. "We need to go."

"Sure, I'll just—"

He stepped forward and picked her off the floor where she'd been sorting shoes. "You'll be back. I promise."

Her eyes filled with moisture as she chewed her lip. "You don't know that. I may never come back to your home."

Our home.

His heart broke.

"Oh, sweetheart." He pulled her into his arms and held her tight. "I'm going to do everything in my power—which is pretty damn considerable—to get you back here. This is our home now, Sara."

There was no greater mission in his life—now or ever—than spending eternity with her and their child. To be a family together.

She sniffed against his chest.

"Now let's go back to our Earth-based home." She gave him a little smile.

Hey, look at me being good at this boyfriend stuff.

He closed the suitcase before she had any second thoughts and started to walk out when he felt Raphael arrive. That he hadn't knocked on the door or even barged in got his attention.

What's going on? he telepathed for speed.

We need to talk before departing.

"Hi, Raph." Sara smiled shyly.

Michael rolled his eyes.

"Bye, Heaven. I hope to be back one day soon," Sara said.

He glanced at Raphael, who had pity in his eyes. Don't, brother. I'm going to fix this. Now, what is it we need to discuss?

"I flashed to Earth to make sure everything was safe for your arrival." He looked between them. "Someone had broken in and gone through your belongings, Sara. Angel energy remained."

"Severial," Michael growled. "Let's go!"

He pulled her into his arms, and a moment later, they were standing inside her house, back on Earth.

CHAPTER FORTY

Sara held onto Michael's arms and just as she was getting her bearings, sudden and overwhelming nausea struck her

"Oh God." She thrust the cat cage into Raphael's arms and put a hand over her mouth. "Let her out, please. I'm going to be sick."

She ran to the bathroom. Or at least she tried, but Michael caught her and flashed her directly to the toilet just in time.

"I guess I have delayed morning sickness."

"You were temporarily immortal in Heaven. Now that we are back on Earth, you will feel the pregnancy as a human again. It may even slow down the growth."

"Ugh, it's freezing." Winter had well and truly arrived in New Zealand, and boy, did she feel the fifty degrees in every one of her bones.

She tugged at her top, which was exposing her skin, and shivered. A moment later, she was wearing a white sweater and a pair of navy sweatpants, maternity waistband and all.

"Thank you." She smiled at Michael, then stood and brushed her teeth.

Then it was time to face the carnage. As they walked through the house, Sara took in the mess the angel had left after rummaging through her stuff.

By the time they reached the living room, she found Raphael swinging a toy mouse around. Tilly was staring at him blankly.

"She's broken. I thought cats liked mice?"

"Anyway," Michael said, shaking his head. "Let's track the path of this energy and see what we can find. Sara, perhaps you should go lie down, babe."

"Pregnant, not incapacitated," she mumbled as she chewed on some plain crackers and waited for the two archangels to head outside before she flopped down on the sofa.

Just as her eyes were closing, her cell phone rang. It was still charging in the kitchen where she'd left it. That the rogue angel hadn't taken it was fortunate.

"You're back!" Lisa squealed down the phone.

"I am! Sorry for being AWOL."

She felt terrible. Her best friend thought she'd cut communication with her, even if just for a week. She wasn't that kind of friend.

The worst part was she had a lot more news to share with Lisa—things she would have normally consulted her on as they unfolded. Unless you fell in love with an archangel, things usually didn't go quite smoothly.

"How was Hawaii? Are you tanned and relaxed? So jealous!"

Heaven. Hawaii. Same-same.

"It was so warm." Truth. Heaven was warm. "I got to meet his family." Also truth.

"How's his dad doing?"

Oh, you mean God? The guy who refuses to give the mother of his first grandchild immortality? He's…

"You know, he's an interesting character, but I think he'll be fine."

Sara lifted her eyes to the ceiling and sneered.

"I can't believe you never shared one photo. You normally drive us all nuts with your Hawaii photos!" Lisa laughed.

Sara chewed the side of her mouth as guilt flushed through her. Still, what could she say? Certainly not the truth—she'd think she was crazy if she tried.

"My phone wouldn't connect. I was going to buy a new SIM card, but in the end, I unplugged. And do you know what? It was so nice."

She wanted to share as much as she could with Lisa, but it would be hard for her to understand. The only person she could talk to was Michael, but as much as she loved him, no one could replace your best friend. Not when you were as close as she and Lisa were.

"I was going to tease you and say he can't be that good in bed." Lisa giggled.

Yeah, he is.

Sara laughed. "Well…"

The two of them giggled, and then Lisa quietened.

"Truthfully though, babes, is everything okay? I know it's a big deal for you to let a man into your life again, so I wanted to check you are okay."

"I am. I'm happy, Lisa."

Oh, and we're technically engaged, and I'm pregnant with his child. We're moving to Heaven, I hope, if we can figure out a way to turn me into an immortal. But first I have to tidy up this house because a bad angel warrior is trying to kill me.

But she couldn't say any of that.

Sara turned as Michael and Raphael walked into the room. She frowned at Michael irrationally, blaming him for having to lie to her friend. He gave her that blank male look that said, what did I do?

She shook her head at him.

"So how's it going with Mr. Hottie anyway?"

"You know how it is after you've spent a week with them. They drive you nuts."

Michael looked at Raphael as if he'd missed something.

Raphael smirked.

Sara moved into the dining room and put her feet up.

Sticking as close to the truth as she could, she told Lisa how Michael's brothers had also been on the island and how close they were. Carefully, she told her about their date at the beach, how she was madly in love with Michael, and then dropped the bomb about his proposal.

"Oh my God! Sara."

"I know…"

"I'm not going to say it's too soon. It is, but you're a grown woman. You make your own decisions."

Sara was speechless.

"Look, life is short. If this stupid pandemic has taught us anything, it's living life now. If you love him and want to marry him, then I'm happy for you."

"Oh, thank you. I do love him," she cried, wiping away her tears.

"So, when can I meet him in person?"

That's where things got tricky.

Michael was an archangel. His presence felt different and overwhelming for humans. While they could work around that for a quick lunch, she couldn't hide the baby growing inside her.

"So, I have some other news."

Silence.

"I'm pregnant."

The gasp was loud.

Michael stepped up behind her and put his hands on her shoulders. She should've known he would show up to comfort her for this conversation. His love was palpable as he ran his hands up and down her arm and leaned down to kiss her head. He knew she was uncomfortable sharing the pregnancy news most of all.

"That's…are you sure?"

"Oh yes, I'm definitely pregnant. Morning sickness and everything."

"Holy shit," Lisa said slowly, then paused. "Sara, tell me honestly, is this why you're getting married? You know you don't have to do that, right? "

Michael squeezed her shoulder. She glanced up, and he

cringed. She had expected the comment. If she had been in Lisa's shoes, she'd have probably asked the same thing. Her friend was just being a good friend.

"No. I know it's a lot all at once, and we're both coming to grips with it ourselves, but Michael is my soulmate, as cliché as that sounds." She smiled into the phone. "Some days, I feel like this is all a dream, but it's very real. This baby is a miraculous gift, more than you could ever know."

She loved her friend very much, but the love she felt for Michael and their baby was beyond words.

"Wow. Sorry. I'm just trying to process it all."

You and me both, she wanted to say. Lisa didn't know the half of it. And it would stay that way.

"You know it's my job to ask those shitty questions, though, right?"

"Absolutely, and I thank you for caring enough to ask them."

"Always."

Michael squeezed her shoulder again and wandered off.

"So enough about me. Tell me what's happening with Dave. Spill."

"I mean, I think things might work out. Since lockdown he's changed, you know. He's been over a few times."

For a quickie, Sara thought, but didn't have the energy to say it for the seven hundredth time. Lisa knew.

The guy was not long-term material. He'd never settle down, and Lisa could do a lot better. Best friends also knew when to step back and let the other one make a mistake because sometimes you had to experience pain before you'd look at the truth of a situation.

They chatted for a bit longer, then Sara signed off, claiming jet lag and needing to unpack. She walked into the kitchen where Michael was pouring himself a glass of water.

He sat down at the breakfast bar, chugging down the entire glass before grimacing. "Gah, the toxins in this water are disgusting. Humans—why do they do this?"

"What's crazier is that taxpayers pay for the chemicals to be put in, and then some of those same taxpayers buy boxed water with the chemicals stripped out," Raphael replied.

"Firstly, that's the least of our stupidity." They both looked at her and nodded slowly. "Secondly, we don't have a choice about the chemicals going in in the first place."

They stared at her.

"Anyway, humanity's stupidity aside, we need to take some photos together. We've just been to Hawaii and gotten engaged, and we don't have a single photo. We need photos. And I might need some sunshine. Oh wait, please tell me you're not like vampires and can't be photographed."

Michael and Raphael stared at her, and both burst out laughing.

"I'll take that as a no."

Michael grinned. "We can get some photos, but when you move to Heaven, I'll be wiping their memories anyway, so does it really matter?"

"Yes, it matters, and that could take years."

His smile vanished.

"You guys go. I'll tidy up here," Raphael offered, looking suddenly uncomfortable.

"Dude, we need you to take the photos," Michael said. "Take selfies!"

Michael frowned at him. "An hour. Don't be a dick."

Ten minutes later, the three of them were standing in Waikiki Beach, clothed in tropical attire. They spent an hour wandering around taking photos, and by the end, even Raphael had chilled out.

"Okay, do we have enough photos, little human?" Michael asked, tugging her in for a kiss.

"Get a room, you two." Raphael rolled his eyes and laughed, then stilled.

Sara followed his eyes and saw he was staring across the road at a woman who had just walked out of the Alohilani Resort—a five-star hotel on the main street in Waikiki. She was tall and graceful, with beautiful tanned skin and long dark wavy hair. She wore a fitted navy-blue dress, and from here, Sara could see she was carrying a designer handbag. The woman was wealthy and classy.

Michael had said Raphael socialized with the rich and famous on Earth when he spent time here.

The woman seemed to stop, as if she had felt Raphael's presence, and she turned. The two of them stared at each other before she carried on walking.

"Do you know her?" Sara asked.

"No." Raphael didn't take his eyes off the woman.

"Let's head back," Michael said, frowning at his brother's obvious lie. "Zadkiel just arrived at Sara's."

"I'll meet you back there shortly." Raphael quickly glanced at them, then turned and walked away without saying another word.

After watching him for a moment, Sara turned to Michael. "What was that about?"

"Sex. Probably."

She was starting to really understand just how unique her relationship with Michael was. Although the way the two of them had looked at each other had felt like more than just sex.

Sara glanced back once more and saw the two of them talking.

Definitely not just sex.

CHAPTER FORTY-ONE

Raphael had returned the next day and refused to answer any of Sara's questions about the beautiful woman—her words, not his. He wasn't that dumb.

Michael had assumed Raphael had just seen something he liked and followed it. Of all the archangels, he was the most promiscuous with humans. He spent a lot of time on Earth blending into their lives and entertaining himself.

Socializing with humans had never interested Michael, but he'd had no issue with his brothers doing so. And look at him now, he was basically living on the planet with his human until he could take her home.

He glanced at Raphael; the guy appeared fine. Sated, in fact.

Gross.

Yeah, his mate was just being a romantic. Raphael had simply found something he liked and acted upon it. Of all the archangels, Raphael was the one he saw having the most trouble accepting a mate.

"Okay, we're all secure," Zadkiel said. He had arranged for their Heaven-based witches to add magical wards around Sara's property. It would keep everyone but angels out, which meant Severial could still get in, though Michael wasn't too worried. He had no intention of leaving Sara's side, so if Severial visited the house again, it would be his pleasure to rip every limb and wing from his body and ask questions later.

If Ares showed up? Things would get a little bit more

complicated. Letting out a long breath, he thanked his brother. "You heading back?"

"Yes. Shout if you need anything. Bye, Sara." Zadkiel waved, then flashed away.

Michael smiled at the quick departure. The guy wasn't a big talker. He was a deep thinker and analytical as hell, which drove them all crazy at times, but he was smart and strategic. They were all so different yet fit together like a beautiful puzzle.

If you sense anything, let me know.

Ditto.

He kept his conversation with Raphael telepathic. He didn't want to worry Sara unnecessarily. She was outwardly taking it in stride, but he sensed her underlying worry. None of them were willing to risk her, or the baby's safety, and that included their mental well-being.

"You staying, Raph?" Sara asked

"Yes, I'll just stretch out on the couch."

"You will not!" Michael grinned at the horror on Sara's face as she fussed and dragged his huge, grumbling brother upstairs to the spare room. Man, if he'd planned this better, he could have changed the wallpaper and linens to pink florals.

In their room, alone at last, Michael pulled Sara into his arms, breathing in her beautiful scent.

Though he felt frustration at God every single minute for not gifting her immortality, he knew she had to choose, and he'd wait as long as it took while also doing everything in his power to help it along.

He didn't doubt Sara's love or commitment to him or her desire to make Heaven her home. She'd loved it there. The question was, was she ready to give up her humanity and home on Earth to be with him?

Only then could he take her and the baby back to Heaven.

Sara's bottom was pressed into him. He ran his hand

over her belly and between her legs. She moaned and her legs opened. Slipping his fingers in further, he felt her moisture greet him. He shifted them, angling his cock into position, and gently entered her.

"Michael," she moaned quietly.

"I need you," he said. "Need to be deep in you like this."

He palmed a breast, flicking her nipple, and held her tight against him.

"More, I need you harder, faster. Please."

Michael loved hearing her plead. Not that he wouldn't give her everything, but her desire for him made him hard and fucking horny.

He pounded harder, moving her body so he could go deeper. Then he thumbed her pussy in just the right spot, grunting as she cried out. Pleasure plowed through them both.

"That's my girl. Come on my cock," he demanded.

"Oh God, I'm coming again," she cried.

He flipped to his back, lifting her so she was sitting on him facing away, sliding her up and down his shaft.

"Keep coming, baby. Come for me again."

She gripped his knees and rode him until he had filled her.

Finally, he had her back in his arms.

Sara laid a hand on her belly.

"Is the baby okay?" He knew enough to know sex would not harm it, but he couldn't help but ask.

"Yes, shaken and stirred, but it's fine." She smiled at him.

He laughed and kissed her nose. "Sleep now, beautiful, knowing you are very much loved."

Sara wriggled into a comfortable position and eventually fell asleep. Michael dozed, enjoying the feel of her and the baby safe in his arms, until something knocked at his senses, waking him fully. His eyes opened as he pushed his senses out.

Raphael.

You feel it too?

What do you sense?

As he waited for Raphael to answer, he looked over at Sara. Her eyes were wide open. Her mouth too, as if she were trying to scream and couldn't. Her eyes started darting back and forth until they landed on him and froze, pleading.

"Sara? Sara!" It hit him—she was paralyzed.

Fuck!

"RAPH!" A second later, Raphael and Gabriel appeared in the room. "Sara! Sara. Can you speak? Breathe. Now."

The three of them pushed their energy through and around her, clearing the thick dark energy which had broken through their wards and was pulsing into her.

He felt it begin to dilute until, finally, Sara gasped. Immediately, the paralysis disappeared, and she grabbed at her throat, spluttering.

"Mich, arhgh, I couldn't, ugh, breav."

"It's okay. Slow down and breathe." He looked around at his brothers, fury rolling off him. "The fuck?"

Raphael looked as furious as he felt. "I'll go."

He disappeared, and Michael felt his brother's aura expand across the property, searching for the source of the evil energy.

Gabriel stepped up to the bed and placed his hand over Sara's stomach. "The baby is okay."

"Thanks." Michael sat back on his knees and ran a hand over his face, then pulled the sheet up over Sara to cover her silk negligee. She shrugged it closer and looked at him with terror in her eyes.

"What the hell was that?"

"Witchcraft," he gritted out.

Raphael flashed back into the room.

"It felt like pins or spiders all over my body. I couldn't move or breathe."

"Witchcraft," Raphael confirmed his suspicion. "Feel this."

As he shared the energy signature he'd picked up outside, all three of them nodded.

"What witch or warlock could have the power to penetrate our wards, though?" he asked angrily.

No one answered immediately. There were only a few possibilities, all of them ugly and unthinkable.

"One with help."

Fuck.

Raphael was right. The god of war was behind this, and he was not alone. Several was helping him, they knew that, but the small-fry angel was not powerful enough to breach through wards set by Heaven's witches, the same ones who created and maintained Heaven's wards. No. Someone more powerful was aiding the god of war.

Time was running out, and he couldn't allow his mate and child to remain so vulnerable.

Michael rubbed Sara's arms and thought of their next steps. Ares didn't know the Pegasus was back in Heaven. "He's coming for the Pegasus," Michael said. "He's run out of patience."

"He knows about you and Sara," Raphael continued. "Word must have reached him, so he's getting desperate."

Michael nodded.

"I say we let it play out and catch him, then we can do something about it," Gabriel suggested.

"I'm not letting anyone play with my mate!" he yelled as Sara cringed. He sent her an apologetic glance.

"What choice do we have?" Raphael interjected. "We can't head to Olympus and accuse him of something we have no proof of."

"We have proof, but we can't use it," Michael snapped, referring to Aria. "It doesn't matter, in any case. The gods follow no laws. Ares simply needs to be stopped."

Michael wasn't leaving Sara exposed on Earth without him, so all he could do was stay put and protect her. The other archangels would have to do the legwork.

"Please don't leave me." Sara gripped his arm.

"Never."

He felt her visibly relax, and he moved on the bed and pulled her into his arms.

"What does Severial hope to achieve by fulfilling this prophecy, anyway?" Gabe asked, leaning against the doorframe with his arms crossed.

Sara flinched, and he wrapped the sheets around her some more. He hated that she was having to suffer because of him. While the Pegasus had been inside her family for nearly two hundred years, he still felt like she was involved in all of this because Ares had some vendetta against him.

The god was an unstable brat.

"Ares will have promised him some bullshit. It was clear Severial thought he was special. To be honest, there's always one or two like that, but it usually burns off over time, right?" Raphael said, and they all nodded.

"I'm less concerned about him than I am Ares. The god of war has been plotting patiently for nearly two hundred years, and that's unlike him. Can he honestly believe the Pegasus's power would allow him to overpower me?"

They all stayed silent for a moment, considering the question.

"Like, truly, what does he think would actually happen if that were possible?"

"Could it be?" his innocent little human asked.

"Fuck that," Raphael snapped.

"He's delusional. He hasn't considered he'd need to take all of us on, not just Michael. The gods truly do not know how powerful we are," Gabriel responded.

Sara turned to him, clearly unsatisfied with their answers.

"No, sweetheart, he couldn't," he said. "The gods deny our Father's existence and believe they are more powerful than us. In the Earth year 1844, they attempted to breach the walls of Heaven, and while they were somewhat successful, we stopped them."

"They could get in?" she asked, her eyes wide.

"Yes. But it doesn't mean we would let them, and we didn't."

Raphael sat down in a nearby chair. "We took offensive action, but the trouble is we aren't permitted to destroy them or any of God's creatures. That they deny Him does not change that."

Sara frowned, but he knew she understood.

"Both Ares and Several are hungry for power and have no idea the realities of the game they are playing. The only reason they've had the upper hand is because we were unaware of the situation until recently," Gabriel said.

Michael nodded.

"And they are using dirty and dangerous tactics," Raphael added.

"Which stop now," Michael declared. "The fucker needs a lesson, and it's been a long time coming."

Sara looked up at him.

"Yeah, it has." Raphael nodded. "A long damn time."

CHAPTER FORTY-TWO

"You don't have to stay, Gabe. It's been two days," Sara said to the archangel lounging on her sofa.

"The service is better here," he replied.

It was a full house having three archangels living with her, but she appreciated their protection after the fright of being paralyzed.

Raphael came and went, and while she'd asked him about it, he'd simply shrugged and said, "Archangel stuff."

Tilly was living the dream, lying tummy up, enjoying her fifth brush of the day. Sara grinned at her fur baby.

"When I become immortal, what will happen to Tilly?" she suddenly asked.

"She's coming."

"We'll keep her."

"She does too."

Surprised, she stared at all three brothers. Then it hit her. "Wait, so Tilly is being gifted immortality, but I'm not? You motherf—"

"Oookay," Michael interrupted. "Let's get to planning our ceremony, shall we?"

"God said he didn't mind blasphemy."

"He lies," Gabe affirmed, and Raphael agreed.

"Ceremony," Michael said pointedly at her.

She groaned.

"Michael, for crying out loud. I love you, but can't we wait until you've sorted out the baddies first?"

Despite the calm look on his face, Sara could tell he

wasn't going to back down. He'd been pushing for days. They had an eternity, in theory, so she didn't understand what the urgency was.

"No, we can't wait!"

The room shook, and an energy blasted through them all. The archangels frowned, and she flew back into the sofa.

Raphael leaped up and grabbed Michael, dragging him outside. "Let's go, big guy."

"Sara, I'm sorry," he said just as the door closed.

"Jeez," she muttered, shrinking into the sofa and looking over at Gabe.

"That's still blasphemy," he replied, and she glared at him.

"Not helpful."

"Go talk to him. He doesn't want to speak to Raphael; he wants you."

"Didn't sound like it," Sara said moodily.

"Pregnant much?"

She sighed.

Gabriel was right. Her hormones were all over the place. She glanced toward the door. Gabriel stood and held out his hands. She let him lift her up, and he nudged her in the direction of his brothers.

"Go. No one likes a grumpy Supreme Archangel. Save us all, please."

She let out a small laugh. "Fine."

Outside, she found the two large brothers standing at the fence, looking out at the ocean. Michael looked stiff and annoyed, likely with himself.

She knew him pretty well now.

It was mid-July, and there was a southerly wind bringing the cool weather from Antarctica. It was bitterly cold.

She'd taken no more than three steps outside when a large white coat suddenly wrapped around her. No matter how frustrated he was, he still loved and protected her.

She smiled.

Being loved by an archangel sure had its perks.

Raphael walked toward her, stopping to touch her arm affectionately before leaving them to talk.

"I'm sorry," she started, stepping under Michael's arm and tucking herself into her favorite place in the world.

"Don't apologize." He turned and wrapped both arms around her. "I should never have yelled."

"It's scary when you do that, Michael."

"And that is why I yelled. I am scared for the first time in my life. Not because of Ares or that little shit, but because I want you up in Heaven with me. I want you in my life for eternity." He ran a finger over her cheekbone. "Because I need to keep you safe."

His overwhelming need for her security was always at the forefront of his mind and in every discussion they had these days. But how their ceremony had anything to do with that, she didn't know.

"And I love you for that. I know you will find a way. I trust you."

He began to kiss her. Gently at first, and then it deepened. His hand threaded through her hair and cupped the back of her head as heat flushed through her. Leaning into him, her nipples hardened.

"I can't lose you." He ran his thumb over her lips, his eyes telling her everything he needed right now.

His hardness nudged against her. Alpha males like Michael had only one way of relieving their frustration when it came to protecting the woman they loved. Total domination, and that included her body.

Just the thought of what he was about to do caused a flood of pleasure to cascade through her. His nostrils flared as his hand gripped her bottom. Moisture pooled between her legs.

"You won't," she said as his blue eyes swirled with lust.

He flashed them to the bedroom, and the door closed.

"No, I won't. You are mine, Sara. Forever," he growled possessively.

From anyone else, those words would have scared her. But when Michael said them, she felt protected, loved, and desired. She was his, and she gave herself freely to him.

The coat disappeared, and he slipped his hands under her top, nudging her bra aside, freeing her nipples. She gasped, her body sensitive as his mouth dropped and began to suckle.

"Lie down and spread your legs," he demanded huskily once he'd had a taste.

Her yoga pants disappeared, along with her panties, leaving her exposed and vulnerable.

"So wet already. Do you want my cock or my tongue?" He kneeled on the bed and ran his fingers through her wet folds. "Decide. Now."

"Tongue. God, I need your tongue."

No sooner had the words left her mouth than his mouth was on her and his fingers sliding inside. She arched and grabbed her breasts, tweaking her nipples.

Michael gripped her hips, holding her in place as he devoured her, nipping at her clit in delicious ways.

"That's it, baby, squeeze your nipples for me."

"Agh, God," she cried out.

"Come, Sara, and then I'm going to fill you with my cock."

Wetness poured out as she threw her head back, crying out his name.

"That's it, my good little girl. More," he groaned, inserting his fingers as she orgasmed again. He undid his fly and pushed down his jeans, lust burning in his eyes. "God, I need to fuck you. Right now."

Michael pushed inside her in a single thrust, grabbing the back of her neck with his large hand. She arched into him, needing to feel the fullness of him.

"You're mine, Sara. Say it."

Grateful that she was so wet and able to accommodate his large, rock-hard member, Sara grabbed his arms.

"Say it," he growled, gripping her knees and flipping her over. Positioning her on the sheets, he bent over her and plunged back inside. Reaching underneath, he palmed a breast, pinching her nipple, and breathed into her hair, "Mine."

With a handful of sheets bunched in her hands, she arched into him, loving the way his huge body enveloped hers.

"I'm yours."

"Mine," he groaned.

"I'm yours, always and forever."

She cried out as his seed burst into her, filling her with his love. After a moment, moving her carefully, he wrapped an arm under her, and they lay gazing at each other. His beautiful blue eyes were so familiar to her now, she now knew what each shade meant. Anger, impatience, lust, protective humor, and her favorite, love.

"Do you have any doubts, my little human?"

Laying a kiss on his gorgeous golden chest, Sara shook her head and smiled up at him innocently. "None. I love you, my little archangel."

"Little?" He raised an eyebrow and smirked. "Now that's not true and you know it."

She giggled.

"What about you, Michael? Do you have any doubts? One minute you're Mr. Supreme Bachelor of the Universe, the next you have a human to protect and a baby on the way. It's a big change for you."

He leaned on an elbow, staring down at her. "Never. You are my greatest blessing, and there is nothing I would change."

Michael brushed her hair back off her forehead and kissed it. "So please, sweetheart, let's do this. It's all I ask of you."

"Okay."

As the words left her mouth, Michael fell back on the bed and smiled for the first time in days. Sara knew he loved her and wanted to protect her, but she couldn't stop feeling like he had some ulterior motive.

Michael ran a hand down her chest and over a nipple. It hardened, and he smiled. "You're a part of me now." His hand dropped to her stomach. "And you have a part of me within you."

That she had nearly missed out on this experience in life gave her shivers. Loving someone was one thing. Creating a life with them and seeing the awe in their eyes as it continued to grow within you was unexplainable.

Michael's blue eyes shimmered as he continued to caress her bump.

"Is it strange to be with someone after being an eternal playboy?"

He cupped her cheek and smiled gently. "It's not strange for me to be with you, Sara. Don't look for problems where they don't exist. I want to exchange our vows—there's substantial power in doing so, my love."

She tilted her head, but he said nothing further.

Perhaps he was right. She was looking for problems after a lifetime of disappointment. For the first time in her life, she really trusted someone. Heck, if you couldn't trust an archangel, who could you trust?

She turned and kissed his hand, receiving one on the lips in return that quickly developed into another beautiful lovemaking session.

After a shower, they headed downstairs, and she was secretly delighted to find they had the house to themselves. It would give them time and privacy to plan out their ceremony.

Sara got out a notebook and started making notes.

"Well, first things first. I'm wearing a big, and I mean

big, beautiful princess dress."
　　Michael grinned.

CHAPTER FORTY-THREE

While he didn't say it out loud, Michael could have written Sara's wish list for their ceremony with his eyes closed. Every day of his existence, he'd heard prayers from brides around the world. But while he may have no experience in relationships, he had enough wisdom to keep his lips closed.

This wasn't a wedding; this was the joining of an archangel to his fated mate, one he hoped would trigger Sara's commitment to him on all levels and make her immortal.

"How about this? We go to a private island and exchange our vows at sunset. We both love the beach, and that's where you proposed to me," she said.

"Perfect. My brothers will be the witnesses."

"And Lisa will be my bridesm—what?"

"No humans." Sara's face fell, and he felt it right in his heart.

No one could attend. If what he hoped and believed came to pass, there could be no human witnesses. God had promised that if Sara chose to give herself to him—body, mind, and soul—freely, she would become immortal, and it wasn't like she'd be given a pink slip to cash in later. It would happen in the moment. Only God knew how that would manifest, and a mortal audience was not something he was going to risk.

But he sensed it was more than just having her friend at their ceremony. Sara would be giving up her entire life, including the people she loved and trusted. It was a small circle, but they were special to her.

"I know you're giving up a lot to be with me, Sara. Leaving your life and all of this behind."

Her eyes slowly widened and swept around the room.

"All of it? I thought…"

"All of it. It will take you time to adjust to being an immortal and integrate into your new home in Heaven. Then you'll give birth to our child and learn how to be a mom. You will no longer belong in the world of mortals."

"Can't we travel between both our homes, like we did last week?"

"It gets complicated. How will you explain your disappearances? Why aren't you on social media? Where do we live? Where do you or I work? Why can't they see our baby? If it has wings, which I highly suspect he or she will, it won't be able to leave Heaven until it is grown."

"Oh."

He knew he was laying it on thick, but Michael wanted her to have all the information so she didn't regret her decision.

He closed his eyes for a long moment, hoping he hadn't scared her off.

"What will I look like?"

"The same." He smiled.

"So no big muscles?"

"No." He laughed. "You'll be the mother of a baby archangel. I'm sure there's no requirement for a warrior's body for that job."

"Sure, but for the record"—her hand landed on her bump—"I don't want to be a kept woman, Michael. I want my freedom and a job or purpose of some kind."

"Raising the first ever archangel baby isn't purpose enough for you?" he asked, raising his eyebrow.

"You know what I mean."

"Actually, I don't."

How could that not be important to her? Did she really

not understand the enormity of what she was growing within her?

"I just want to know you won't tuck me away like a little wife in Heaven. No friends, no freedom." She shook her head and gritted her teeth. "I've been an independent woman all my life, Michael."

He groaned.

He wanted nothing more than to tuck her and the baby away in his chambers, lock the door, and know they were safe every single day for eternity. He was the Lord Protector, for God's sake.

Yet, goddamn it all, he knew his little human, with all her spark, would shrivel up inside if he did that to her. He loved her spunk, her attitude, and the way she teased him. Her passion was part of his attraction to her.

No doubt their child would also be a little firecracker with a mix of their personalities and grow up to be a wild little warrior himself. Assuming it was a male.

Gods, he hoped it was a male. Having a daughter would likely drive him mad. Two females to protect to within an inch of his life? Yes, he'd go mad.

Reaching out, he pulled her onto his lap and laid strong lips on hers. "Sara, I would never dampen your flame. It's one of the things I love most about you."

"Good," she said stubbornly.

"This is still so new to me, but I promise, as much as I want to protect you, you will have complete freedom. You'll tell me when I get too over the top, and remember, you have my six brothers to keep me in line."

She grinned.

"Yeah, you already have a few of them wrapped around your finger, young lady."

Her blush undid him.

"So," he said, controlling himself. "Tell me before I rip your panties off you again, are you ready to do this?"

His heart pounded, waiting for her answer.

"I'm terrified, Michael." She held his face in her hands. "My life is with you now. Just remember, you aren't the Lord Supreme Whatever with me. This is a partnership."

He went to respond to correct her use of his title, but the look in her eyes made him stop.

Sara was right.

"In our relationship, yes, we are partners."

"Okay, so then, first vow," Sara said, grabbing her notepad. "Lord Michael, do you promise to obey Sara for eternity."

"Unlikely," he replied, tickling her and grinning as she wiggled in his lap. "But probably."

Michael felt a new and delicious energy building inside his chest. It was working. Sara was committing, and her immortality was manifesting within him.

His faith grew. He glimpsed their future for a moment. Sara in their home in Heaven, their child being birthed and lying in her arms. Right now, his job remained to simply keep her safe. There had been no more energetic attacks, and while he was happy, it did beg the question as to why. Had they sensed the Pegasus was gone?

"I'm going to ask Raphael to officiate the ceremony in God's name. Obviously, Father cannot come down to Earth."

"I guess so." She chewed the end of her pen, then added, "I never thought I'd marry in a religious ceremony. Then again, I never thought I'd meet God either."

"Or believe that he existed."

"No."

"Yet you believed in me."

"Yes. I did."

He simply smiled at her.

"Are you mad about that?"

"No. It matters not what people believe. We still exist." He shrugged.

"Wait, do you think that's why God won't grant me

immortality?" she gasped.

Standing up, he pulled her to her feet, grasping her face. "My darling. God loves all his children unconditionally. He is not vengeful. The universe has laws, yes, but believing in your creator does not mean you get special privileges."

She chewed her lip, unconvinced.

"Do you really think he would have paired you with his Supreme Archangel if he was unhappy with you?" he asked with a grin.

"Well, then perhaps it's a punishment in disguise," she teased back.

Shaking his head at his smart-mouthed little human, he turned back to the table where a large leather-bound book appeared. The cream leather looked ancient, and inside were dozens of blank pages.

"Oh, that's beautiful," Sara exclaimed.

Opening the cover, on the inside front page, in calligraphy-style font were the words "The Union of Sara Jacobson and Saint Michael, Lord Protector, Son of God."

"Hey, I need a title."

"You will have one, my little immortal-to-be." Michael laughed at the surprise on her face.

"I will?"

"Of course. You'll be my mate. See here"—He pointed to the Saint Michael wording and grinned—"I'm important."

"Sure. I guess I just thought I'd be your, well, your…I guess partner. Wife. Soulmate. I didn't think about what I would be. So will I be an angel then?"

"Well, that's up to God. And you."

She gasped. "I get to choose? Could I be a goddess?"

"Noooo." He cringed. "Angels trump goddesses, trust me."

"A princess?"

"Well, we have the Queen of the Angels, who you, er,

met. So let's just see what God proposes."

"This is harder than I thought," she muttered, and he laughed, kissing her forehead.

"You'll survive, gorgeous. Now come on, let's choose an island, and I'll get it booked for tomorrow."

"Tomorrow?"

"Yes," he said firmly. "Tomorrow."

He was done waiting.

CHAPTER FORTY-FOUR

Raph and Gabe appeared suddenly in the kitchen a moment later.

"Gah!" Sara jumped beside him in surprise.

"Sorry, beautiful," Raph apologized, winking at Michael, just waiting for a bite.

He was out of luck tonight.

Michael had made love to his beautiful Sara and spent an enjoyable evening planning their ceremony. Nothing could rile him up.

Gabe pulled up a chair and leaned down to pat Tilly while Raph leaned against the wall, arms crossed. Damn, they were in warrior mode, and that got his attention.

"What did you find?"

"We've found the source of the attack from the other night," Raphael said. "It was a warlock. An incredibly old and powerful one."

"And?" Michael stood.

"He's dead."

"You killed him?" Sara asked, surprised.

As archangels, they didn't go around killing humans, warlock or not, even if he had attacked the Supreme's mate. That wasn't their M.O.

"No. He was dead when we found him. Likely killed not long after the incident by the state of his decomposition. We tipped off the authorities, so they'll find him tonight."

"We found a notebook. He'd been working with Ares

for nearly two centuries, keeping notes," Gabe added.

"Wait. Centuries? You said he was human," Sara said.

"The gods can gift a type of immortality," Raphael explained, tapering off at the end as Michael cursed out loud.

"Seriously? The fuck?!"

"Sara, it's not the same. It's an extension of life, and it comes with a price. Believe me; it's not a gift," Michael said, shaking his head.

"Fine. But how did he die if he's…"

"Not immortal. Also, immortality doesn't mean you can't die. It's just more difficult to die."

His human looked around the room until finally Gabe ran his finger over his throat and gasped dramatically.

Her eyes widened.

"Oh." She leaned into him unconsciously for safety, and Michael nearly purred while simultaneously glaring at Gabriel.

Raphael, still leaning against the wall, got them back on track. "Anyway, there was nothing in the notebook that implicates any of our angels, at least not at first glance, but we'll go through it in more detail."

"Someone must know something."

There was no giving up. Until they knew who was behind this, Sara would be in danger. Potentially, even when he got her back to Heaven. He wasn't going to spell that out right now, though. He needed her to feel safe and open to becoming an immortal at their ceremony. Once it happened, he'd whisk them up to the heavens and hunt down everyone responsible, especially that fucker Ares.

As his mate, she'd always have a target on her, he realized, as would his child. Life for him had now changed. It wasn't just about leading God's army anymore; he now had a family to protect.

"Well, I'm not sorry that warlock is dead after all the pain and suffering he's caused Sara's bloodline, but he was likely manipulated by Ares, as many have been."

They all nodded.

"Tomorrow, though, my brothers, we celebrate. Sara and I are exchanging our vows."

Their faces lit up with big smiles.

"Tomorrow?" Raphael asked.

Sara nodded and faced Gabe shyly. "Would you, um, manifest my dress for me tomorrow? I've got photos, but I want it to be a surprise for the big guy."

"Abso-friggin'-lutely!"

Michael placed an arm around her shoulders and looked over at Raphael. His first brother; his closest friend. "Raph, would you officiate on behalf of God for us?"

"It would be my honor, my lord," Raphael said, using his official title in a rare moment of respect.

Michael nodded his thanks.

Gabriel then announced he was leaving and would update Uriel, Chamuel, Jophiel, and Zadkiel. "I'll be back in the morning to assist our bride." He leaned in and kissed her cheek.

"Thanks, Gabe."

Watching the friendship she was forming with his brothers warmed his heart—he just wished they'd keep their damn paws off her. While he trusted his brothers explicitly, the desire to knee them in the groin every time they smiled, winked, or kissed her was one he was only just keeping control of. And he was only able to do so because he knew they were doing it to test his resolve.

Gabriel caught his eye and grinned.

Shithead.

You'd both be wise to find another form of entertainment, brothers.

They both laughed out loud.

Their time would come, and he would rejoice in their anguish. He pulled Sara onto his lap and kissed her neck. She turned in place, brushing his cock, and he groaned quietly into her hair.

Life was good.

Tomorrow, he could finally take his beautiful Sara and their unborn baby home.

CHAPTER FORTY-FIVE

"Oh my goodness, we're getting married today," Sara said, smiling against his lips as she lay warm and snug in his arms.

"We are." Michael grinned and nipped at her bottom lip playfully. And thank goodness. He wanted her and their growing child safe in Heaven as fast as possible.

"Oh God, here we go." Sara scrambled out of bed as morning sickness struck again. Michael rolled over, feeling as useless as any human father-to-be could. She'd asked him to stop healing her because apparently morning sickness was a good sign her hormones were doing the right thing, so he had to watch her feel unwell, which went against every protective inch of his being.

Uriel.

No sign of him, sorry, Michael. And no one is talking.

He'd sent a few of the archangels to Olympus to find Ares or whatever they could about his plans. So far, nothing. Michael was finding it hard to believe the god of war could stop himself from boasting about his plans for so long.

Michael climbed out of bed and focused on his priority. The one brushing her teeth with more vigor than he believed was necessary.

Sara had finally found an image of the perfect dress for Gabriel to manifest. Knowing she could have anything she wanted was every bride's dream; however, she couldn't budge a nagging feeling.

She wasn't getting cold feet. She loved Michael and didn't doubt their love. It was the finer details she was concerned about. She knew he was determined to get her up to Heaven, but without God's help, was it really possible? And if not, what was the plan?

Would it mean he'd be tied to Earth for the next forty something years watching her age? Or worse, would he come and go with their child as she remained stuck on Earth?

It was time to face the truth.

There would be no immortality for her. If God wouldn't and Michael couldn't, then it simply wasn't possible.

What a fool she had been.

Glancing across the room as Michael sat in a meditative state, she wondered if she should set him free. A twinge in her abdomen reminded her that, even if she had wanted to do that, she couldn't.

He wouldn't.

Michael would never walk away from her or his child. It wasn't like he could pay child support and visit on the weekends. She blinked and realized Michael was staring at her. She could see the slight frown on his forehead.

"You would stay here with me, wouldn't you? On Earth. If there was no other choice."

"Yes," he answered without missing a beat and walked over to her. "I'm not leaving you. Ever. But we haven't run out of options yet, sweetheart."

Sara ran her hand over his broad shoulders and gazed up into his beautiful blue eyes. Some days she had to shake her head and remind herself how blessed she was to be loved by such a magical and powerful being.

Today, she would focus on that. And dig deep in her faith in him. And pray for a miracle.

"Gabriel is here," he whispered against her lips.

"Hey, kids!" he called from downstairs, and they wandered down. The archangel was looking sharp in a pair of dark blue denim jeans and a tan sweater. "You ready to create a masterpiece?"

"Good luck. You've seen his house, right?"

"Hey, my décor is stunning."

If she didn't intervene, the brotherly bickering would never end. No matter the subject or if their comments made any sense, they just loved winding each other up.

"I have a bunch of photos ready upstairs."

Michael grinned and bit into an apple which suddenly appeared in his hand. Then he flicked his finger in the air and the back door opened.

In walked Tilly.

"Hey, she has a cat door! You're creating bad habits."

"She doesn't like the long walk down to the garage," Michael replied as if that was a good explanation. She raised an eyebrow, and he winked at her.

Jophiel appeared.

"What's up?" He walked up to Sara, wrapping her in a big brotherly hug that lifted her off her feet. Sara giggled and saw Michael shake his head and throw his apple core in the waste.

"Keep the Grumpster busy while I help Sara, bro," Gabriel said, slapping Jophiel on the back.

Sara laughed, leaned up to kiss Michael's frown, and pulled her dress designer upstairs with her. "Come on, Gabe, before you poke the bear too far."

Upstairs, she flipped open her iPad and showed Gabe her photos. He nodded patiently while she described the exact color, design, and fabric she wanted. After flicking through them one last time, he handed her back the device and said, "Okay, I've got this."

She watched as he closed his eye then waved his hand in front of him. A clothes rack appeared with three dresses. "How'd I do?"

Walking up to the dresses, she ran her hand over them. "Oh gosh, they're so beautiful."

Sara had always known she wouldn't have her mom with her on her wedding day, having lost her as a little girl, but she had never expected to be without her friends.

Sure, she'd given up on finding true love, but in the back of her mind, she had always thought that if she ever did get married, Lisa would be her bridesmaid. She had imagined them giggling as they tried on gowns and danced around in veils.

Suddenly, she wanted to cry. Quickly, she grabbed a dress and walked into the wardrobe to change.

"Sara? What is it?" Gabriel surprised her, laying a hand on her shoulder and turning her. "What is this sadness I'm sensing?"

She dipped her head, knowing she should be grateful, but unable to keep her emotions in check. A tear slid down her face.

"You can't read my mind?"

"Do you want me to?"

She shook her head. "It's nothing. I just wanted to share this day with the people I love. My mom's not here, nor is my best friend. It's just sad."

Gabriel took the dress out of her hands and pulled her into a giant hug. "I'm sorry you can't be with them today. Life as one of our mates is not easy, is it?"

"No, but he's worth it."

Sara looked down at the dress when the archangel released her. She shook her head. "You know what? This big fancy gown doesn't feel right. Can we change it?"

He sent her a knowing smile.

Damn archangels.

"Close your eyes and visualize what you want."

She closed her eyelids and imagined standing in front of Michael as he gazed upon her with the unconditional love she had become so familiar with. She glanced down at her imaginary self and saw the dress.

"Perfect," Gabriel said. "Open your eyes."

Ten minutes later with her hair and makeup done—courtesy of the mind-reading archangel—she was standing in front of the mirror, grinning.

"You missed your calling, Gabriel."

"The one I have is pretty cool, thanks—it comes with wings." He grinned from his Cleopatra-style pose on their bed. "So, we ready, princess?"

She looked in the mirror and let out a huge breath. "Yes."

"Incoming…" he warned.

They were getting good at reducing the amount of heart attacks she had at their sudden appearances. As if on cue, Raphael appeared behind her.

"Whoa!" he cried. "Holy smokes! Michael is going to be speechless, and that's saying something."

Sara laughed.

"It's time. Michael has just left, and I'm to escort you to the venue."

Gabe climbed off the bed, and she carefully stood on tiptoes and kissed his cheek. "Thank you for everything. I feel so beautiful."

"You look absolutely radiant."

Having seven huge and powerful archangels in her life was taking some getting used to, but she loved it. Gabe pecked her cheek then flashed away, leaving her with Raphael.

He held out his arm, and as she took it, he glanced down. "You doing okay?"

"Yes."

"Then take a breath, Sara Jacobson. No pressure, but you're about to be bound to the first archangel in the history of forever."

CHAPTER FORTY-SIX

A moment later, Sara was standing on a lawn overlooking the ocean with the sun setting in the distance.

"Oh, it's beautiful," she gasped.

Around them, hundreds of fairy lights glittered against the glowing orange sky. She could hear the waves gently brushing the shore below as birds called out in the distance. The air was warm—that dry, tropical heat with a soft breeze.

Under her feet, a short path had been laid with white rose petals which led toward five of the archangels who were standing in a half circle.

Dressed in long white shorts, shirts, and gray waistcoats, it looked like a GQ photoshoot, or maybe their muscle edition.

As they walked, Michael appeared in long white pants, a white shirt which stretched across his chest and arms, and the same gray waistcoat. His eyes glistened with love as he watched her take step after step toward him.

"Told you," Raphael whispered.

When she was only a couple of steps away from him, Michael began to glow. She froze and gripped Raphael's arm in surprise.

"It's okay." Michael held out his hand, and she stepped into him. "God, you look fucking gorgeous."

The white chiffon, empire-style gown which gathered under her breasts flowed to the grass. Tiny diamonds on the bodice matched her diamond bracelet and simple teardrop earrings. Her hair was pinned loosely, letting her curls fall around her neck.

Sara felt the world disappear as Michael held her eyes with his.

"Brothers," Raphael started, and a subtle green glow surrounded him. "We stand today in ceremony for Saint Michael as he bonds with his mate. On behalf of God, our heavenly Father, as his witness, I have the privilege to join you both for eternity."

She gave Michael a wobbly smile, and he squeezed her hand. It was the sweetest moment, and she'd forever remember it. It was as if they were just a boy and girl, nervous while taking this next step in life together.

Raphael continued.

"In this first ceremony of an archangel bonding to his mate, we create history. Sara and Michael have written their vows, but before we begin, I ask, do you each come freely?"

"I do," Michael answered, not taking his eyes off her.

"I do."

Glancing at Raphael, she noticed he was holding a large white candle that had three wicks burning. A glance to her other side, and she saw the others were also holding candles.

"Lord Michael, your vows."

He said nothing for a long while, and it got awkward. Then he took her hand and let out a breath.

"Sara, my beautiful human, you are the single greatest surprise of my life. Had I known this love was possible, I would not have stopped until I had found you. I have been blessed with the purest love from our Creator, and holding you in my arms finally feeling worthy of my title as Lord Protector is the greatest gift I have ever received."

His white energy flowed around them, wrapping around her in a warm kiss.

"I see you. I feel you. I hear you. I know you. Sara, I

pledge to you my body, my heart, my soul, my eternal life, and all who I am."

She could barely breathe at the depth of his words and the power of love that flowed from him. Then Michael took a half step back, surprising her by lifting his hand in the air.

A large white sword of light appeared. The Sword of Michael. With force, he plunged it into the earth beside them.

"My heart. Everything I am, is yours."

Her mouth fell open as she stared at the awe-inspiring, divine tool of God.

Sara had heard of Archangel Michael's famous flaming sword, but nothing had prepared her for its magnificence. As tears filled her eyes, she gazed upon his celestial face. Even the brilliance of the sword couldn't dwarf this incredible being who adored her.

How she deserved him, she didn't know, but damn, she loved this guy with everything she was.

"Sara. Your vows," Raphael prompted.

She cleared her throat. "Well, I don't have anything as fancy as your big sword, but here goes."

Sara heard Jophiel snigger as Michael took a deep breath. She took a long look at him. He looked worried.

Did he not believe she felt the same way?

"I've waited all life to truly be loved. I don't believe I knew the meaning of the word before I met you. The way you look at me, whether I'm washing the dishes or we're making love, is the same."

At his raised eyebrow, she let out a little laugh.

"When you look at me, I feel like the most beautiful, precious thing in existence. Which is funny, because to me, you are."

His eyelids became heavy.

"Letting myself love and be loved by you has been the most terrifying and vulnerable thing I've ever done, but I know my heart is safe with you. You may be the Lord Protector, but you are my protector, my love, my mate."

Sara felt her throat tighten as her emotions became too much. Michael's eyes followed her hand as it naturally made its way to her round belly. She glanced down, then back up at him. He was still staring at their child.

Of course, she realized suddenly, everything falling into place.

It was the child.

She looked away as her heart broke into a million pieces. She'd been right. She would never become immortal. The moment he had discovered she was pregnant with his child, he had suddenly confessed his love for her. Before she'd become pregnant, they'd gone around in circles about their relationship.

Oh, she knew he loved her; she didn't doubt that. But it had been the baby that had cemented his commitment to her. Her life flashed before her eyes. Michael would stay with her, taking the child and training it until it became obvious he or she could no longer stay on Earth. She had years, not decades, with him.

She smiled sadly, understanding.

How could she hate him for loving their child?

She couldn't.

He would do his best to be part of her life, but it was as she feared. He would be a part-time fixture once their child was in the heavens, returning for visits as she aged on Earth.

Sara's heart broke, quietly and painfully.

Even if he let her, she could never love another. Michael owned her heart. Her future would be filled with lonely days and lonelier nights.

As she drew in a sob which everyone would just assume were her happy emotions, she calmed herself. She wrapped her heart in a protective hug and closed down. She had to. It was how she survived.

This, she was very experienced at.

Sara loved him, but she couldn't give her whole self. She had to keep herself safe. And so, as she spoke her last words, she did so with only a half truth.

"I pledge to you my heart, body, and soul for all eternity."

Then she closed her eyes.

CHAPTER FORTY-SEVEN

Michael released his white wings, ready to provide the protection and privacy she'd require as the immortality entered her body. They hung straight up as he wrapped his arms around her and kissed her. As soon as his lips touched hers, he knew something was wrong.

Panic filled his whole being.

What the fuck?

He scanned her emotions and found a solid block wall with echoes of sadness and love blending into one.

As if he were standing in a tunnel, he heard echoes of Raphael's voice as he made some statement of their joining and it being official.

Michael dropped his wings and stared into her cold, fake, smiling face. He stared at her blankly. She held his gaze for a moment before turning away from him, accepting hugs from his brothers.

"Congratulations!" Back slaps, hugs, and kisses were exchanged while Michael nodded, feeling completely stunned.

"You okay?" Raphael asked.

He turned and glared at his brother, fire in his eyes. "She didn't choose."

"No," Raphael replied. "But she loves you, and that will need to be enough."

Michael watched as his brothers spun her around, dancing as they officially welcomed her to the family. They all knew, though; they could feel his tension and were giving him glances. They'd all been expecting the change and immortal fireworks.

Yet for her, they pretended, because they loved her too and knew she had free will.

Sara had had the choice and not fucking chosen him. Why?

Michael faced the ocean and took a breath, wondering what had changed.

Raphael glanced at Uriel. The archangel nodded, and music filled the air as he took Sara's hand and invited her for a dance.

She curtsied, laughed, then took his hand.

Raphael stood patiently at Michael's side.

"I don't know what happened. I was sure she would declare her feelings, and her immortality would enter her body."

Chamuel poured glasses of champagne and started handing them around. Michael took one mindlessly and threw it back.

Dom Perignon. Humans had gotten a few things right.

He accepted another glass.

"Why don't you go take a moment?"

"I can't leave her." Pain and disappointment were pouring off him in spades.

He didn't understand what he'd felt. Or why. She had closed off her heart to him moments after being utterly open and vulnerable.

Sara loved him; he knew that. Something had changed, and he wanted to know why. He pushed aside his hurt feelings and looked at Raphael, who dropped his eyes.

"You saw it?"

Without looking at him, Raphael nodded.

"Fuck."

Pushing aside his disappointment and hurt, Michael was now increasingly worried about how he would get her and the child into Heaven.

He watched as she danced and avoided his eyes. Her brick wall was solid. She needed time, something they didn't have. The longer she was down on Earth, the more vulnerable she became.

The pain in his chest grew.

What if she never chose him?

What if she never became an immortal and eventually died in one of the innumerable ways humans could?

Not knowing you had a soulmate was one thing. Knowing you had one, loving her, and then losing her was a totally different one leading to a life of emptiness and heartache.

How could she do this to him? To them? To their child? Didn't she understand?

He had so many questions, and yet, he had to honor God's rule. Free will.

"Go. Take a flight. Get this out of your system. I'll keep an eye on her."

He nodded then flashed into his chambers and let out a scream that shook the foundations of Heaven.

CHAPTER FORTY-EIGHT

Sara stopped to catch her breath after the third dance and wandered back to Michael. She looked around, confused, when she didn't see him.

"Father called him back to Heaven. He won't be long," Raphael informed.

And so it begins.

"Great timing, God," she said. "Do you know what it's about?

He shrugged. "God's business, whoever knows?"

"Well, I thought you might because you're an archangel," she replied rudely, and then instantly regretted it. Just because she felt like she'd lost her one true love didn't mean she had to be rude to everyone.

"Heck no, I'm just winging it most days." Raphael smiled, and she gave him an apologetic smile.

"He didn't say goodbye," she said.

"No."

Sighing, she turned and looked out at the now dark sky. It felt like there were a million conversations not taking place right now and a tension she didn't fully understand.

"I wish I could walk off this hill and directly into Heaven," she spoke without thinking.

"You should tell him that."

It wasn't often she saw Raphael so somber. He was usually lighthearted and playful, but as she turned to look at him, he was very serious and staring at her with a mix of disappointment and pity.

"The ceremony was beautiful, thank you."

Raph nodded.

She wanted to cry. She felt as if a gaping wound had replaced her heart.

"Guys, I think we should tidy up here and head back to Sara's house," Gabriel interrupted.

"When will Michael be back?" she asked, and Raphael shrugged.

Raphael nodded at Gabe, and the archangels began to quickly clear all evidence of the ceremony away in a matter of seconds.

"Take Sara back to the house," Raphael instructed them. "I will go get Michael and meet you back there shortly."

Sara watched as Raph flashed away without another glance. She swallowed down her emotions and wrapped her arms around herself.

"Come on, Cinderella, let's get you safely home." Gabriel took her arm, and a moment later, they arrived in the kitchen. Tilly meowed at them and she picked her up, watching as the other archangels arrived one by one.

No Raphael and no Michael.

"Give them a few minutes," Chamuel said, taking one look at her expression. "In the meantime, should we have some wedding cake? I've always liked that human tradition."

She nodded and gave him a sad smile. "Sure. You do your angel magic stuff, and I'll put some music on."

She didn't really feel like listening to music, but Sara needed a minute to herself. Crouching in front of the stereo, she buried her face into Tilly's fur and cried.

Maybe it was a good thing Michael wasn't here. What would they have to say to each other?

She'd been a fool to trust him. No man—angel or otherwise—had truly loved her for who she was. She'd thought this time was different, but when his eyes had dropped to her belly, she had seen the truth. It was the child. She hiccupped with the need to have a really damn good cry, but now was not the time.

This was her life now. Surrounded by archangels as the Archangel Michael's mate and mother to his unborn child. She had lost him today—on an emotional level—by realizing the truth. And yet she was now stuck with him for the rest of her life, assuming he didn't take their child from her.

There was nothing she could do right now. He would return eventually, and she would have her answers soon enough.

Sara stood and saw Jophiel, Uriel, Chamuel, Gabe, and Zadkiel admiring their creation of a three-tier wedding cake. It was absolutely beautiful. Despite everything, she was grateful for their kindness and for keeping her safe.

"It's chocolate and vanilla," Chamuel informed when he saw her enter the room.

"Chocolate is perfect." She smiled.

"I've changed it to red velvet on top," Uriel said unapologetically.

When she blinked, the top layer changed to a cream cheese icing. She let out a little laugh. "Why didn't you just make a cupcake cake, then you could all have any flavor you wanted?" She looked back at the open mouths staring back at her. "No, wait…"

Too late. One of them had turned the cake into a tower of multicolored cupcakes.

"Do we have to wait for the groom?" Chamuel asked, eyeing the cakes.

"Nope!" she answered as she took the top cupcake and stuffed it into her mouth. It felt like the most passive-aggressive action she could take right now.

She ignored all the sideway glances as she munched on her chocolate cupcake with vanilla icing. They soon joined her, and the five of them dug in with the same vigorous appetites she'd witnessed over the past few weeks.

Zadkiel, true to nature, cleaned up around them and

stacked her dishwasher, even if he could wave his archangel fingers and make it all disappear. She gave him an appreciative smile, and he gave her a small nod.

Sara knew they were all aware of the situation, even if they didn't understand it exactly. Or perhaps they had known all along. She didn't blame them, though.

Nor did she really blame Michael.

They had both gotten pregnant by not taking precautions because, hello! they didn't know they needed to. She was the one to blame. Right from the beginning, she had known she should keep her distance. She had wanted to tell him not to return, but he had pushed.

With her experience in love, she should have been stronger and wiser.

No. She was to blame here.

Falling for a damn archangel was a mistake she would have to pay for for the rest of her human life. She had to make the most of this situation. Enjoy being a mother, hope she had as many years as she could with the child, and protect her heart for as long as Michael remained in her life.

Perhaps he would bring the child for visits to Earth from time to time.

Her head was spinning. Until they talked it out, she was never going to know what he would do. He had the power and she hated it. She would do what she could to live as happy a life as she could, but she would be clear with him—their intimate relationship was now over.

She had to protect her heart; he no longer owned it. And she had seen the look in his eyes—he knew it.

"How much would you all hate me if I turned on MasterChef right now?" Uriel asked.

"Are you for real?"

"It's the finals!"

Zadkiel shook his head and turned to Sara as they all followed Uriel into the living room.

She shrugged.

Uriel grinned and had the remote in his hand before anyone could disagree. As all five of the oversized males plopped into chairs and the sofa, she walked up to the French doors and looked out across the yard. Still winter in Auckland. She wasn't inclined to step out in her sheer dress, but she really needed a moment alone.

"Guys, I'm just going to step outside for some fresh air."

They all looked up as if she'd announced she was a unicorn. Okay, bad example, given who they were.

"Just out here." She pointed to the garden.

"That's cool," Joph said. "What?" he added when Zadkiel glared at him.

"Wait a minute," Gabe indicated, and the next minute she was wrapped in a faux fur white coat. "Stay close."

She smiled and nodded, then stepped outside.

She wandered around the yard, keeping the beautiful coat wrapped tightly around her. When she reached the fence, she leaned against it, staring out at the ocean.

Despite everything she had thought and felt today, she knew she loved Michael deep in her heart. And that's what hurt the most.

She had truly thought he loved her just for her. Not their child. Just days ago, she had stood here with Michael, his arms around her, telling her she was his. Tears poured down her cheek as memories of their time together flashed before her eyes. His words of love, their bodies connecting, the way he'd been so protective and bossy.

A small sound escaped her that could only be described as raw anguish. Her head dropped into her hands as she let the sobs escape. She was grateful the archangels were giving her space. Michael would return soon, and she needed to grieve.

Eventually, she looked out over the ocean again and wrapped the coat tightly around her. After three long deep breaths, she went to turn to head back to the house...

...but couldn't move.

She was paralyzed.

Oh shit.

She tried to call out for help but couldn't speak.

"Human," a deep, dark voice called from the beach below.

She squinted her eyes and saw the outline of a tall, large man. Her heart raced, and she knew without a doubt who he was. As he took a few steps forward, she could see his long dark hair and broad chest. He was a warrior.

"Yes. I am who you think I am," he sneered. "Do as I say, and you will not be harmed."

She stared at him blankly, mostly because she couldn't do anything else.

"In a minute, I will return your ability to move. You will do exactly as I say, or your neck will be snapped in half. Do you understand?"

She couldn't nod, and he let out a dry laugh.

"When I say go, I want you to open the gate and step down onto the beach."

She had no choice. If she tried to run or call out, he would kill her, and her baby would die. Even if the archangels heard her call, they wouldn't be fast enough, would they?

Why hadn't they sensed the god of war?

"Now, human."

She grabbed her throat as soon as she could move and fumbled with the gate.

Oh God, oh God. Michael, Gabe, someone, can you hear me? Help!

"Now, human!"

The gate opened, and she stepped down onto the sand, falling to her knees. He took a few steps forward, reached for her, and suddenly, she was flashed away.

The last thing she saw was five furious archangels

crashing through her windows, wings spread.

CHAPTER FORTY-NINE

Raphael found Michael flying through the sky somewhere between Heaven and Olympus.

"Why has she shut me out? I fucking love her," he roared.

"You need to talk to her and give her more time, Michael. Patience is not your strong suit."

"What more can I do? I've given her everything, Raphael!"

He stretched out his green wings and tilted toward his brother. He hated seeing Michael like this. God, he hoped he never met his mate; it all looked like hell, if he was being honest.

"Where is your faith?"

"Oh, fuck off. Wait till you have your balls in a vise and see how you like it."

He grinned.

"You haven't lost her; you just need to find another way. She's hurting, Michael. Something's triggered her. I think you both need to talk this out."

"I need to go to her."

He nodded. "You do. They are back at her house..."

Michael.

Raphael.

They've got her.

Get your ass here!

"WHAT!" Michael screamed, and his light exploded out around them.

Raphael returned to pure energy to withstand his brother's mighty blast, pushing his divinity out to reflect it.

Michael. Fuck. Get it together, or you'll destroy something. Like me, for fuck's sake!

They have SARA!

As the Supreme Archangel regained control of his power, they looked at each other and immediately flashed to Sara's house.

Michael landed on the back lawn and did a one-eighty turn to take in the situation. Light sparked around him as his celestial power rolled off him.

His brothers marched up to surround him, holding their hands out in a shield to protect the planet and its inhabitants.

"Where is she?" he roared in the deepest, darkest voice he was sure he'd ever used.

"Michael, breathe," Raphael demanded.

He glared at his brother despite knowing his instruction was wise.

"Ares has her," Chamuel informed. He was scanning the lingering energy Michael could sense now that he was in control of his fury. Without it, he was no good to Sara. "He used mind control to get her down onto the beach."

"And yep, he used some kind of magic to block his presence from us," Chamuel added a second later.

"How? He doesn't have those abilities," Gabriel said.

"Who the hell is helping him?" Raphael asked.

They were all thinking the same thing. Someone powerful was helping the god of war.

"It's a witch. We know he's had warlocks and witches helping him. But who?" Michael pondered.

"Who do we know with those powers and a reason to want Sara out of the equation?" Raphael asked knowingly.

"No. She wouldn't, would she?" Zadkiel piped up, horrified.

"Yeah, she would," Uriel answered.

"Fuck." Michael ran a hand through his hair.

Regina. Former witch.

She had been warned about using her powers in Heaven; however, for decades, she had been bitter he had refused to be her lover any longer, and more so, her exclusive lover.

Ares, the snake, had obviously connected with her via Severial. It wouldn't take much to get heavenly gossip out of the young warrior—everyone in Central City knew about her obsession with him—and the Olympic god would have devised a way to tap into her fury. Nothing like a woman scorned.

He'd known from the moment he'd met her she was untrustworthy. Still, this was long after Ares had cursed Sara's line and Aria, so she was just one pawn in his evil plan.

"It has to be her. Chamuel, any tracks to follow?"

He shook his head. "There's an echo, but it's not solid enough to follow."

Michael stepped down onto the beach and pushed his energy out across the planet. Nothing. He felt fucking nothing. Since Sara had become his mate, he'd been able to sense her energy even from Heaven. Now, he couldn't feel anything.

Was it magic blocking him or was it because she had closed her heart off to him?

Pain sliced through his chest at the thought of losing her. He needed her to know he truly loved her. He needed to know she felt the same. He believed she did.

What a fool he had been to leave her unprotected. If it was the last thing he did, he was going to get her back.

Michael. We will find her.

He glanced at Raphael and nodded.

"Alright. What do we know?" he asked, looking around at his powerful brothers. "He cannot take her off the planet because she is mortal. If he thinks the Pegasus is still within her, he will want to keep her alive."

Nods.

"Gabriel. Uriel. I want you both on Olympus. Demand answers, no discretion required. Ares has taken my mate; Zeus can kiss my ass if he has a problem with that."

"I want Chamuel to come with us. If Zeus gets snotty, we'll need more backup," Gabriel said.

"Agreed." He nodded at the tall, chocolate-skinned archangel who was well-known for his speed, but also his diplomacy. It might come in handy, although Michael couldn't give two fucks right now about keeping any of the race's relations in harmony. Not until he had Sara back in his arms.

And fuck God and his refusal to give Sara immortality. Fuck all the rules. He was going to war for the woman who owned his heart.

"Get the information. Report back and return immediately."

The three of them nodded and flew up into the air with the urgency and speed he expected.

He rubbed his hand over his face. Zadkiel, Jophiel, and Raphael stood waiting for his instruction.

"We need to speak to Regina," Michael said.

"Where would Ares take her?" Jophiel asked. "He's somewhere on this damn planet."

"Yes, and he can't stay masked forever. Jophiel, stay here and search the area for any energy leaks. There's a possibility the wards protecting her location aren't perfect. Regina hasn't used magic for a long time, and she isn't a master like our witches."

Joph nodded and, masking his presence, flew around the area.

Michael turned to Zadkiel and Raphael and let out a long sigh. Archangel he may be, but he was Sara's soulmate and a father first and foremost. Michael wasn't sure when his priorities had shifted, but they had. He would destroy anyone that harmed them.

But first, he had to find them.

"Come. We have a witch to break."

They flashed directly into the Hall of Angels.

"Regina!"

CHAPTER FIFTY

Whether it was because of the cold, damp floor of the cave underneath her or the absolute terror running through her veins, she didn't know, but Sara couldn't stop shivering. Violently.

She did not know where she was, but outside the mouth of the cave, it was dark and stormy—and given it was only twenty feet away, she was feeling much of the cold.

Around her stood three celestial beings, all bickering. If her life hadn't been at risk, she would've told them to shut the hell up. It was like listening to a bunch of incompetent fools trying to run a circus. That one of them was an Olympic god made her realize it wasn't just humans who were a bunch of muppets. They were in every race.

Ares had flashed them into the cave, dumped her on the ground, and turned his back on her as if she were no more important than a bag of rice. Which wasn't exactly true, because he still believed she housed the Pegasus within her.

Still. All he wanted was to get the soul out of her, so Sara guessed her body didn't need to be in great working order to do that.

The thought sent a cold chill down her spine.

A tall young man with a strong athletic frame had given her a long glance then had begun debating with the god of war.

"Don't test me, Severial," Ares growled.

So this was the warrior prophesied to kill her and her

child.

As she glanced around her, it was hard not to start believing in the prophecy, even if Michael hadn't.

Michael.

Her heart clenched in her chest.

There was a huge damn chance she would never see her archangel again, and regret poured through her. God, how she loved him, and now, he would never know how much. The last time they had looked at each other, there had been a haunted look in his eyes.

Please, don't let it be the last, she prayed.

The woman standing with the two males finally turned, and Sara recoiled as she realized it was Regina. Dressed in a long black, regal-looking dress, she took a step toward her and stared down at her as if she were nothing more than dirt.

"Human," she said in a sultry voice that made Sara feel sick.

Knowing the woman had shared Michael's bed made her hate her, regardless of their situation.

"You didn't think I was going to let you have what is mine, did you?"

"Regina!" Ares growled behind her, and the queen closed her eyes as if searching for patience. Her face changed to one of serenity before she turned.

"Need I remind you of our arrangement, Ares? She dies at my hand tonight. What is he doing here?"

"No. I am the one who will kill her," Severial said.

"We had an agreement," Regina repeated angrily.

"Stop. Both of you. I am sick of the sounds of your voices."

The arguing continued as Sara lay in the cold, shivering. She continued to call out to God, the archangels, and directly to Michael, but without Aria inside her, she didn't have the ability now.

Not that she knew how she'd done it in the first place.

"Ares, regardless of what you believe, I am destined to destroy this woman, and it must come to pass."

Pacing the floor, the god hissed, "Neither of you are going to kill her. Inside her is the soul of a Pegasus; I trapped it over one hundred and seventy years ago. To gain possession of it, she must take her own life."

Suddenly, she snapped.

She was cold, pissed off, and wanted to be back in Michael's arms. "I hate to interrupt your plans, you crazy fuckers, but I am not committing suicide, and you can't force me."

"That was not our agreement, god!" Regina screamed. "I will fucking kill her, or you will no longer have my help."

Sara frowned.

Think.

If she told them Aria was now in Heaven, would they simply return her home? No. The queen and the angel still wanted to kill her for different and equally crazy reasons. It was only Ares who wanted the Pegasus, and for that reason alone, she was still alive. If she no longer held any value, he'd allow the others to kill them, especially if it hurt Michael. She was beginning to understand the animosity that existed between the two males.

Would he avenge her death?

Michael. Where are you? Please help us.

Sara was cold, tired, and terrified. A tear escaped down her cheek; she knew she was in real trouble. Even if she could contact him, she didn't know where they were to direct him, anyway.

Ares ignored Regina, sending her a dark look, and glanced down at Sara. "You will do as I instruct, human." Then he turned to the angel. "And why the hell are you here, Severial?"

"I don't believe your story about the Pegasus. They haven't existed for nearly two centuries. The Oracle has predicted I am the one to kill the Supreme Archangel's mate, and you will not take that from me. You can't fight fate, Ares."

Ares glared at the young angel. He should have killed the little shit decades ago. Truth was, he had kept him alive because he was as wary of the Oracle's warnings as the next god. But looking around him now, he could see no need for him.

He had the human.

He had the Pegasus, and with Regina's spell hiding their location from the seven archangels, all he needed to do was assist the fucking human into committing suicide, the edge of the cave mouth being the perfect opportunity for her to do it.

He'd run out of patience and was running out of time, especially if Regina was threatening to jump ship. Her fury and desire for revenge was strong, though; he didn't believe she would leave until she saw the life leave the human's body.

When he'd heard Archangel Michael had formed a relationship with Sara, Ares had been furious. The archangels had never had mates, and yet, of all the beings in the universe, the fucker had chosen the one he had trapped the goddamn Pegasus in to bond with.

It was like he was the cursed one.

So the time for patience was over. He needed the soul back and the power to take Michael out. That way, he would be able to breach through Heaven's wards and prove his worth to Zeus.

Regina had been a last-minute addition to his plans. Her fury at Michael finding a mate was palpable. She'd turned up at The Fat Angel demanding a private audience with him. They'd come to an arrangement. She would help him claim the Pegasus, and when Ares took down the Supreme and stepped into the position of power in Heaven, she would retain her role and Michael would be given to her.

A sex slave, if you will.

Of course, none of that was possible because he needed the human to commit suicide to extract the soul, but the witch wouldn't have helped him if she had known that. She wanted revenge in the form of murdering the female who had won the Supreme's heart.

Besides, Michael would die.

He didn't exactly know how the Pegasus's powers worked, but he had been told they were powerful enough to destroy an archangel. And his six brothers? Well, when he was in charge, they would have to fall into line or follow the same fate. He was the god of war; strategy was his strength. Playing too far ahead when you didn't know the full extent of your armory wasn't wise.

"And what of your God's free will, angel?" he sneered at Severial.

"Oh, please, do I look like an archangel?" Severial raised an eyebrow at the god. "I don't give a flying fuck about free will. I am the prophesied one, so step aside and let me kill her."

Then all hell broke loose.

The angel suddenly drew out a knife and lunged past both him and Regina at a speed that surprised them both.

He was fast.

Regina held out her hand to stop him, but Severial slashed at her. Crying out, she grasped her hand. "Ah, you little shit. Stop him!"

"The field, Regina, hold it!" Ares yelled, feeling the protective wards slip.

Sara uncurled as she saw the angel coming toward her, her eyes wide in horror. She began crawling with speed toward the entrance of the cave.

Oh. Maybe this will work out after all. Ares slowed his approach to the angel. If Sara jumped or fell, he would fly out and grab the soul. He smirked.

Then the angel came to a stop.

What the hell?

"I told you. She's mine to kill."

Severial fell to his knees as the dagger in his back poked out the front of him.

Oh, well. The queen had good aim; he'd give her that.

He sighed and watched Sara grip the edge of the cave floor.

That's it, little human. Just a bit closer.

CHAPTER FIFTY-ONE

Michael marched through the building.

"She's not here. Let's join the others on Olympus. One of the gods must know where Ares is."

They had searched Heaven for Regina, and she was nowhere to be seen. The angels were crying and hiding in the doorways as the three furious archangels demanded any information that could help them.

He would deal with their emotions another day.

Today, he would find Sara and kill Ares.

They flashed to the city of the gods, and if he hadn't had been so desperate to find Sara, he would have laughed.

"Christ," Raphael groaned beside him.

"Leave this to me." Zads marched ahead of them.

"I will not," Aphrodite screeched as Gabriel held her in a neck lock. "Uriel, you better—"

"Gabe," Zadkiel started, calmly gripping his brother's forearm and holding Uriel away from killing Gabriel. "Put her down."

"I've been fucking telling him that for the past ten minutes," Uriel yelled. "She knows nothing!"

Michael watched as more gods and goddesses amassed around them. Artemis walked out of The Fat Angel across the courtyard and crossed her arms, glaring at him.

He was about to look away when Apollo stepped out beside her. Her protective twin brother looked his way, then back at the altercation with Aphrodite, unimpressed.

He could go fuck himself.

The gods did not intimidate him, and while Michael

may appear to just be standing there quietly watching the scene, he was ready for whatever was needed to find his mate.

"We need to clean this up," Raphael said beside him.

"Where is Chamuel?"

As Gabriel dropped the goddess and took a step back, the tension around them did not lessen.

"Behind Apollo."

Chamuel walked out of the drinking establishment, looking as furious as he felt. Catching Michael's eye, he made his way over. "The queen was here recently. Ares met with her privately in his home."

Most of the citizens had cleared the area, leaving the archangels and gods alone. Michael noted Uriel's protective stance near Aphrodite and groaned.

An issue for another day.

"Listen up!" he roared across the courtyard. "Ares has taken a human hostage, and I want her back. If any of you know anything, speak up now, or there will be consequences unlike any you've ever seen before."

Apollo took a step forward and put his hands on his hips. The guy was big; muscular and powerful. But he was no challenge for any of the archangels, even if the gods denied their power and the archangels could not destroy them because of their Father's laws.

"You come into our city and make such a claim about my brother. Where's your proof?" Apollo yelled.

He had no time to fuck around with the gods' games today. He had to find Sara before Ares harmed her or the child growing within her. He only hoped she'd had the wisdom not to tell Ares the Pegasus was in Heaven. It would be the only thing keeping him from killing her, and who knew what Regina was capable of.

Fury poured through him as he released his wings. The white feathers of light stretched to their full size on either side of him in an expression of his enormous power. He noticed the subtle shift in the body language of the Olympic gods.

Finally, he had their fucking attention.

"The human is my mate. If I find out, either today or in a thousand years, that any of you were involved in harming a single hair on her head, I will kill you myself. Slowly."

A stillness fell around him. He felt the tension coming from everyone, even his brothers. Archangels didn't kill, not unless it was in defense. God did not give them permission.

But this was his mate.

His love.

His heart.

His child.

The rules had now changed. His brothers would one day understand.

Looking around at their faces, he saw their fear and surprise.

Try me, Apollo, you little fucker.

The god took a step back and nodded.

Love. Soulmates. Life partners. It was an interesting concept; one everyone seemed to understand, whether or not they had one, you didn't mess with. That and children, but he would not inform the gods of his child's existence. He was furious, not fucking stupid.

Time was running out.

Michael's voiced boomed across the courtyard once more. "Thirty seconds or I am dropping bodies!"

"They're on Earth," Artemis muttered.

"What?" he roared, barely able to hear her.

"He's with the queen. Regina, not Hera," she repeated louder. "On Earth. That's all I know."

"Where are they, Artemis?" Raphael pressed, his voice full of fury.

"I don't know. I walked in on them and overheard them saying they were heading to Earth. Honestly, that's all I know."

Apollo stepped protectively in front of his twin, and Michael respected the guy for it. Marginally.

"Anyone else has any damn information they'd like to share? The clock is ticking!" Raphael demanded.

Zeus and Hera suddenly flashed into the courtyard.

Oh, fucking great.

Waves of power rolled off the father of the gods as he stood in his usual legs spread power stance dressed in a black toga. "Supreme, it's time you—"

Michael held up a hand as his large wings lifted higher and he bellowed, "Do not test me today, Zeus. My threats are real."

Zeus's face turned red.

Hera clasped her hands in front of her. She was draped in a long navy gown that fell from one shoulder, looking as queenly as she always did.

Michael shot a dark look her way. "That goes for both of you."

Hera was the epitome of femininity and had an endless love for her children, but she was as cunning as a snake. Michael respected her intelligence, sure, but he didn't trust her. Not one bit.

"Michael," she said calmly, placing a hand on Zeus's forearm to stop the step he was taking. She reached out an upturned hand. "We feel your pain; we truly do."

Like fuck she does.

"I am not here for your empathy, queen. Your son has my mate, and when I find them, he will pay with his life if hers is not intact."

She held his eyes for a moment before turning to Zeus and saying something privately.

"Do it," he heard her say quietly yet firmly.

Everyone knew who wore the pants in that relationship. For her to do it so openly was unprecedented, but then again, her son's life was being threatened, something he had never done to the gods. Ever.

They knew it was only a matter of time before he found Ares. The god couldn't stay hidden forever, and Michael would never forgive any of them if she was killed.

Zeus flipped his palm over in front of him, and a vision appeared. Michael stepped forward and saw Ares and Regina inside some kind of cave.

Michael, I've found Sara! Jophiel's voice boomed in his head.

Where? Michael glanced around at all his brothers. They were all receiving the same communication.

Mercer Bay Cliffs in Auckland.

"Jophiel has her. Let's go!" Michael ordered.

His brothers lined up to either side of him.

"We wish your mate a safe return, Lord Michael," Hera said. He was sure she was trying to sound sincere, but she didn't.

"Keep your children in Olympus, queen. Anyone who interferes will not live to see another day. You might want to start praying to God I find my mate alive, or you won't see your son again."

This wasn't over. They all knew it was just the beginning, and the next few hours would dictate all their futures.

The archangels simultaneously spread their wings—an intimidating sight—and lifted to the sky. Michael's large white wings sat center stage while Raphael's emerald green and Cham's black wings flew to his right. On his left flew Gabriel, with his stunning silver-and-blue feathers, Zadkiel in dark blood red, and Uriel's beautiful turquoise wings.

How the knowledge of the Pegasus had leaked, which had started all this, was still to be determined. Had he become complacent in recent years? Did Heaven have a spy or a traitor?

A matter for another day.

First, he had to save Sara.

CHAPTER FIFTY-TWO

All of them flashed to the location Jophiel had shared with them. The moment he saw her, Michael's heart nearly left his body.

Fuck.

"Oh God."

"Fuck me!"

"Let me kill him first."

Sara was sitting flush to the edge of the mouth of a cave, one hundred feet above jagged rocks with crashing waves in the bitter cold. Ares stood three feet away from her, and behind him, he saw Regina.

Michael flew as close to the mouth of the cave as he dared, his wings flapping. He glared at Ares.

"Michael," Sara cried out, terror pouring off her. "Oh, thank God you are here."

Behind and around him, his brothers hovered, also keeping their distance. Until he got a handle on the situation, he wasn't risking anything.

Hold back, brothers.

Yep.

Absolutely.

Motherfucker.

"Don't move, Sara. Just stay still," he said calmly, not looking her way. He couldn't. Not only did he need to keep his eyes on Ares, but he needed to analyze the situation, and fast.

The wrong move could end her life.

He wouldn't risk it.

That was the thing about enormous power. Sometimes, it meant jack shit. Sure, he could flash in and grab her, but he didn't know what kind of magic the witch had set up. That might be exactly what they wanted. This whole scenario could be rigged, and in the middle of it was the one person who meant the most to him, not to mention his unborn child.

He would approach with caution.

"Ares, you have something which belongs to me." His voice was dark and threatening.

"You can have the human when I'm finished with her. She has something I want locked inside her," Ares said. "And if you come any closer, I will kill the angel queen." The god moved fast, gripping Regina by the throat. Michael glanced to the side of them and saw Severial lying on the cave floor.

"Please, be my guest," Michael replied. He glanced down at Sara, and his heart throbbed.

"Stay very still, Sara," Raphael repeated from beside him.

He heard a little cry leave her throat, and it took all his strength to stay where he was. She was deathly close to the edge of the wet, slippery cliff, and the winds were blowing dangerously around her.

Any of his brothers could move fast enough to save her if she slipped, as long as there was no magic to interfere.

He would save her if it was the last thing he did.

Grab her when I give the go-ahead, he instructed Raphael.

You don't think it's a trap?

Yes, I do, but we may run out of options.

"You asshole," Regina sneered. The ground of the cave began to shake. "Both of you. Let go of me, you lying god of shit."

He watched as Sara wobbled and cursed. The witch was using magic to shake the cave in an attempt to dislodge his mate.

Ares laughed. "You know what they say about a woman scorned."

Fortunately, without the use of her hands, which Ares had clasped, Regina's witchcraft was limited. Michael glanced at Sara and knew he had seconds to make a decision that would change the course of his life.

Of all their lives.

CHAPTER FIFTY-THREE

Sara nearly lost her balance as the cliff shook. Below her, waves crashed angrily against the rocks below.

Desperately, she stared at Michael, wondering why he didn't just fly in and flash her out. He had barely looked at her. Her heart bled to have his arms wrapped around her, to feel his comforting love. He looked back at her, angry and cold.

She let out a little sob, trying to steady herself. Instead, she slipped, crying as she clawed at the muddy floor.

"Go!" she heard Michael roar.

Sara looked up as he flew into the cave, his enormous white wings brightening the dark space. Suddenly, a dark shadow covered her.

"I am the prophesied one!"

Sara turned and saw Severial, whom she had presumed dead, falling over her. Something sharp struck her chest.

"NOOO!" Michael screamed.

She lifted her eyes to his and knew in that moment nothing else mattered. Her life was over. The prophecy was right. Sara felt death come upon her and knew that nothing could stop it. Pain of a different kind filled every inch of her being. Utter loss and sadness. She cried out silently, her eyes begging him to help her, though she knew it was hopeless.

She saw the horror in Michael's eyes, and with it, she saw the truth.

He loves me.

His soul reached out, connecting with hers, as she

realized it had been her holding back. She had not trusted him enough to give herself fully to him.

Regret filled every inch of her being as she saw into his soul. So with what time she had left, she opened herself fully and gave him her heart. Her soul. The very essence of who she was. If it was only for one second or half a second, it didn't matter; Sara gave him everything. And it felt like the purest, most beautiful thing she'd ever done.

Through the pain and tears, a smile formed on her lips, and she mouthed, I love you.

"NOOO!" Michael screamed again as he landed and pulled her into his arms.

Then the world faded to black.

"FUCK! SARA, NO!"

Michael wrapped his wings around them as he roared. He pushed his powerful celestial energy into her body, but there was no life.

How?

He hadn't mistaken the energy of her heart and soul connecting with his. Sara had chosen him. It had only been for a brief second, but she had chosen him.

God!

Around him, he heard his brothers restraining Ares and Regina with angelic handcuffs made of celestial light. They were unbreakable and would disable the powers of both the god and witch.

Several had not survived the blast Michael had shot at him when he'd stabbed Sara. Nobody rose from a fatal blast from the Supreme Archangel's sword.

"Release me, you fucking angel!" Ares screamed. "If that Pegasus is released, it's mine! I've worked for centuries to claim it. Let me go!"

He saw Raphael kick the god's legs out from under him and watched the god fall to his knees. "You fool. The creature is already back in God's kingdom."

"What? For how long?" he screeched.

"All you need to know, Ares, god of war, is that there will be consequences for this, and right now, I'd be begging the Supreme for your life."

"He can't kill me."

Michael heard the doubtful murmurs.

"I'd pay to watch it."

"Uh, yeah, I think he will."

"If he doesn't, I will."

Michael buried his face in Sara's hair and felt himself go numb.

His mate. Void of life.

He faced an eternity without her. Before Sara, he hadn't been able to contemplate having a mate. One lover forever? It had been unthinkable. Now, a minute, a century, an existence without her was the worst kind of agony.

His heart began to bleed and ache unlike anything he believed possible. An animalistic cry built inside him, but knew he had to contain his pain or risk harming billions of humans.

Michael gasped into her hair, holding her against his chest, wrapped in his wings. He'd flash her to Heaven and let out his agony in private.

And then he felt it.

A flicker.

Michael jerked.

At first, he thought it was the child, but then he felt a second sign of life. Keeping his wings wrapped around her, Michael pulsed energy through her body in search of more. He felt the other archangels begin to contribute. They had also sensed it.

His heart pounded as the sparks grew stronger and stronger.

Sara?

"Get these cuffs off me, you Neanderthal," Regina screeched. "I want to speak to God."

"You answer to Michael," Uriel reminded her. "And do not believe yourself worthy of our Father's presence, witch. Especially after this betrayal."

The spark lessened.

"Shut up, all of you!" Michael yelled as the spark disappeared. "No. Fuck. No!"

His brothers surrounded him as he dropped his wings and let Sara's body rest in the ground in front of him. Michael threw back his head and screamed.

Suddenly, light burst out of Sara's chest and lit up the entire cave, shocking him out of his roar.

"Holy shit," Raphael said. "Michael, look."

He gazed in shock and awe at the bright white light which poured from Heaven, through him, and into Sara. The powerful energy of immortality flowed through his heart and into the woman he loved.

Sara began to arch off the ground, her body vibrating. Then suddenly, her eyes burst open. White heavenly light poured out of them as she stared emptily ahead.

Michael took her face in his hands. "Sara? Can you hear me?"

The divine light began to subside until finally Sara's beautiful hazel eyes blinked and found their way to his. She smiled. "Yes."

"You are immortal, my sweetheart," he said, tears sliding down his cheeks.

"I am."

"You did it. You chose me. You chose us."

She nodded knowingly.

Just as God had promised, when she gave herself to him completely, she became immortal.

By him.

Michael felt the life force still pouring through him and into her as he held her. Suddenly it stopped, and she lay in his arms, a hazy glow still burning off her.

An eternal bond now existed between them, similar to

the one he had with his brothers, but brighter, stronger, and so damn powerful it took his breath away.

He knew, like his brothers, he would be able to locate her anywhere in the universe, and she him.

Pulling her into his arms, he lifted her to her feet and kissed her. "How do you feel?"

Sara gripped his forearms to steady herself. "Better by the minute. I'm no longer cold, thank goodness."

He glanced down and placed his hand on her stomach.

"Gabriel." Michael turned to find his brother and saw all the archangels staring in awe at his mate. He gave them all a small smile.

"The baby's heartbeat is rapid. She needs to rest. In time, we will know if it will survive," Gabriel said, his voice somber.

"I'm taking them back to the house. Take these two and lock them in the dungeon. I will deal with them later."

"I'm immortal," Sara mumbled. "You made me immortal."

"We need to get you home. You may be immortal, sweetheart, but our baby is at risk. I want to get you into bed and let you rest."

"Our baby?" Regina growled. "That's not possible."

"Get her out of here."

The former queen of the angels spat and cursed as Jophiel and Zadkiel flashed her and Ares away.

Michael glanced down at Sara and kissed her on the forehead. Her color was returning. Immortal or not, she would need time to recover.

"Uri, you and Gabe go to Olympus and deliver Zeus a message. Tell him I have his son and he's being charged with kidnapping and attempted murder of the Supreme Archangel's mate and unborn child. Trial date pending."

There was no precedence for his claim, but he would deal with those finer details another time.

"Raphael, you're with me."

"Thank you," Sara said, smiling at Raphael.

"No need. You are part of our family," Raphael replied. "I'm grateful we can now take you home."

Michael wasn't sure what had passed between the two of them, but he was overflowing with love for his closest brother and his mate.

"Home." She smiled.

Michael pulled her in close, still feeling the need to hold her tight, and flashed them away.

CHAPTER FIFTY-FOUR

Sara lay on the bed in her bedroom and ran her hand over her belly. She had showered and changed into everyday clothes and was now being doted on by three gorgeous archangels: Chamuel, Raphael, and Michael.

The latter was her favorite.

So far, the baby's heartbeat had been stabilizing, but Michael still wouldn't let her get off the bed. After the past few hours, she was happy to stay snug inside the warmth and comfort of the covers.

"I need everything," she had told them when they'd asked what she wanted packed.

"Well, we can take the whole damn house if you really want," Michael had answered.

Now, as she watched him packing her clothes into her suitcases, she questioned the rules of her immortality one more time. "Can we really not ever visit? Surely, I can pop down and hang at the beach without it being that big of a deal? You guys are on Earth all the time."

"After the baby is born, perhaps. I think you need time to adjust to your new world and role as a mother, sweetheart," Michael said, glancing up at her from the floor. "And your new position in Heaven."

"What position?"

"The mate of the Supreme Archangel," Cham piped up from his leaning spot against the door. "You pretty much just have to do what he says all the time."

Michael and Sara glanced at each other before they

burst out laughing.

"You'll find your place, Sara, and we'll all help you," Raphael said, grinning.

"I guess you have a point. It's like moving towns; you can't keep going back. I've got a new life to start."

Which brought up a question that was forming in the back of her mind. What was she? Sure, she was immortal, but what did that mean? Was she an angel? She didn't want to ask in front of the brothers, so she kept the question to herself for now.

The important thing was she could now spend her life with Michael, and when the baby arrived, they would never be separated.

Michael had explained she'd had the power to choose her immortality all along and that he hadn't been able to tell her, as it would have interfered with her free will. Or worse, her ability to choose it.

She wondered if it was really worse than being stabbed to death, but kept those thoughts to herself. God was not her favorite…well, God right now.

Sara rubbed her stomach. She could feel the baby on a more energetic level now. It desired calm and peace, and they were in total agreement on that.

"So what if we pack up my belongings but still keep the house? When you guys are on Earth, you can stay here or just check on it. Then if I want to, once I'm settled, I can visit."

Cham looked at Michael, who nodded. "That's a fair compromise. I know you love this place, so we can do that. But Sara, for the love of God, please tell us what you want so we can get it packed."

She laughed. "Tilly. The rest doesn't matter."

"On it!" Raphael turned and went to get the cat.

"I'll take these boxes back now," Chamuel said and disappeared.

Michael stepped up to the side of the bed and pulled the blanket up around her. He leaned down and kissed her. "What is it with the cat and my brother?"

She grinned and shrugged. "She's a cool cat."

Tugging his face closer, she deepened the kiss, enjoying the feel of his large, warm body.

Being an immortal felt different. She had thought she'd feel like a warrior princess, but she didn't. Perhaps it was because she didn't know how to use any of her powers.

Wait. Did she have powers?

You have some, my love.

Her eyes flew open. "You're in my head!"

He nodded and smiled, kissing her forehead. "Try it."

"How?" she asked.

"Just talk to me in your head. Just think it."

Like this?

Just like that.

Sara whooped and wiggled on the bed. "That's so amazing." *I mean, that's so amazing!*

Michael laughed and kissed her some more. "Oh, this is going to be fun."

She went quiet and stared at him. "I love you, Michael. So damn much."

"I love you too, baby." He brushed a few strands of hair off her face, lowered to the bed, and pulled her closer into his arms.

Desire flushed through her, and she suddenly felt the need to feel his naked skin against hers.

"No," he growled. "Rest first, then when we are in Heaven, we can play."

She sighed. He was right. She was tired and needed rest. They had eternity to enjoy one another's bodies.

But before she left, she had something she had to do.

"I need to say goodbye to Lisa."

"You can't," Michael said softly but firmly.

"I won't tell her, but I want to have one last girly human chat," she pleaded. "I know she won't remember me afterward; I get it. But please, Michael. I'm leaving behind everything."

He groaned, but nodded.

"Just remember, all her memories will be scrubbed, but not her emotions. So try to keep it light for her sake."

She agreed, knowing it was kinder for her friend.

She picked up her phone.

"Hey, you," she greeted as her friend answered on the second ring.

"Hey, girl, everything okay?" Lisa asked. "You're normally well asleep by now."

It was late. She hadn't thought this through properly.

"Yeah. I couldn't sleep. Wanted to see how you were."

Lisa yawned loudly, and Sara smiled.

"Well, I'm okay. Kind of. I ended things with Dave. Like, completely this time," Lisa replied. "Hey, maybe you can introduce me to some of Michael's hot brothers. I saw the photo you put on Instagram."

Nope. That was so not happening.

Ever.

"Sure. They're kind of idiots though," she said, smiling because she knew Michael could hear. There was silence. "Lisa. I just wanted to say, um…"

"You okay? Sara, what is it?"

"I'm just feeling emotional. Probably these baby hormones. I just wanted to say thanks for being the bestest best friend ever."

"Definitely the hormones." Lisa laughed.

"And that I love you."

"Okay, now you're scaring me. Also, I love you back."

That was all she needed to hear.

Michael stood in the doorway with a small smile on his face. "Hang up, sweetheart. Let her go."

She nodded, tears in her eyes. "Okay, sleep well. And…talk soon."

Look after yourself, my beautiful friend.

"Night, babes," Lisa said, and the phone clicked dead. Tears fell down her cheeks.

"I'm fine. Honestly, I'm fine. It's totally fine."

She held up her hand, but Michael knew her. He walked to the bed, pulled her into his arms, and she fell apart, sobbing. Some people had a big loving family, and for others, their friends were their family.

Blood was not always thicker than water. That was total rubbish. Sara felt blessed to have had one person she genuinely loved and trusted during her human life. Sure, she could have rung a whole list of friends, but none of them had ever compared to the friendship she'd had with Lisa.

Wiping away her tears, Sara curled up in a ball and felt Michael layer her with his calm, magical energy. She dozed on and off, and a few hours later, she stood in her kitchen, ready to depart her life as a human.

She'd stared out the window at the beautiful beach for a long while and imagined not living on the planet any longer. It was impossible.

But she wasn't human anymore. It was time to go

"Am I an angel?" she finally asked Michael.

"Yes."

"An archangel?"

"No." He kissed her nose.

"Why not?" She tilted her head.

"Well"—he shrugged—"I don't know. Perhaps you can discuss that with your new Father-in-law."

"Ah, no, I'm good." She shuddered.

She took one more look out the window as the sun rose and smiled. "Thank you for being a wonderful home, Earth. I'll see you again one day. Please, please, don't let the humans destroy you."

She turned to Michael, and he pulled her into his arms.

"Now. Finally. Let me bask in this moment, my love. I get to take my mate and child home."

They flashed into his chambers, and as Sara looked around at the heavenly décor, one word entered her mind.

Home.

CHAPTER FIFTY-FIVE

"Why do we all need to be there?" Raphael asked him as they stood in the middle of his chambers.

"You questioning God?" Michael said, his eyebrow raised.

"Yes. On the daily."

Michael laughed.

"I do not know. At least he gave Sara and I a few days to settle her in before demanding an audience. If I had to guess, it's about our new guests in the dungeons."

Sara was adjusting very well to her new life in Heaven. Tilly, much to her frustration, kept disappearing over to Raphael's place. She always came home in the evenings, but his pregnant mate was not happy.

He hadn't told her yet, but Raphael had installed a sneaky cat door.

Yeah, he definitely wasn't going to tell her.

It still weirded him out. The guy was cooler than a cucumber, yet he had a weird affection for the cat. Tilly was an awesome cat, but still.

"Our noisy guests," Raphael added. "It's like The Real Housewives of Orange County down there with the two bickering at each other."

Yeah, and that was a shit show he now had to deal with; his message to Zeus had gone as expected. Michael crossed his enormous arms. "Good, they deserve all the punishment I can serve up."

Sunshine poured into the living area, and Raphael

walked to the glass doors, lifting his head to the golden globe. "Where are we going to hold this trial?"

Michael frowned. It was a damn good question. No way he was doing it on Olympus, since he didn't trust the gods at all.

Having them in Heaven was not an option.

"I'm not sure." He waited a moment to drop his next bomb. "I'm going to demand the death penalty."

Raphael's eyebrows nearly hit the ceiling.

"Before you say it, I know, but Sara is my mate, Raphael. He's lucky I didn't kill him in the cave and dealt with the consequences later."

"You would never have done that."

"Before Sara, maybe. One day you'll understand."

Michael watched Raphael try to hide the twitch in his eye and fail.

He sighed.

Maybe Raphael was right. To kill one of Zeus's sons would create a war, and he had no idea if God would punish him.

"This will not end well," Raphael said, shaking his head. "Father will not let you kill him, Michael. We both know that."

"This time, I'm not giving him the choice."

CHAPTER FIFTY-SIX

All the archangels plus Sara stood inside the Great Hall after being summoned by God. Michael stood protectively beside her.

"Father, we're all here," Michael said loudly, an echo bouncing around the hall. A moment later, they were all transported to a sunny garden with an array of outdoor furniture as if they were going to have a tea party.

Another one of God's self-humoring moments.

"Welcome, my sons," God greeted. "Sara, immortality looks stunning on you, my dear. Welcome to the family."

"Um, thanks," she answered and accepted the seat Michael pulled out for her.

The Deity took a single chair, running his hands down his white linen pants and Hawaiian shirt as if he'd not ironed them properly.

Michael saw Raphael narrow his eyes at God as the Deity grinned at him. Raphael shook his head.

What is that about, Michael wondered.

"Not happening," Raphael muttered.

"What's not happening?" Zadkiel asked as he sat down next to Raphael on the deep wicker couch.

"Nothing." Raphael shook his head and glanced at Michael.

Michael raised an eyebrow, but Raphael looked away. Something was definitely going on. Had this something to do with that woman in Hawaii? Was that what this theme was about?

Interesting. Very, very interesting.

He smirked.

The thought of one of his brothers meeting their mate was highly desirable. He hoped their experience was smoother than his and Sara's, but anything was possible.

But Raphael? Of all the archangels, he saw him as the least likely to settle down with one female.

God was grinning at him.

Michael frowned back.

It was time to get down to business.

"So."

"So," God repeated.

A stare off ensued for a few minutes.

"You're not killing him. End of story. On to the next subject."

"You don't get to make that decision," Michael boldly replied.

Everyone just stared.

They'd had some arguments over the years—God had created him as the Supreme Archangel not because he took orders but because he was a leader.

"I am God. Pleased to make your acquaintance, Archangel Michael. If you need reminding of the order of authority, please refer to your induction manual."

Uriel snorted.

Gabriel tried to hide his smile but failed.

"So, matter number two," God continued, lifting his china teacup with little yellow flowers all over it.

"No, the fuck—" Michael started to say.

"Would you like to know what you are, Sara?" God asked, ignoring Michael, and it was only because he knew it was of great importance to his mate that Michael held his tongue.

"I do!" Sara piped up as he'd expected.

She placed her hand on his leg affectionately, but he knew it was also a message, namely: I need to hear this.

"Excellent," God replied.

Suddenly, a flash of white light rained down over her, and she froze. They all froze, except for Michael, who moved into a protective position. But then they all felt the pure essence of the energy. One they all recognized.

"Oh, my…"

"Yes, God. I know." The Deity grinned.

"Is that…?"

"So, is she…?"

"What did you do?" Michael asked, his mouth gaping.

White wings, much smaller than Michael's, glowed from her back. Sara twisted her head to look and held up her arms. Her whole body was glowing from head to toes.

Slowly, it faded.

"Sara, I bequest you here today with celestial powers. You will be known as an archangel; not a warrior like my sons, but one of creation. Pure feminine energy."

Sara opened her mouth but was speechless.

"If you wish, I would like you to look after the angels." He looked at Michael and lifted an eyebrow. "It appears we have a vacancy."

"Hey, don't look at me. Regina chose her actions. Free will and all that," Michael defended himself, holding up his hands while throwing God's number one rule right back at him.

As Michael and God did a bit more glaring, Sara continued to run her hands over her body.

"Thank you. It would be my honor."

"You have wings," Jophiel declared.

Of course. They could all see them, but she couldn't.

"I do?" Michael manifested a mirror and she gasped. "Oh my God—er, goodness." Sara glanced apologetically at God. "Michael, look."

"They're beautiful." He leaned forward and kissed her. "You're beautiful.

"Get a room," someone muttered.

They grinned at each other.

"I don't know what to say. Thank you. I do not know what I'm doing with these wings, but I'll learn."

"I'll teach you, sweetheart." Michael cleared his throat of emotion and turned. "Thank you, Father. I mean it."

God nodded, their disagreement put aside for the moment.

"Cool, you can fly with us now," someone called out.

"Can she flash?"

"Are they white to match Michael's? That's so Bennifer."

God leaned forward, shaking his head, giving Michael and Sara his full attention. "You don't have the same level of power or all the same powers as the warriors. That's unnecessary. You can transport from location to location—or flash, as these goons call it—and you can fly. You'll also learn to manifest things out of energy."

"Oh yes!" Sara jumped in her seat.

"Did he just call us goons?"

Raphael tried to imagine the woman he'd met sitting with them in God's presence. Sara had given up her entire life as a human to be here with Michael. His girl would never do that.

His girl?

What the fuck.

God glanced at him and smirked.

Nope. Nope. Nope.

No way. He wasn't smitten like Michael.

"So who's up for flying lessons later?" Raphael asked, and Sara lifted her hand in the air like a first grader needing the bathroom. "Cool…and to other matters, why can't we kill Ares?"

Sure, call him an asshole, but anything to distract from his little cough problem.

Michael narrowed his eyes at him, then started in on

his argument. "Look, our laws dictate that we have to hold a trial. We know that. I'd also like to point out that there's a clause that says if they cause death to an archangel, then we…"

And in ten, nine, eight…

Zadkiel cleared his throat. "Well, Sara has only just become an archangel. There's also no mention of our mates, because at the time of drafting, we didn't know we would have mates."

Zadkiel may be the Archangel of Benevolence, but the guy's attention to detail was second to none. Also pedantic, but whatever.

"So that needs amending. Unless, of course, you're going to make all our mates archangels?" Michael asked.

They all looked at God.

And waited.

Finally, "Not necessarily."

Well, that was interesting.

"Oh." Sara looked up at Michael in surprise, who leaned down and kissed her nose.

He groaned.

Enough already with the rainbows and puppies with these two. Raphael loved seeing them happy, but it was like damn Valentine's Day twenty-four seven.

"Hold the trial, present your evidence, and let them present their argument. Then, I will rule," God concluded firmly, as if the discussion was now closed.

"And the queen?"

"Someone already stripped her title."

Michael shrugged, and Raphael didn't blame him.

"Then it is decided. The trial shall be held in ten days."

Shit.

Raphael looked away. There were tense days ahead of them. And yet, his mind once again flashed to the dark-haired beauty he couldn't stop thinking about.

Or at least, his cock wouldn't.

CHAPTER FIFTY-SEVEN

"I'm an archangel." Sara grinned as she skipped into the bedroom.

Michael grinned. "Come here."

She spun around, and he caught her in his arms. He pulled her against him, and he groaned with need. He had been giving her space to heal and adjust to her new life.

Now, he needed to be deep inside her.

"Michael," she purred.

He took one of her breasts in his hands, rubbing his thumb over her nipple, and ran his tongue over her neck when she arched back.

They were so familiar with each other now, her beautiful curves his to possess for eternity. Michael lifted her up and laid her on the bed underneath him, not harshly, not gently.

He held her gaze for a moment to make sure she was okay. Despite Sara now being an immortal, he still felt the need to be gentle with her. When her lids lowered, he knew she was on board.

Removing her clothing, he spread her thighs and let his tongue circle her clit, nibbling. She moaned, making his cock twitch.

"So wet and ready for me, Sara."

"Yes, please, yes," she pleaded, her body preparing to climax.

He felt selfish, but he stopped. Tonight, he needed to be in her, to love her, to become one with her when they both released. Kissing her inner thigh, he moved up her body, careful of her swollen belly, and pressed his cock to her entrance.

"You are mine," he growled in her hair as he pushed inside.

"Forever."

Michael pulled back so his head was still inside and then thrust harder, faster. Sara clung to his arms, her fingers digging into him.

He looked down and saw love flowing from her bright hazel eyes. Their mouths found each other, and it was as if their souls connected. He couldn't get enough of her.

He never would.

Sex with his mate was not the simple, physical act he'd had with every other lover before Sara. There was a loving and spiritual passion. Every touch, every kiss was savored. He lived to give her pleasure. Together, their passion was explosive.

Michael ran his mouth over her arched neck as he tilted her hips. He needed to go deep to feel every inch of her around his cock. She clenched around him, moaning. He knew her body, her nuances, and the signs. She was close.

"Sara, my beautiful archangel, God, you are so hot and moist."

"Yes, God, yes!" she cried out. "Michael, I'm going to come."

His cock pulsed inside her. He was ready, too. As she tightened around him, he poured his seed into her willing body.

After a moment, he slipped off her and pulled her into his embrace. He loved having her here in Heaven, in his bed, where he could protect her.

One day soon their baby would arrive, and he would have two incredible beings to love more than he could ever have imagined. He felt blessed beyond his wildest dreams.

He recalled the nightmares he'd had for two centuries, where he'd seen the female now lying in his arms dying on the floor of what he now knew was that fucking cave.

But he'd saved her.

He did not know, back then, how or if he would save the beautiful female from those nightmares. But here she lay in his arms, not only as his mate, but as an archangel.

Now they got to spend eternity together. As a family.

"Thank you for believing in us and never giving up," Sara said, laying a hand on his cheek.

Michael pushed the hair off her face and gently kissed her lips.

"I will always fight for us, my love. You are my heart."

And now he was going to do everything in his power to make sure both his mate and his child were safe and protected for eternity.

* * *

If you loved Michael and Sara's story, then I would love a review on your favorite book retailer. Book three in the Realm of the Immortals releases late 2021.

Have you read my Moretti Blood Brothers series?

Turn the page for a taste of chapter one, then jump online and download the story...
for FREE!
www.juliettebanks.com/books

THE VAMPIRE KING

CHAPTER ONE

1891 England. 20th Century

Bram Stoker sat at the end of the bar and lifted his ale to his lips, watching as four large men walked across the room and sat at a table.

They had a look of aristocracy about them, however, there was something more. Something that made a man keep one eye on them.

As a writer, he would describe them in one of his novels as menacing-looking fellows, dressed in the high quality tailored black suits of the time, with bodies far too bulky and tall to go unnoticed. Their demeanor was dark, confident, and dangerous.

The men winked at the barmaids playfully, which did nothing to lessen the dark aura about them, and yet the women were tripping over themselves to serve them.

Women.

He gave his head a small shake and returned his attention to his notebook.

Bram was currently staying in Whitby, on the Yorkshire Coast, to write his novel. His wife and family would join him in six months, and he was determined to have a first draft ready by the time they arrived.

It was plenty of time. If he knew what he was going to write. The seaside town had a moody feel to it, which was perhaps why he was projecting menacing characters onto the men across the room from him.

"Another ale, sir?"

"Thank you, yes," he replied to the barman.

"Don't mind them." He tipped his chin at the new arrivals. "They're regulars, and usually no trouble despite their appearance."

He glanced behind him again and let out a little laugh. One man had pulled a woman onto his lap and was nuzzling into her neck. Heat flushed through his body as he noticed his hand slip under the woman's dress and push her legs apart.

Bram's pants tightened when she arched in the way women did as they were being penetrated.

"Good to hear." He cleared his throat. "A question, if I may. Am I mistaken in my summary of their attire? They appear to be aristocrats."

He was now questioning his judgement after his observation.

"Aye, you're right. They are. However, I'm not about to complain about their patronage."

He took the beer from the barkeep and thanked him. Lifting the glass, he peered over again and noticed one man watching him. There was a warning in his dark eyes, which looked as if they belonged to someone far older, despite his youthful appearance.

Sloshing his beer on the counter, he looked away.

A chill ran down his spine, and Bram considered hastily retiring for the evening. He wasn't a coward, but in his experience, when one ignored their instincts, it was never wise.

It was late, in any case. He folded his notebook and placed it in his inside pocket, taking a last swig of his drink. He then picked up his hat, nodded farewell to the barkeep, and made his way to the entrance.

As he reached the nondescript brown door, it came flying at his face, followed by three men. He fell on his ass and caught himself before his head followed.

"Moretti!" One of the men boomed in a strong Italian accent.

The table of men snarled and jumped to their feet. Standing with their legs wide, the menace he'd perceived was now on full display.

"Step back." The shorter of the men said, holding up a hand in warning.

"I lay down my challenge. Here and now."

All the men froze.

"Fuck, here we go. Are you jesting, Russo?" one of the cheekier men said, rolling his eyes.

"Brayden." The man placed a hand on the others shoulder, quieting him. Then he stepped forward. He had a fatherly vibe despite appearing of similar age. "Roberto Russo. You choose this public place to challenge me?"

He had a quiet, powerful aura about him as he spoke in a calm, deep voice. Bram noticed it was the same man who had caught his eye across the room.

"You have increased our taxes yet again, and now my sister has mated with one of your males. It's the last straw." the man growled.

Two of the men sniggered.

"Hey, you brought Lucinda to the ball. Not our fault." one of them said.

"Poor Tom."

"No, she's not an idiot like her brothers."

"Quiet." The powerful man said, not bothering to glance behind him.

He was obeyed.

Bram got to his feet and brushed off his pants. The conversation was making no sense whatsoever. What was mating? Aside from the marriage bed act, and if so, it was outrageous these men were discussing it so loudly in public.

"If you wish to follow through on your challenge, then come to the castle an hour before dawn, and you shall have your opportunity."

Did he mean a duel?

Bram was about to draw to their attention such an act was illegal, but he thought better of it.

"The throne will be mine, Moretti. Mark my words,"

"Hello. Am I invisible?"

"He has two sons, remember." The cheeky one pointed between himself and the man next to him, grinning. "Princes. Heir to the throne. Do I need to talk slower?"

"Brayden, for god's sake." The man shook his head, frustrated. "Shut. Up."

Princes? Son's?

They looked nothing like the royal family, and more to the point, all the men looked the same age.

Bram looked from face to face then landed on the apparent father. He held Bram's stare for a moment, then slowly looked back at Roberto.

"Go. Leave now. We will clean up your mess and see you at dawn."

The men plowed out the door after throwing out a handful of curses and threats. Bram scrambled on the floor to find his hat, and without looking back, he headed for the door. His hand was an inch from pulling it open when he heard the click.

Bother.

He slowly turned and found the supposed father standing directly behind him with a regretful expression.

"I'm sorry, my friend, you cannot leave just yet."

The Vampire King is book one of four (currently) in the Moretti Blood Brothers series – a fresh new steamy paranormal romance.

You can download The Vampire King for FREE on www.juliettebanks.com/books or your favorite online book retailer.

Printed in Great Britain
by Amazon